# Nancy Screw & The Case of the Dirty Benjamins

## ALSO BY JANE LABOUCANE

*50 Worst Dates*

# Nancy Screw & The Case of the Dirty Benjamins

JANE LABOUCANE

First paperback edition June 2025

Cover design by Bailey McGinn

ISBN: 978-1-7390491-4-0

*This book is dedicated to my sister, Megan.*

# CHAPTER 1

"I'm not sure what I saw." The elderly woman brought a pink-tipped finger to her mouth and began nervously chewing. Small, stylish spectacles rested on her wrinkled skin and framed her soft brown eyes. Her hair had that voluminous, blown-out look so fashionable amongst the moneyed crowd and there was an air of confidence about her—a trait so ingrained in those from well-to-do families that it almost seemed to be there at birth. The nail-chewing continued, the woman's obviously well-mannered upbringing notwithstanding, and her hair bounced as she tittered with the finger in her mouth. It took a couple of seconds for her to realize what she was doing and her hand dropped into her lap as she banished the nervous tic. "I'm not sure what I saw," she repeated. "But something seems off and I don't want to involve the police."

Nancy nodded a silent encouragement for Ms. Elena Fineberg, the pink-nailed woman who was seated across the table from her, to continue.

Soft beams from the overhead light bathed the elderly woman in a warm glow. Not a fan of fluorescent, Nancy's office had been designed to exude warmth—like stepping into a steamy bubble bath. The look she had gone for was cozy, calm, and comfortable. When clients came to see her, she wanted them to feel relaxed. Well, as relaxed as they possibly could be, given the circumstances. When people sought out her services, it typically wasn't for anything good. In that sense, it was helpful to have a space that made people feel at ease. It also helped Nancy to assess her clients. The number of things you could pick up on from a person just by observing them or listening to them talk was infinite. And sometimes what her client *didn't* say was just as important as what they did say. Not that reading between the lines was always helpful. It added layers and gave Nancy more things to think about, but what wasn't said could never be considered concrete. Although, what *was* said couldn't always be considered concrete either.

There is a myth that truth is objective—but in Nancy's view, that couldn't be more wrong. Like any kind of story, truth is subjective—tainted by feelings, twisted by motives, and told from different perspectives. Nancy's job was to take the story, tease out each part, fill in the blanks with an impartial eye, and then come to a conclusion. Often the conclusion was one the client was dreading, but there had been the odd instance of a happy ending. Which was ironic given Nancy's other job, in which happy endings were what she exclusively dealt in. Not literally, of course—the figurative kind. As a full-time private investigator and part-time dominatrix, probing people was what she was paid to do—finding out people's deepest, darkest secrets, getting to the bottom of their motives, and figuring out the missing pieces to their puzzles.

Like her clients, the cozy, oatmeal-coloured space that served as the office for Nancy's detective work actually held a secret: through a locked door that looked nothing so much as a janitor's closet was a dungeon. Calm and cozy on one side of the building, cold and crazy on the other. Each business had its own entrance—one in the front, and one in the back, and the door in between was kept locked at all times. It was a division that kept Nancy from getting her two lives intertwined.

Well. Mostly.

As a detective, she had solved some of the city's most high-profile cases and, as a dominatrix, she had serviced some of the city's most high-profile men.

All done discretely, of course.

In the office, she wore contact lenses and minimal makeup. In the dungeon, she wore a latex mask and heavily made-up eyes. But the disguises didn't stop there. When it came to her detective work, she was a chameleon. It was wild what a bit of makeup, coloured contacts, wigs, and some clothes could do to disguise a person. Her closet was full of wigs in different styles, cuts, and colours, and her wardrobe ran the gamut from librarian to socialite, housewife to scientist, and everything in between. She had lucked out when she had found her condo. It was a quiet, low-rise building full of retirees. The elevators were mostly empty in the evening, which is when she conducted most of her detective work, and the odd time that one of her neighbours did see her sporting a strange outfit or a wig, they either didn't recognize or didn't remember her. As for her dominatrix getup, that was something she only ever put on in the dungeon. One could easily excuse a woman wearing a lab coat or spike heels and a short dress in the elevator. A latex bodysuit, fishnet tights, and black platform heels, however, was a different story. That, she knew, would stick out like a sore thumb and probably attract the attention of her neighbours and their Board.

Quietness aside, her condo was within walking distance of her Queen Street office—a space she had found just before she had purchased her tenth-floor home. Her two offices were wedged in the middle of a rowed block of buildings and she had spent several months getting both spaces just right. Calm, quiet tones and soft lighting for her private investigator office; heavy wood, blacks, reds, low lighting, and soundproofed walls for her dungeon—which she privately thought of as 'The Cell'. Clients who were interested in her private investigative services were given one address and entrance, and clients interested in being sexually dominated were given another. It suited Nancy well.

Not just the office, but her two careers.

It spoke to the dichotomy of her character—she was smart, reserved, kind, and caring on one hand; on the other, she was sexy, dominant, cold-blooded, and cruel—all qualities that bled over into both of her jobs.

Elena Fineberg adjusted herself in the plum-coloured velvet chair and Nancy stayed silent while she waited for the formidable woman to continue. It wasn't the lady's no-nonsense gray pantsuit or the Birkin that made her intimidating—it was the air about her. A self-confidence that money *could* buy. With one word, she had the power to cripple a company or revive it from the dead.

Elena shifted uncomfortably in the chair but didn't say anything else.

"What happened, Ms. Fineberg?" Nancy asked gently.

Elena paused a second to collect herself—a testament to just how rattled the normally self-assured woman was.

"I was approached by one of my dear friends about investing in a private equity fund," she began. "A real estate fund. I met with Barron and Theodore Benjamin, from Clover Capital, at my office and they explained the fund's strategy: they would purchase multi-family apartment buildings, buy out the tenants, renovate the units, and then rent them out at a higher rate."

Nancy nodded. Simple enough.

"On paper, the numbers were great—5.8% return on your investment after three years with the ability to roll your investment and returns into other funds. I showed it to some of my financial advisors and there weren't any that advised against it. In fact, they all told me that they thought it was a great model."

Elena took a deep breath and let out a sigh.

"Who am I to question brilliant financial minds?" She made a slight shrug of her shoulders. "One doesn't get to be a top dog on Bay Street by being bad at his job. So, I brought it to my foundation's Board of Directors. We have big plans for the foundation and need a substantial amount of money in order to complete them." She paused to make sure Nancy was following. "The foundation does charity work with disadvantaged youth," she said proudly. "We work with schools, youth organizations, and families to provide youth with support, opportunities, and training."

Nancy nodded and Ms. Fineberg continued.

"The Board voted to invest in the fund and, five months ago, I wrote a cheque for $20 million of my foundation's money and gave it to Clover Capital. After that, I didn't give it a second thought. They sent out monthly updates, but they didn't consist of much aside from telling me which buildings had been purchased, the price, and the work that would be done along with the timelines. Everything seemed tickety-boo. Until the other day." She paused again before continuing a little more slowly.

"I'm not sure exactly what I saw." Confusion clouded her face as if she were still trying to make sense of it. "But something seemed off. I know one of the buildings that the fund bought. It's close to a school that our foundation does some work with. I was leaving the school and saw the contractors at the apartment building and thought I would stop by to see it." She paused again and drew a breath—the poor old woman looked troubled. "But there was something about them that seemed . . . off." She was choosing her words carefully now. "The contractors."

Nancy murmured an "hmm" in encouragement for Ms. Fineberg to continue.

"I . . ." The woman looked down and then she met Nancy's gaze. "They didn't seem like the kind of contractors that would be hired to renovate a building by Barron and Theodore Benjamin. Their work vehicles looked like they were on their last legs and they were sitting around smoking cigarettes and what smelled like marijuana."

Nancy's expression had morphed into one of empathy as she tried to understand where Ms. Fineberg was coming from. She didn't think the elderly lady had any knowledge or experience when it came to renovations, but she was sharp. And it didn't take a rocket scientist to detect when something might be wrong in the state of construction. Still, Nancy didn't see how a couple of broken-down vehicles and some weed meant that there was something going on. Surely Barron and Theodore Benjamin would have properly vetted anyone who was working for them. They were dealing with hundreds of millions of dollars and she couldn't see either of them risking their reputation or financial ruin to save the equivalent of spare change. *That* fall from grace wouldn't just be hard—it would be cataclysmic. Reputation was everything in the world of finance. Although if there was something untoward occurring, goodness knew that the brothers wouldn't be the first people who had become too intoxicated by money and corrupted by power. There was more than one financial genius who had been taken down by their own greed. Starting off with good intentions but transformed by the temptation of riches along the way. It was understandable, of course, when you were dealing with massive amounts of money. It didn't take much sometimes—once you started cavorting with the rich and powerful, it took a lot to keep up. And sometimes it wasn't just keeping up, but it was the motivation to overcome and one-up. But broken-down vehicles and marijuana-smoking contractors? If that was the bar for suspicious activity and fraud, she imagined that there wouldn't be a construction company in existence that couldn't be accused of hiding something.

Nancy could see some hesitation in Ms. Fineberg's eyes—the elderly lady wanted to tell her something more, but there was something that was stopping her.

"What else, Elena?" Nancy asked gently.

"Well," Elena hesitated, "there were only three of them. Workers, I mean. And I saw the countertop materials."

Nancy stayed silent and Ms. Fineberg continued. "Something about it didn't sit right. I was very interested in the renovation work that was being done to each of the units, having a design background myself. And the mock-ups that the

Benjamin brothers showed me when they presented their fund to me was not high-end, but it had the look of luxury. Which results in a more lucrative return because the apartment building is able to be rented out at a higher price."

Nancy thought she had an idea where this was going.

"The material at the site looked cheap. Like laminate. I tried to get a closer look, but the workers shooed me off of the property." Ms. Fineberg pondered a moment. "Now that I think about it, technically I partially own the property so I really should not have let them shoo me away."

"It's understandable that you left," Nancy reassured her. "I'm sure you were taken aback by what you saw and being asked to leave only added to it."

Elena nodded, looking at Nancy's desk.

"That's why I came to you," she said suddenly. "If there is something going on, I can't very well ask Barron or Theodore about it. And if there isn't anything going on, I don't want to raise any alarms by inquiring or asking around. As far as I can tell, the brothers are very successful in business and all of their previous deals have been without any issues. But I've also invested a large sum of my foundation's money with them and I can't risk losing it if there is a chance that things are not above board."

The hesitancy had fallen away from Ms. Fineberg and now distress was written all over the poor wealthy woman's face. It was usually a relief for clients to tell Nancy the story of why they had sought her out and Ms. Fineberg's tear-glistened eyes pulled at the detective's heart strings.

"I understand, Ms. Fineberg," Nancy said gently. "I will get to the bottom of it one way or another. If there is something going on, you will know. And if there's nothing going on—no harm, no foul, and no one needs to know."

Elena smiled regretfully. "I wish it hadn't come to this, but you were recommended to me by a friend. You helped her out during her divorce a year ago. She said you are the best."

Nancy smiled back.

"I wish we were meeting under different circumstances, but I will keep my fingers crossed that my investigation turns up nothing. But if it does," she added, "I will do everything I can to ensure that your investment is found and secured."

"Thank you." Elena mustered a grateful smile before pulling some folded-up papers out of her purse and sliding them across the desk. "These are the records of my investment and the updates that Teddy and Barron have sent out. I don't know whether they will help with your investigation, but I thought I would bring them just in case."

Nancy unfolded the papers and glanced at the first few pages. "Any information is helpful," she nodded with a smile. "Thank you for bringing them."

Elena stood up then and Nancy got up to walk her client to the door. She put her hand on the woman's shoulder.

"I'll keep you updated on what I find."

Elena, her eyes glassy from holding back tears, thanked her again before she turned and hurried out of the office. Nancy watched her walk to her car—a Mercedes, of course—across the street, before turning back to her desk. The papers that Ms. Fineberg had given her littered the top of her desk and Nancy gathered them up into a pile. She was going to get to the bottom of this case, no matter what it took. If there was one thing that Nancy disliked, it was well-to-do men taking advantage of women. Even well-to-do ones.

# CHAPTER 2

A glance at her desktop confirmed that there were no clients scheduled for a domme session that day. She'd blocked the afternoon off several weeks ago for a massage and some personal time, but that had been before this morning's last-minute meeting with Elena. Now it looked like the few hours she had before her weekly therapy session would be consumed with the Benjamin brothers. Not that she was complaining. While she loved her dominatrix job, detective work was where her heart really lay. And she didn't have an assembly line when it came to clients of either business. Neither her detective nor dominatrix services were widely advertised; she was happy to keep it to word of mouth. Her high domme prices kept out most of the creeps and she made sure to vet each client before allowing them to avail themselves of her services. With her private investigator skills, it was something she managed to get done quite quickly.

Most of her detective clientele were one-offs, given people typically weren't looking for investigative services on an ongoing basis. But most of her dominatrix clientele were regulars. Not every man was into the same thing and Nancy got to know them—intimately. She had rules for things that she wouldn't do and had turned people away because of it. Aside from that, she loved her job. The men weren't the only ones who derived satisfaction from the sexual play. There was something so intoxicating to her about being in total control of a person. Like a drill sergeant in latex and heels, she meted out orders and punishments to men who were only too happy to oblige.

"Yes, Mistress," they would say. "Please, Mistress." "Thank you, Mistress."

It was an odd thing to have someone thank you for walking all over their groin in your sharpest stilettos. Odder still was to have someone pay you for it—handsomely, at that. But it hadn't taken her long to get used to it. One of the things that most people don't understand about being a dominatrix is that it isn't about sex. It's about power. And surrendering total power over your body to someone else. That was what makes it erotic. It is an experience—a fantasy lived out that most people are unable to encounter any other way.

Did her clients go home and get off on reliving their encounter? Probably, but she didn't care nor care to think about it either way. Nancy turned their fantasy into a reality and what her clients did with it afterwards was none of her concern. She never slept with any of the men and, in terms of her job, it was ironic that the hand and blow varieties were considered out-of-scope services. On a good day, she could bring in more than $1,300. The tips were tax free, but, otherwise, Nancy had a legitimate business. She might hate the government digging into her coffers as much as the next person, but she paid her fair share at both of her jobs.

While her BDSM business had been built up over several years, her detective career was still in its infancy. Her P.I. storefront had remained empty for the first few months and her first client had fallen, literally, into her lap. Sitting in her office one August afternoon—an office that contained everything a P.I. needed except a client—Nancy was feeling frustrated by her failing detective endeavour. On a whim, she decided to pop into a restaurant a few blocks away. While nursing a martini at the bar, a middle-aged blonde-haired woman had stumbled on the floor, tripped, and fallen into Nancy's lap. The woman looked distraught and apologized fervently, which Nancy brushed off—she was more concerned with whether the woman was okay.

Grace, Nancy soon learned, was a fifty-six-year-old mother of two who was married to a high-profile mergers and acquisitions lawyer. She had booze on her breath and told Nancy a tearful tale of her failing marriage. She was convinced that her husband, Bruce, was having an affair. There was no tangible evidence that she could point to but she had a hunch and it was eating her up inside. She'd had her hair blown out that morning and had spent most of the afternoon drowning her sorrows at the bar. Her kids were spending the evening at their grandparents' house and she had come downtown with simultaneous thoughts of stalking her philandering husband and finding a one-night-stand out of spite.

Fortunately, Grace had chosen to do neither and had instead gotten floor-licking drunk. Not a good look at 3 p.m. on a Tuesday, but who was Nancy to judge. Liquor wouldn't have been her first choice if she suspected that her husband of thirty years was having an affair. Nancy would have gone into work mode, found the evidence, and then extracted her revenge. Not that she was a vengeful person, typically. But there were some situations where the crime deserved a punishment. And a hypothetical husband hypothetically cheating on her with his hypothetical young and bubbly new secretary at work?

That would require a punishment.

A big one.

Nancy had ordered Grace a water and offered her investigative services for free. Wobbling in her chair, Grace had taken Nancy's card and examined it closely, closing one bloodshot eye and squinting with the other as she tried to read what was scrawled across it.

"*Nancy Screw*," she slurred, one eye still closed, the other trying to focus on the card. "*P.I. I'll do whatever it takes to solve the case* . . . You're a detective?" Both eyes opened and she looked at Nancy.

Nancy smiled: "I am. And if you want me to figure out what's going on with your husband, you can call me at the number on the card or send me an email. No cost and no pressure. I know you're under a lot of it already."

Grace smiled gratefully. "Thank you. And I am so sorry again for tripping into you. I don't know what's gotten into me," her face flushed and she looked flustered. "I'm usually very composed. Everything with my husband just has me in such a mess."

Nancy put a hand on her bar companion's arm.

"It's okay, Grace," she empathized. "I'm sure anyone would feel the same way in your shoes."

Shortly after, Nancy had ordered the woman an Uber and packed her into the back of a white sedan. Less than twenty-four hours later, Nancy was sitting in her office reading *Page Six* when her P.I. line rang. On the other end of the phone was a seriously hungover Grace who requested Nancy's services. She provided Nancy with all of the information that she had needed and, that afternoon, after putting on one of her wigs and dressing up in corporate clothes, Nancy walked into one of Bruce's favourite after-work watering holes—a Japanese-fusion resto-lounge that was done up in red velvet. She spotted her target as she sauntered up to the long black bar, hardly believing that Grace's case could be this easy. Bruce looked like most of the balding, middle-aged men who were part of the after-work crowd—the high-powered lawyers, bankers, and hedgies who worked hard and drank even harder. But there was one thing that set Bruce and his middle-aged counterparts apart: the other corporate, middle-aged men were either drinking and bullshitting with each other or with scantily clad women of questionable employment at the bar. Bruce, however, was seated with his young, blonde secretary at a corner table. She recognized the woman from the law firm's website.

Nancy took a seat at the bar and ordered up a martini while

she watched the couple out of the corner of her eye. Bruce was clearly enamored with the blonde. The restaurant could have burned down around him and he would be oblivious—the fire department would probably find him still sitting there with a lust-sick expression on his sooty face, his charred body still smoking. But Nancy could kind of get the appeal. Mindy, the lackey, was attentive, smiley, and her skirt had a big side slit that went all of the way to the top of her thigh. She figured that either the law firm didn't have any kind of professional dress code or Bruce, as a senior partner, had bent the rules in addition to Mindy. She watched the blonde flick her hair over her shoulder and lean in closer to her boss, Bruce. This case was going to be a piece of cake.

Nancy took a sip of her martini and tucked a sheet of her blonde-wigged hair behind her ear. Bruce's hand suddenly went up the slit in his secretary's skirt and Nancy pulled out her phone. She was pretending to be checking out the lighting for a selfie while her camera zoomed in on Bruce when her view was suddenly blocked.

"Is this seat taken?" came a deep voice.

She glanced up into the face of a striking, blond-haired, blue-eyed man who had a five-o'clock shadow and a devilish grin. A shock went through her body at the sight of him—holy hell he was hot. Visions of her and blondie tangled up in bed flitted through her head and she had to stop herself from turning her full charm and focus on him—she couldn't let her libido get the best of her now. Grace was counting on her.

"Apologies," she smiled warmly, resisting the voice in her head that was telling her to just get his number "I'm actually waiting for someone."

To blondie's credit, he didn't scowl. But he did look a little put out.

"No worries," his smile dimmed a little. "Whoever is joining you is a lucky guy."

Nancy demurred and took another sip from her martini. When the man moved around to the other side of the bar, she was surprised to see that Bruce had apparently requested the bill. She did the same and discreetly followed the duo to a hotel that was two blocks away. She took a seat in the lobby bar that had a view of the check-in desk and snapped some photos of Bruce pulling out his credit card and renting a room. She kept taking photos as the duo took their room card and, instead of heading for elevators, started walking in her direction. *Because of course they are*, she thought to herself. Bruce was a heavy drinker. He would have to fortify himself with a few beverages before they went upstairs to do the deed. Room service was too long of a wait when he could get immediate bar service from the lounge. She didn't know much about the man, but it was interesting to see what took priority in Bruce's life. His wife, Grace, was playing second fiddle to his secretary, Mindy, but neither of them could compare to Bruce's one true love—liquor.

Thirty minutes later Bruce had downed two drinks and ordered one for the road. Nancy had gotten enough photos and video footage to confirm Grace's suspicions and she left the hotel shortly after the duo had disappeared upstairs. She held off on sending the evidence that evening, reasoning that Grace's hangover could hardly be improved by photos of her cheating husband. The next morning, she had gone to her office, put everything together in an email and sent it off to the poor woman. Thirty minutes later she had received a phone call. Grace sounded composed, all traces of yesterday's gravelly voice were gone, and she was resolute. She thanked Nancy profusely and insisted on paying her usual rate, which the detective protested.

Two days later, a couriered cheque for $5,000 arrived at her office.

She was floored and immediately phoned up her first official client.

"Not at all," Grace's voice sounded stronger than it had the last time they had talked. "I feel so relieved to finally know what he's been doing and to be able to make a decision about my marriage. That's worth five thousand alone. And if you don't cash it, I will drop it off in bills."

Nancy demurred at that point: "Thank you," she said sincerely. "And if you know of anyone who is in need of a private investigator, please give them my number."

What followed was a trickle of referrals from Grace's friends and *friends* of friends who all suspected that their partner was having an affair, and Nancy soon found her business transformed into a less-trashy version of *Cheaters.* Less trashy, she reasoned, because she wasn't posting it online for people's entertainment. While she was glad that she was able to help so many women find answers, it was a little disconcerting to know that her work had directly contributed to so many breakups, canceled weddings, and divorces. It was almost enough to put her off of dating. After all, if you lay down with dogs, you're going to get bit. But if she were honest, she didn't really have time for dating. Her careers kept her too busy. Which wasn't a bad thing. Her ex-boyfriend Jamie had broken her heart—had smashed it into a million pieces. He'd taken a proverbial sledge hammer to the organ but somehow it kept beating.

She shook herself out of her daydream and clicked open a new tab on Chrome. *Barron and Theodore Benjamin,* she typed out and then hit 'Search'. The first page of Google filled with results about the brothers, touting everything from their good looks to their financial prowess. She clicked onto Google Images and let out a breath. Whether the Benjamin brothers were embroiled in any shady or illegal business dealings, she didn't know, but what she did know was that it should be a crime to be that good looking.

As a detective, she pledged to do whatever it took to solve her client's case, which also included a silent pledge to do *whomever* it took to solve her client's case. If Barron and Theodore Benjamin were half as attractive as they appeared to be in Google Images, she was looking forward to putting the second half of her pledge to good work.

# CHAPTER 3

"I'm Nancy, and I'm an alcoholic."

She glanced at the people seated in the circle around her. Seven addicts with varying vices and one do-gooder therapist. Two alcoholics, two sex addicts, one druggie, one gambler, one addict unknown—and a partridge in a pear tree. Eric, the newest member of the group and the one unknown, gave her a small, friendly smile.

*Damn*, she thought to herself. *He's hot.*

Nancy had been coming to this group for the past six weeks and she still wasn't sure how she felt about it. The meetings hadn't done a thing to curb her urges, and at this point she wasn't sure if she was actually hoping to get help or hilarious stories from her fellow addicts.

She checked out blond-haired Eric with his knife-edge nose and chiseled jawline. He looked like he had just stepped out of an advertisement for a surfing company. His lips were soft and full and his skin had that golden, beach-tanned perfection. His gaze was focused on Rhys—sex addict number one—who was, in typical form, giving a long-winded introduction of himself.

Aside from Eric, she had only seen the others six times, but already felt like she knew them. And she knew that Rhys liked to tell a tale. It was still unclear to her why he attended the weekly meeting because he sure as shit wasn't taking any steps towards toning down his sex life.

In other group therapy sessions, they had a sharing circle. In this boundary-challenged support group, they had an over-sharing circle. Their therapist, Carmella, was working on her PhD in addictions. Part of Carmella's work was focused on using talk therapy to tame uncontrollable urges and she wasn't too strict, which often resulted in the group going off of the rails. Privately, there was nothing about Carmella's theory that Nancy believed in. She didn't see how Rhys gloating about his sleazy encounters was going to cure him. It was like going to Alcoholics Anonymous and trying to entertain attendees with your drinking stories. Although it was an interesting view into the mind of the male psyche.

Well, one of them, at least. She hoped that Rhys's mind was one of a kind.

Which wasn't a compliment.

Nancy's own addiction, fortunately, didn't get in the way of her work, which was more than she could say for some of the other group members. Poor Theo—sex addict number two—had gotten caught polishing the proverbial pole during an all-staff Zoom meeting and been put on an extended leave. The way Theo told it he had walked off-camera during the director updates and started doing the kind of thing priests warn will make you go blind. The illusion of privacy was shattered by a well-placed mirror, and the rest of the meeting was treated to a full-frontal performance by Theo—a cinematic masterpiece or a horror show, depending upon your tastes.

Initially, Theo had been facing termination, but he had blamed it on addiction and lawyered up. Employment laws obligated the company support him while he sought treatment, and that was what had landed him at the weekly meetings. Nancy didn't think Theo actually had an addiction—he just didn't want to lose his job. He hadn't divulged anything since his first meeting where he had laid out his whole story, which included the humiliation of having to discuss his 'disability' with the HR department.

She grimaced at the thought of him having to face his colleagues after completing his treatment and thanked her lucky stars that her own issues had never interfered with her life to that level. Still, she could scarcely believe she had ended up here amongst the likes of Rhys, Theo, and surfer-boy Eric—previously the Shameful Six, now Seven.

She was curious about Eric's backstory—what had led him to the Tuesday group. From the outside, none of the men around her looked like people who were suffering with various addictions. Hell, Nancy didn't look like someone who was suffering from an addiction.

Truthfully, she still didn't think she had a problem with alcohol. She drank, yes. But it wasn't like she was hitting the sauce first thing in the morning. Her situation was a little more nuanced. In the same way that an unhealthy relationship can be detrimental without being dangerous, that was her and liquor. It hadn't always been that way and Nancy could pin-point how it had happened. The moment that things spiraled out of control and landed her in Carmella's Tuesday-night therapy group started with Jamie. Jamie, the handsome, long-term love of her life had dumped her after three years of dating. She had loved him. She had thought that they were going to live happily ever after and grow old together. Instead, he broke up with her. The fallout dragged her down a dark hole and, for six months, alcohol was her only escape.

Blackouts had happened with regularity and had regularly resulted in her waking up next to strangers. She never drove drunk, didn't pass out in odd places, and, curiously, never appeared messy in public. The hangovers, ironically, had actually made her a better domme—the cruelty of a woman in a latex suit sweating out last night's vodka, with a splitting headache to boot, could not be overstated. Her detective work, however, was a different story. When she was on the clock, she kept her consumption in check, and it had never affected her investigations. It was between cases and in the intervening hours when things went sideways.

She introduced herself as an alcoholic every Tuesday night—not because it felt true, but because it was easier. Tied up her situation in a nice little bow, even if she felt it wasn't entirely accurate.

The group had been good for excising Nancy's demons and lately she had been mostly managing to keep her consumption in check. A martini or two, a couple glasses of wine—those were no bother. It was when the anxiety overtook her and she felt everything closing in that the drinks became a way to numb the noise, to push back against the mounting pressure.

She surveyed the faces around the room as the introductions continued. Nancy's friends, few as they were, were oblivious to her six-month bender. It was ironic, really—the people who knew her the best, the people who knew her deepest, darkest secret, weren't those who were closest to her—they were complete strangers.

During that night's meeting Eric shared a brief overview of why he was there, but most of the time was dedicated to Rhys who talked about his experiences the past week, one of which involved a cucumber, a corkscrew, and some Gorilla Glue. The mind boggled and the evening concluded, as it always did, with Carmella wishing them well and reminding them that she would see them all next week.

Nancy had kept careful, but inconspicuous, watch of Eric's face during the meeting. She was curious to see what surfer boy's reaction would be to the outlandish group. As someone who rolled with the proverbial punches and typically didn't find much of anything to be surprising, the first meeting that she had attended had left her nonplussed. It had taken her a couple of days to process the experience and she had been better prepared for the next session.

Eric, the group's newest addition, had remained expressionless the entire time. Still, she couldn't help but wonder what secrets lay beneath that surfer-calm exterior.

*

The twenty-minute drive home left Nancy's mind swirling. She was on autopilot as she maneuvered the vehicle through Toronto's busy streets—all of her thoughts were on Elena Fineberg's case.

That afternoon, she had done some cursory research into Barron and Theodore Benjamin, their firm, Clover Capital, and familiarized herself with the basics of private equity. She had heard the term before, of course, but what it actually meant and how it actually operated had always been a mystery. It was one of those financial phrases like 'hedge fund', that gets thrown around a lot. Everyone knows it's money-related, but that's where the understanding stops.

Over the next few days, she planned to immerse herself in the world of the Benjamin brothers to find out everything she could about them and their business. When it came to criminal activity, she had a few advantages over the police: while they were often hamstrung by red tape, Nancy wasn't bound by the same restrictions. As a private citizen, she didn't need to worry about warrants, Charter rights, or entrapment. She could do whatever she wanted as long as it stayed within the confines of the law—something that she played fast and loose with on occasion. When you were facing unconventional crimes, solving them sometimes called for unconventional measures. Often, it required her to put a toe across the line of what's considered 'legal'.

# CHAPTER 4

Black bob? *Too Pulp Fiction.* Blonde bouncy curls? *Too risky.* She intended to spend more than one evening with Barron and she didn't want him to discover that she was wearing a wig. Nancy flicked through her closet and finally decided to go au naturel. Her long black locks could be hot rolled to within an inch of their life and then tousled to give her that sexy, just-blown-out look that was popular amongst the influencer crowd.

Tonight she was going to attempt to catch Barron Benjamin unawares. She had done her homework over the past few days and, after some Googling, she had called in a few favours to find out more information. According to her contact in the entertainment industry, Barron was still clinging onto the party phase of his youth. Though almost fifty, he still, apparently, found joy in loud evenings out at the club. Or, maybe, Nancy thought, the joy he found wasn't in going out, but in going home. With a woman.

She had heard rumors about the Benjamin brothers' behaviour—they had a reputation for being a bit lecherous, but Nancy was confident she could handle them.

Barron and Theodore Benjamin, she discovered, were two of Toronto's most eligible bachelors—high-flying financiers who managed money for some of the city's wealthiest families and corporations. Born minutes apart, the twins were virtually indistinguishable—tousled black curls, ice-blue eyes, and wide, easy smiles that left the ladies swooning.

She had spent a few days surveilling Clover Capital's offices—a sleek, 47-floor skyscraper that was set back from the street. By loitering in the lobby, she was able to watch the brother come and go. While they were indistinguishable to her, the building staff greeted them by name. Eventually she realized it was the brothers' routines that gave them away.

Barron, she had learned, typically left his office around 6 p.m. and then stayed in the area for after-work cocktails with his crew. He would be throwing back Patron and sipping Manhattans for hours without it seeming to affect him. If he didn't head to a club around 10 p.m., he would zero in on one or two women and would be in an Uber back to his place at the Ritz-Carlton by midnight. Ever the gentleman, the women were sent home in an Uber by 2 a.m.

Theodore, by contrast, was in the office early and typically worked late into the night. He seemed to be the more responsible twin, but was still a fixture on the party circuit, just less inclined to bring home women. How the two kept up with their schedules was beyond Nancy, but she was looking forward to seeing one of them in action that night.

Her deep dive had turned up more than just their party habits. Barron had started out on Wall Street, having taken his first job at J.P. Morgan. Theodore, on the other hand, had cut his teeth in Asia, working for Goldman Sachs before returning to Toronto to join a hedge fund. Both of them were financial whizzes. She didn't know the details of their past jobs, but she knew they were smart enough to start their own PE firm and raise hundreds of millions from investors.

She glanced at the latest issue of *Toronto Life*, taking in their rock-hard abs and mischievous smiles. The twins towered over a sea of scantily clad women who had more filler than a Canada Goose coat.

*TWin-ning with the Benjamins: Two of Toronto's Most Eligible Bachelors*, the headline read.

Nancy sighed and tossed the magazine onto her desk. She didn't know if the brothers were attracted to plastic or if that was just the aesthetic of the photoshoot. Either way, she wasn't going to slap on a pair of silicone cutlets for this part of the investigation. Her lack of enhancements was nothing that a push-up bra and a little confidence couldn't fix.

*

Drops of condensation rolled down the side of her martini glass as Nancy, prim and proper in her sexy, skin-tight red dress, lifted the glass and took a sip. A tang of olive juice and gin flooded her taste buds—extra dirty. Just how she liked her martinis—and her men.

Her inky locks were styled to a tousled bed-head perfection and her features were contoured into a supermodel-worthy face. She'd topped off the look with red 'Lady Danger' lipstick and paired her body-con red dress with her highest heels. She had been playing it cool at the bar, brushing off the advances of several men who had approached her with bad one-liners or offers to buy her a drink. Cool, calm, collected, unattainable, and uninterested was the aura she was projecting.

And Barron, whom she had discreetly spotted when she first walked into the busy lounge, had been throwing glances her way ever since. He was leaning back on one of the short, black couches in the lounge, his signature Manhattan in one hand and one ankle crossed over his knee. Nancy could tell that he had been distracted by her entrance when she walked in and found an empty seat at the bar directly in his line of vision.

Well.

'Found' might be a bit of a stretch. What she had actually 'found' was that the head bartender at Louix Louis was very bribable. And very cheap. Twenty bucks got her the information that Barron had booked a table there that evening. Another twenty got her a guarantee that he would save her a bar seat next to it.

In the thirty minutes that she had been there, she'd watched a parade of women all try and squeeze their way to his table. His three friends—bankers, by the looks of them—had welcomed the attention, and squeezed over to make room. Barron had been the only one who looked disinterested. And Nancy knew why. He had his sights set on someone else.

Namely, her.

She suddenly felt a presence beside her and glanced sideways to see the handsome face of Barron Benjamin.

"Hi," his ice-blue eyes locked on hers.

Nancy paused.

"Hi," she replied, holding his gaze.

"Benjamin." He extended his hand. "Barron Benjamin."

Nancy stared at his outstretched hand and then back at his face.

"What are you, James Bond?" she asked playfully.

Barron laughed, a bit taken aback. Nancy took in his attire—a slim-fit, tailored black suit, French cuffs, and the top two buttons of his shirt undone.

"What's your name?" he asked, amusement dancing in his ocean-blue eyes.

"Larissa." She smiled, gently placing her red-manicured hand in his.

They spent the next hour bantering and trading barbs—Nancy could see why Barron was so popular with the ladies. He gave as good as he got. Of course, his big blue eyes didn't hurt matters either.

Eventually, Barron suggested that they go to his place for a drink. Code for: "let's fuck."

She gave a small smirk, and he asked for the cheque. Minutes later they were in a black Cadillac Escalade, courtesy of Uber Black, headed to his home.

While Theodore lived uptown, Barron lived in the Financial District, in the residences of the Ritz. It didn't take a sleuth of Nancy's skills to figure out the appeal—on-site housekeeping, room service, security, and maintenance. She had delved far enough into the twins' past to find out that their bachelor lifestyles were fueled by their upbringing. A doting mom who catered to them hand and foot and gave them every luxury she could afford. When it came to settling down with a prospective partner, no woman could live up to that; no one was ever good enough.

The vehicle pulled up to the imposing building and two valets opened their doors.

"Good evening, Mr. Benjamin," an olive-skinned valet greeted Barron with a grin.

"Hi, David, how is your night?"

"Pretty quiet tonight," the valet replied, opening the door to the building.

Nancy walked ahead of him into the hotel lobby and took a right towards the private residences entrance. She and Barron exchanged flirty smirks on the elevator ride up until the lift stopped at floor 52.

When Barron unlocked the door and Nancy stepped inside, she was taken aback. She knew that his firm was successful and that he was wealthy, but the size of the condo was astonishing. He didn't give her a tour, but the walk from the foyer to the living room alone told her that the place was massive.

"Have a seat, I'll go get us some drinks," he gestured to the large, gray sectional that sat in the middle of the living room.

Nancy took a seat and watched Barron head through a set of doors and off, presumably, to the kitchen. He was a sexy specimen of a man and Nancy had no doubt that his big, strong hands would be able to give her exactly what she desired.

But this was strictly work.

There would be time for play later.

While Barron busied himself with drinks and making a late-night snack, Nancy went to work. Ostensibly, she was looking for a washroom. At least that's what she would claim if Barron caught her. What she was *actually* looking for was his office.

There were five doors in the hallway. She felt like she was on a gameshow—did she want what was behind door number one, two, three, four, or five? On a hunch, she went for door number two, grasped the brass knob and pushed the heavy, dark-stained door forwards and took a purposeful step inside.

Right into a linen closet.

*Jesus.* She backed out quickly and pulled the door closed behind her, then she eenie-meenie-miny-moe'd her way to door five.

The heavy wood made a faint creak as she pushed the door open. After feeling around for the light switch and flicking it on, she was rewarded with his office.

Bingo.

The dark colours that surrounded the rest of Barron's penthouse extended into his office, which was done up in masculine tones of black and gray. A large rug covered the black herringbone floor. Two stiff-looking leather chairs sat in front of an imposing black desk topped with a Bloomberg terminal, a Mac laptop, notepad, and a stack of files. Behind the desk, a floor-to-ceiling bookshelf spanned the wall from one end of the room to the other, brimming with an array of books whose titles were too far away for Nancy to read.

*Interesting.* She knew that Barron was a financial whiz, but she hadn't taken him for the well-read type. She turned her head to listen for any hint that Barron knew she was missing but was reassured by sound of silence.

Taking careful steps into the office she treaded lightly on the plush white rug. Sheer curtains covered a wall of windows to the right of her right, pulling double duty by keeping out any prying eyes. Snapping open her velvet purse, she pulled out her phone and launched her hidden camera detector, then scanned it in a circle around the room.

Detective work hadn't exactly become harder in the 21st century, it had just become a little different.

A green light flashed on her screen signaling that the room was clear, but she didn't put her phone away just yet. She crept over to Barron's desk and began snapping pictures of the paper files, scribbled notes, his computer terminal, and the bookshelf.

Then she did a quick sweep of the room to make sure that she hadn't left anything behind or moved anything out of place. Like most type A personalities that she'd encountered, Barron appeared to be a meticulous clean freak. All orderly, no knick-knacks, and "not a sheet of paper out-of-place".

Stepping out onto the hardwood, she pulled the door quietly closed behind her and paused outside the kitchen. Her ears were met with the reassuring sound of wine glasses clinking.

Moments later, Barron strode into the living room balancing a tray with wine, glasses, and a delectable looking charcuterie board. Nancy was comfortably perched on the middle of an oversized sectional, pretending to be engrossed in an *Economist* magazine she had fished out from between the cushions.

"Read anything interesting?" he asked with a raised brow and a flirtatious smile as he set the tray down on the table in front of her.

Good lord, he was handsome.

She felt a tingling sensation creep through her as she smirked back.

"Oh, you know," she said breezily. "Money laundering and Mexican drug cartels."

She studied his face for any flickers of nerves at the mention of illegal activities, but Barron kept as cool as ice.

Setting the glossy magazine down on the table, she angled her body towards him as he opened the bottle of cabernet and poured two generous glasses of the burgundy liquid.

"Cheers," he said, passing Nancy a glass as he shifted himself back on the couch.

"Cheers," she echoed, clinking his glass against his. A seductive smile flashed on her face before she took a sip.

The tannins, blackberry, and currants burst on her tongue as Barron took a deep drink and settled his arm across the back of the couch, his hand just brushing the top of her shoulder. They engaged in idle chit-chat for a few minutes before the conversation took a turn for the suggestive, punctuated with double entendres and sexual innuendos. It was obvious that

Barron was into her.

Not that it appeared to take much to end up in Barron Benjamin's bed. And not, of course, that she didn't want to. But she had no intention of letting things get that far tonight. Leave Barron wanting more and she would end up with ample time to solve the mystery of the missing money—and maybe even hunt down the big O.

She pretended not to notice Barron's fingers gently caressing the top of her shoulder and she snuggled closer to him on the couch. Close, but not too close. She didn't want to give him the wrong impression. Which was a difficult task given how her body was presently betraying her. Every time their eyes locked she felt a jolt of arousal go through her, tingling in all the right places.

Barron clearly felt it, too—he shifted ever so slightly to hide the growing bulge in his pants.

"So, tell me, Ms. Larissa," he said casually, his eyes focusing on her shoulders as his fingers worked their way up from her shoulder to her neck and jaw. "What is it you do?"

God, he was good. She was really going to have to be careful around this one. It was no wonder he had a revolving door of women that rivaled popular King West clubs.

"I'm a researcher," she lied smoothly as her face followed the movements of his touch. A wrinkle of ecstasy teased her forehead—a miracle, given the generous helping of Botox she had had the previous week. Her eyes narrowed and her lips parted as Barron traced his finger across them.

"A researcher," he repeated, sounding amused. "Brains and beauty." He slid one finger into her mouth. Nancy gently nipped at it before wrapping her lips around it and sucking slowly.

She felt a jolt go through him as his pulse quickened and she flashed him a sly smile. But she wasn't going to give him the pleasure of her pleasure. At least, not yet.

Still, the bulge in his pants gave her pause. The tailored black wool could barely contain him.

*In for a penny, in for a pound*, she thought, reaching over to cup him through the fabric. She began to massage him slowly, drawing a deep groan from the black-haired financier. He moved his hand from her lips, trailing it down to the red elastic hem of her dress, sliding his fingers towards her swollen, quivering heat. The surprise on his face when he discovered she wasn't wearing any panties made her smirk. She gave him a mischievous look and pressed her hips into his hand.

A sexy smile spread across his face as he parted her soft, wet lips and slipped a finger deep inside. Nancy gasped, tossing her head back in pleasure as he worked his thick digit in and out of her throbbing core.

"Look at me," he commanded.

Her head snapped forward, eyes locking with his, breath quickening. She clenched around him as he picked up the pace, their breathing syncing in a rhythm of heat and desire. A moan of ecstasy escaped her lips as he drove deeper and faster.

*No wonder he's so popular with women*, Nancy thought, losing herself in the waves crashing through her. Gasps burst from her with each thrust until, with a strangled cry, she climaxed—moaning low and long as pleasure coursed through her. Her eyes stayed fixed on his as he slowly withdrew his finger. He'd barely slipped out from underneath her dress when Nancy caught his hand and brought it to her lips, still holding his gaze. Then, without breaking eye contact, she wrapped her mouth around the finger that had just been inside her.

Now it was Barron's turn to groan.

She licked up and down his finger, alternating between sucking and deep-throating it until they were suddenly interrupted the sharp ring of a phone.

Nancy froze.

It was her ringtone.

She let his hand go and reached into her purse.

"Sorry," she said quickly, pulling out the phone and checking the screen. "Hello?" Nancy paused. "Oh my god," she said, voice suddenly panicked. "Okay, I will be right there." She ended the call and tossed the phone back into purse. Standing quickly, she tugged her dress back into place.

"Barron, I'm so sorry, but I have to go," she said breathless and apologetic.

He looked concerned. "Is everything alright?"

"No," she shook her head. "It's a lot to explain, but I have an elderly neighbour who I look out for—Mrs. Jones just called and she's at the hospital."

Barron stood up. "Can I help?"

Despite the fact that she was investigating him, Nancy was touched by the look of concern on his face. Barron wanted to help her—even though she was leaving him with seriously blue balls.

She gave him a sad smile and shook her head as she reached down to put on her shoes.

"That's very kind of you," she said straightening. "But I think that would complicate things."

She walked towards the door and Barron followed in hot pursuit.

"I had fun tonight," she smiled. "Thanks. Sorry I have to leave like this."

Barron placed his hand on her arm. She could still see his erection straining through his pants. Shame she had to leave him like that.

"Don't apologize. Just give me your number."

Nancy paused.

"How about I take yours?"

Barron looked taken aback. She was sure that he wasn't used to a woman taking control.

"Okay."

Nancy pulled out her phone and he rattled off his number.

She turned the handle on the door, slipped into the small elevator lobby and pressed the 'down' button. Barron walked out behind her and grabbed her hand.

"Hey," he said gently.

She turned to look at him before he drew her closer and

planted a tender kiss on her lips. His lips were pillow soft and it was the gentlest of kisses. It was a stark contrast to how dominating he was when they were starting to get hot and heavy. She melted into him.

When the elevator door opened, Nancy pulled away with a smile.

"Have a good night, Barron." She pressed 'G' and watched his lustful gaze as the doors slid shut. She typed up a quick "thank you for the drinks and company last night – L" text and scheduled it to send tomorrow afternoon.

One less thing for her to remember.

It was hard for Nancy (even harder for Benjamin by the looks of it) to turn down the handsome and dominant financier, but it was essential that she kept her pants on tonight—even if she had left her panties at home.

In addition to getting inside of his condo and getting a good look at his office, her other aim for the evening was to leave him wanting more. Well, that and to see what he was hiding under all of those clothes. And that, she had found out, indeed. He was hard-bodied with a tantalizing package that she would be delighted to find under the Christmas tree.

*Oh, Santa, you shouldn't have. My new favourite toy.*

*Mission accomplished*, she thought as the lift began its descent.

Barron was hooked.

And her neighbour? Cute old Mrs. Jones? She was elderly, yes. But infirm? Not even close. She was the only mother figure in Nancy's life and one of the few people who knew that she was a detective. Nancy gave her a monthly stipend for helping her out when needed. Nothing too onerous, usually just the odd phone call. The little old lady got a kick out of being able to help with Nancy's investigations. Mrs. Jones had told her that it brought a bit of excitement to her life.

After she had gone exploring Barron's condo, Nancy had texted Mrs. Jones with a request to call her in precisely twenty minutes. It was late for an older lady, but despite her advanced age, which was hovering somewhere in the seventies, Mrs. Jones was a night owl.

*Thanks Mrs. J!* she texted. *I will be over for coffee tomorrow morning.*

Nancy received a smiley emoji in reply. Mrs. Jones lived two doors down from her. She didn't have any family around and her husband, Mr. Jones, had passed away more than a decade ago.

She arrived home fifteen minutes later and quickly removed all of her makeup. Her purse and dress were strewn about on her dining room chair and her sky-high heels sat discarded just inside of the door. Despite the late hour and Nancy's fatigue, she wasn't about to drag herself to bed. She wanted to go over the photos that she had taken in Barron's office before calling it a night.

After uploading the pictures to her laptop, she zoomed in on the images that she had taken. There had been several scribblings on Barron's desk. One hastily written note referred to Barron's firm. Other scribblings, from what Nancy could deduce, appeared to reference the firm's different funds.

In all, the firm had eight funds that they were actively raising capital for—a lofty and atypical approach in the industry. It was a seedling of a company, having only been started by the brothers in the last year. Yet somehow, they had managed to launch eight funds, each with different specialties for individuals, companies, family offices, and organizations to invest in.

That was also unusual. Most firms focused on their niche and raised capital to invest in one specific asset. Sometimes it was real estate, sometimes it was companies—but the overarching theme was for the firm to narrow in on one asset or commodity and offer it to investors.

She wrote the funds down and put the paper aside for later with plans to do some more sleuthing on Theodore Benjamin. She didn't want to 'run into' him just yet, but she needed to familiarize herself with the man. She doubted he had the same personality as Barron, but she was pleased that he was identical in appearance.

Two Barrons. Be still her heart. What she wouldn't do to have a night with the two of them.

She thought back to Barron's big, capable hands rubbing up and down her body as he towered over top of her. She had gotten off, yes, and she did feel a bit bad about leaving him hanging, but she knew that the allure of the chase would soon pay off in dividends, to use an appropriate financial term.

## CHAPTER 5

"Nancy!" Mrs. Jones pulled her door open with a forceful manner that contradicted her advanced age.

"Hi, Mrs. Jones," Nancy smiled at her neighbour. "Do you have time for tea?"

"Of course!" Mrs. Jones opened the door a little wider and beckoned Nancy in. The little old lady was a flurry in bright florals, and Nancy followed her to her kitchen. The condo mirrored Nancy's—it was a two-bedroom with an open layout, kitchen with an island, a dining room table with seating for six and a spacious living room. But the layout was where the similarities ended. Where Nancy's condo was minimalist and done up in dark tones with white accents, modern art and designs, Mrs. Jones's condo was squishy furniture, lace doilies, and chock-full of knick-knacks and photos of her and her late husband. The couple never had children, but they had spent several years taking in foster children, some of whom were still in touch.

Cupboards banged closed and dishes clanged together as Mrs. Jones busied herself in the kitchen with preparing the tea. In any other situation, Nancy would have offered to help, but she knew by now that Mrs. Jones would accept no help and valued her independence. So she took a seat at the antique oak table instead.

The chalky, high-pitched clink of porcelain pierced the air as Mrs. Jones placed the cups and saucers on the table before she returned with the steaming kettle. Nancy wrapped her hands around the mug and let the warmth from the liquid soak into her hands. Her neighbour took a seat across from her and Nancy watched as the teabag seeped into her cup.

"Well?" Mrs. Jones said expectantly. "Don't keep me waiting! What was last night?"

Nancy grinned. "Last night," she pulled the tea bag up and lightly dunked it up and down into the water. "Last night I was with one of the city's most eligible bachelors." Mrs. Jones looked delighted. "At least according to *Toronto Life*."

"Is it a case?" The elderly lady was eager.

"It is." Nancy couldn't share all of the details but she could share enough to keep the older lady entertained. She felt like Mrs. Jones's own personal gossip site. "Tall, dark, handsome, and a banker."

A glimmer of excitement danced in Mrs. Jones's eyes.

Nancy went on. "Muscles like a boxer and stomach like a washboard—he's an irresistible mix of perfect gentleman and bad-boy financier."

"Did he put the moves on you?" Her neighbour looked elated.

Pausing for dramatic effect, Nancy took a careful sip of her tea and set her cup down gently.

"Let's just say that we made it to third base," she allowed a sly smirk and Mrs. Jones broke into a fit of giggles. Nancy loved this part—she knew that the old lady didn't get out much and hearing about Nancy's escapades brightened up her day.

They spent the next forty-five minutes sharing stories and swapping building gossip.

"You know Leslie Richards?" Mrs. Jones asked. Nancy nodded. "She went to the rooftop yesterday and forgot Muffin up there."

Nancy was surprised—Leslie, a long-haired, sixty-year-old

vision in glitter who lived two floors above them, was never seen without her dog, Muffin. She couldn't imagine the poor corgi stranded eighteen floors up in the heat of the sun.

"But it was okay," her neighbour continued, "someone called security. They went upstairs to sunbathe and found Muffin swimming in the pool alone with not a human being in sight," Mrs. Jones took a sip of her tea. "Leslie claims she had an emergency, but I have it on good authority that the 'emergency' was one of the men on that cougar dating app that she uses."

Nancy burst out laughing.

"Poor Muffin," Mrs. Jones shook her head. "Kicked to the curb so that Leslie could get her rocks off."

She left her neighbour shortly after with a promise to keep the little old lady updated on the case and to let her know if there was any way that she could help. Mrs. Jones, bless her heart, said that she was going to bake cookies that afternoon and that she would leave some at Nancy's door. Nancy, for her part, was headed to her office. She had one client that she needed to get dominatrix-ready for and then for the rest of the day, she was working on Ms. Fineberg's case. Aside from any potential dirty business dealings, Barron Benjamin had her intrigued and she needed to formulate a plan to find out more about his brother.

She gathered up the designated bag for her dominatrix work after a quick stop inside her condo. Typically, she did her makeup and got into her latex and leather when she was at The Cell. She brought her outfits home for washing and then brought whatever outfit she wanted to wear that day with her. The Cell was only a few blocks away and no one was any the wiser as to what was in her nylon blue Longchamp bag.

With most women there would be the essentials—credit cards, lipstick, Advil, tissues, and a book. With Nancy, the essentials were a little bit different—shiny, skin-tight latex suits, blindfolds, and restraints. Sometimes she liked to bring her accessories home and play. Although she had had a dry spell ever since she had started therapy. With men, she was always the dominant. The only time she had ever been submissive was with her ex, Jamie. There was something about him that made her want to submit to him in every way possible. Outside of the bedroom they behaved as equals, but once their clothes came off, Nancy was deferential and obedient. She loved it. She craved it. The feeling of Jamie having total control pushed her over the edge. During sex, there was nothing that he would be denied, and Nancy was eager to acquiesce to it. The orgasms that she had with him were out of this world. After sex, he was as sweet as could be. Holding her close, caressing her. Letting her know, through his touch, how much he cared about her—it was an attentiveness that she had found endearing.

She shook away the thought.

It had been seven months since she had last seen Jamie, but the wound felt as raw as if the breakup were yesterday.

Not that it had really been so much as even a breakup.

They had been fighting a lot the month it happened, which was just past the three-year mark of their anniversary. Nancy wanted to settle down together—whatever that meant—and Jamie just kept refusing. She wanted to cohabitate and share their lives together, but he didn't see it the same way. In his late thirties, Jamie still wanted to sow his wild oats, and he didn't want anyone or anything to tie him down. As a successful tech entrepreneur with a GQ face and personality to match, he could have had any woman he wanted. For a time, Nancy had thought that *she* was what he wanted.

But, alas.

After their last argument, on the phone, where Nancy had expressed her frustration at the state of their relationship, Jamie had started yelling. She yelled back and both of them said awful, heat-of-the-moment kinds of things that they didn't mean. Upset over their never-ending battles, Nancy had uttered the verbal coup de grace and Jamie had hung up on her.

She had poured herself a stiff drink after that, cried for a bit, and then went to bed. When she woke up the next morning, she was ready to make amends, ashamed that she had let her emotions take control. But before she steeled herself to pick up the phone and apologize, she had received a call from her concierge. There were some packages downstairs for her. Several boxes that had just arrived.

Perplexed, given that she hadn't ordered anything, Nancy had quickly gone downstairs, half expecting to see a bouquet of apology flowers and Craig's Cookies from Jamie. Instead, she discovered several boxes full of her belongings that she had kept at Jamie's place.

In public, she made a rule of being stoic, but in that moment, the fortress that she had built around her feelings failed and the poor concierge had front row tickets to her downfall. The next few days she had spent in a haze. Life was happening all around her, but Nancy felt like she was stuck on pause. All of her ensuing calls, texts, and emails to Jamie had remained unanswered, and two weeks after the breakup, she had received a text message from one of her close friends. It was a picture of Jamie. In Mykonos, holding hands with a tall, thin, blonde in a barely-there bikini.

Nancy's resulting spiral was what had spurred her into the Addicts Anonymous meetings. She had gone on a drinking bender and a casual sex spree that would put a player to shame. She wasn't sure if it was to heal her hurt, punish herself, or just feel something aside from sad. Every time a memory of him would pop into her head she would crumble—the scab ripping away from the barely healed wound he had inflicted upon her. She had tried her best to keep herself composed enough to ensure her businesses stayed afloat, but it was a struggle. As a dominatrix she became more steely, and as a detective she became more focused. It was when she drank herself into oblivion and hit the bars that the true damage was really revealed.

Seven months later, Jamie rarely entered her thoughts, although when he did, it was like a punch to her stomach that left her feeling ill. It was crazy that he could still do that to her so many months later. But she knew that the best thing to do when Jamie popped into her mind was distract, distract, distract.

When the lock to the back-alley door of her dungeon clicked open, she had already fallen out of the Jamie headspace. She had a client coming in one hour and there was work to do before then. The space, which was outfitted into what looked like a modern-day torture chamber, was kept neat and clean, which was exactly how she liked it. Her client that morning, Wyatt, was into getting caned.

She pulled the shackles out of her Longchamp purse and placed them on the long wooden table that Wyatt would be strapped to shortly. Then, she made sure that all of her gear was in place before she headed for her office at the back of the room and got into costume. She favoured a heavily made-up black eyelid when she was doing her domme work. Her lips would be painted a candy-apple red and a black latex mask would cover most of her face. A ponytail, placed up high near the crown of her head, shot through the top of her latex mask and lent an even more severe look to the outfit. A latex bodysuit—long-sleeved and legless—hugged her torso, which was complemented with fishnet tights and thigh-high boots with stiletto heels. Ten minutes before Wyatt was slated to arrive, she went around the dungeon and lit candles before turning the lights down low. A short time later, there was a knock at the door, and Wyatt walked inside. He stood just inside the door with his head was down, as Nancy instructed all of her clients to do. They wouldn't speak to her unless spoken to, and they would do exactly as she said.

"Wyatt," Nancy purred as she walked towards him with a cane in her hand before sharply changing her tone. "Clothes off."

Wyatt was in his late forties and had curling brown hair and a bit of a beer gut. Obediently he began removing his clothes, starting with his shoes. Seconds later he was standing in front of her imposing latex form with his eyes downcast, buck-ass naked.

Nancy was Wyatt's first domme experience and he had been a fast learner. She walked around his naked body and tapped the cane against the floor, rhythmically interspersing the clacking sound from her high heels. He stood there and flinched as she forcefully smacked him with the cane and circled around hitting his calves, thighs, knees, buttocks, back, pelvis, arms, and shoulders.

She stood back and surveyed her handiwork. There were red marks all over Wyatt's body where the cane had connected with his flesh. Not too soft, not too hard. There was a Goldilocks Zone when it came to BDSM and Nancy knew how to get it just right.

Wyatt's gaze was still downcast, but she could tell from the energy he was exuding that he was excited.

"Get on the table," she commanded in a steely voice.

Nancy always liked this part. The part where she got to bark out orders and exercise control. It helped her when she felt out of control in certain areas of her life. Like that old saying went, "the best way to get over someone is to get under someone", for Nancy, the best way to deal with a lack of control was to exert it. And right now, with regards to Ms. Fineberg's case, she wasn't out of control, but she didn't feel in control either. Especially when it came to Barron.

A crack exploded in the air and Wyatt let out a painful grunt. He had been taking too long to follow her orders so Nancy had given him a good whack on the back of his thighs. Wyatt, for his part, sped up and climbed onto the wooden plank.

"Thank you, Mistress," he mumbled, as he lay down on the smooth wood.

"Good boy." Nancy approached him and gave a gentle whack to each of his limbs so that they were spread appropriately for her to secure them to the table. As she yanked the buckles tight, she taunted her client.

"You poor, pathetic piece of trash," she said sardonically before standing back and surveying him.

Naked and vulnerable on the wooden slab, Wyatt begged for

her approval. He craved not only the sting of the cane but also the sharp edge of verbal humiliation. As a *RuPaul's Drag Race* fan, Nancy would admit that her insults weren't entirely organic. But nor were they entirely borrowed either. Modification was key, given her goal was to humiliate rather than have her client doubled over in laughter.

"Please, Mistress," Wyatt pleaded until Nancy silenced him with a sharp smack of her cane near his groin.

Wyatt's cries echoed around the room with every strike and Nancy allowed herself a small smile.

She loved this feeling of being in control. Savoured it.

*

Later, in her detective's office, a totally different-looking version of Nancy sat at her desk. Her high ponytail from The Cell was now low and loose; all traces of her heavy domme makeup was washed off, replaced instead by concealer and a simple swipe of mascara on her top lashes. If one of her clients from The Cell ever walked into her office on the other side of the building, they would never recognize her. She would deny any knowledge of the business there. A dungeon? A dominatrix? How odd. She had no idea—the two offices were completely closed off from each other.

On her computer, she pulled up the pictures that she had snapped in Barron's office and looked at them again. She had mapped out the eight different funds that the brothers were raising capital for as well as the targeted amount that they had for each. Amongst the various other scribblings that had been on Barron's desk were two phone numbers and two names: Aaron W. and Kerry Killen. A quick search revealed that Kerry was the head of a large family office for the Shudalls—a billionaire family that had made their fortune in construction. That made sense. Kerry was either an investor in the fund—which seemed unlikely given that her name was scribbled down on a notepad and not, presumably, in Barron's contacts—or, more likely, she was a lead Barron was pursuing.

Aaron W. was a different matter. There was a phone number

beneath his name that had a Toronto area code, but none of her advanced internet skills helped her to figure out who Aaron W. was. The phone number merely showed up as the contact information for a numbered company. In Nancy's experience, the numbered company was likely a holding company—typically used as a shell company to shield the investor from various things—taxes, visibility, responsibility.

She had seen this tactic before—in a case where an ex-husband was trying to weasel his way out of paying for child support. His ex-wife, Moira, had come to Nancy hoping to find out what her lawyers could not—where all of the money had gone. The man claimed to be penniless, but he was living lavishly—driving a Porsche, flying private, and shelling out thousands on his new girlfriend.

The case had given Nancy a crash course in financial forensics, which had proved invaluable. Most of her clients were wealthy and where there was wealth, there were people looking to find ways to hide it. With some tech work, she had discovered exactly what Moira's ex-husband had done: the self-described 'momma's boy' had hidden his cash in several shell companies, all controlled—at least on paper—by his mother.

The judge in their divorce case was pissed, to put it mildly. Moira had walked away with more than half of his assets and child support payments of nearly two-and-a-half times higher than initially requested. To top it off, her ex-husband had been named and shamed in the news, and his Bay Street reputation was left in ruins.

All in a day's work.

Nancy scribbled a 'to do' list.

*1. Get a look inside of Clover Capital—talk to staff if possible.*

*2. Start surveillance on Theodore.*

*3. Check with Angus about the brothers.*

She sat back and sighed before picking up her phone and sending off a text.

What she had uncovered about the Benjamin brothers and their glossy private equity firm was still anyone's guess. Elena

Fineberg had seemed uncertain and almost reluctant to have Nancy dig into Clover Capital and the handsome duo behind it. But Nancy had a niggling feeling that Elena was onto something.

Elena was sharp. She was a smart and successful woman with a no-nonsense head on her shoulders. She was not the type to be rattled with no reason. If something felt off to her about the firm, it probably was. With enough digging Nancy believed that the story would eventually come out. There was a reason why the cliché about trusting your gut existed. Oftentimes, it turned out to be correct. The truth was just a little matter of investigation.

## CHAPTER 6

*Time for a quick chat?* She sent off a text.

A reply came in minutes later: *For you, always.*

A short smile passed Nancy's lips and she hit the 'call' button on her cell.

Angus MacDonald, her source at Toronto Police Services, was a one-time potential boyfriend who had turned into a full-time friend. He worked in the I.T. department at the cop shop and his slight bending-of-the-rules had helped Nancy in more cases than she could count. It wasn't that she asked him to do anything illegal. Unethical, maybe. But he had offered her his services any time she needed. And if it helped her to catch a bad guy, then, as someone who was sworn to serve and protect, he was willing to lend a hand. Nancy never abused the privilege and usually went to Angus as a last resort. This time, she was reaching out to him first. It would be helpful for her to know if either of the brothers had ever had any kind of difficulties with the law, and to get a full background check on the duo.

"Good morning, my gorgeous friend," Angus's melodious voice came through the speaker of her phone.

"Hi, Angus," she smiled back. "Thanks for chatting. I need your help with something."

She went on to describe what she was looking for, leaving

out the specifics of the case.

"No problem-o," he replied. Nancy could hear typing in the background. "Barron and Theodore Benjamin." The keyboard clicking continued and Angus let out a short whistle.

"Is there a lot there?" she asked.

"There isn't a lot, but what is there is . . interesting. Can you meet me at Fran's at 3:30 p.m.?" he asked.

She looked at the time on her computer—it was just past noon: "Perfect. See you then."

"Great," Angus replied. "Looking forward to it."

Nancy pressed the 'end call' button and crossed off item number three on her to-do list.

Just then her phone pinged and a text message from Barron appeared on her screen.

*Larissa, I had a great time last night. When can we do it again?*

A smile spread across her face, which, she was dismayed to realize, was accompanied by a few butterflies.

That wasn't good.

But what *was* good was that it had only been ten minutes since her pre-scheduled text had been sent and Barron was already calling. Well, texting. But still. It meant that she had left a favorable impression. She put her phone down. There was time enough to respond to Barron later. Nancy didn't want him thinking that she was too eager.

She spent the next few hours digging into Clover Capital. Their website was run-of-the-mill finance. Bland, stock photos, blank spaces, and buzz-words touting the firm's mission, values, and expertise. She scanned the 'About' section.

*Clover Capital is a client-centered investment firm that delivers exemplary returns from a broad range of businesses. Founded in 2024 by prominent financiers Barron and Theodore Benjamin, with more than 50 years of combined experience, Clover Capital invests in some of the most advanced technology, pharmaceutical, and infrastructure, which is exclusively available to Clover Capital's select set of clients.*

Nancy clicked 'Meet our Team' and scanned through the employee photos. The firm was smaller than she had expected.

For some reason she had assumed that to be raising the kind of money that the twins were, they would need a large outfit. But aside from Barron and Theodore, they had two analysts, one associate, and one administrative assistant. The two analysts, Josh and Brian, looked young—she clicked on each of their bios. Both analysts were graduates of prestigious business programs who had interned at two of the big banks before being hired by Clover Capital. The administrative assistant looked too uptight to have any loose lips, and the associate looked a little too wizened for her to pull out her sexual charms. But Josh and Brian?

Easy marks.

They were both young and just starting out in their careers. Their photos revealed a youthful hint of naivety. Nancy knew that they were likely enjoying the fruits of their chosen career path and would probably be receptive to an attractive woman. She took a screenshot of their photos and saved them in her 'Benjamins' folder.

Three hours later, having scoured the internet for all of the background information she could find on the firm and the people who worked there, she texted Barron back.

*I had a great time last night too,* she wrote. *I'm free this Friday.*

Stretching out the date that they would meet she knew would build up the anticipation on Barron's end. Although if she was honest with herself, she was looking forward to spending another night with him. Not that she planned to sleep over. As much as the man gave her butterflies, she wasn't even sure if she would sleep with him. Butterflies were a dangerous territory for her to tread.

*

She spotted the back of Angus's head in the back corner booth that he typically chose as their meeting place. Fran's was close to the police station he worked at, but not close enough that he would run into any colleagues. Which was perfect for today's purposes. On occasion they ventured out to other locales, but Fran's Diner would always be their spot. The milkshakes were thick, the fries were greasy, and there was a thin film of grime on the floor—it was a classic diner. Burgers, shakes, fries, warm apple pie; coffee that looked and tasted like sludge; and no nonsense wait staff who took orders and didn't take any bullshit—a trait that came in handy given the restaurant was open twenty-four hours a day and often catered to the inebriated bar crowd.

She gave Angus a gentle pat on the shoulder as she passed and slid into the booth across from him. The squishy green plastic stuck to her bare legs, and she inwardly cringed realizing her fashion faux pas. It was a warm summer day, which necessitated shorts. But at Fran's, you didn't want any of your extremities touching the seats without a buffer layer of clothing. The general consensus amongst people was that the restaurant hadn't had a good wipe-down since at least the turn of the 21st century. Not that the filth served as a crowd deterrent. What the diner lacked in cleanliness, it made up for in character and food.

She pushed the thought of the grimy booth to the back of her mind and made a mental note to give her legs a good sanitizing when she left.

"Nancy!" Angus's brooding brown eyes lit up at the sight of his friend.

"What do you have for me, Angus?" A slight smile slid across her face.

"I have a Diet Coke and French fries," he quipped with a grin.

She let out a laugh. "You know me too well."

Seconds later a white-aproned waitress appeared with two Diet Cokes. They stayed silent until she walked away, with the only sound coming from the other diners and the fizzing of their drinks.

"So?" she urged her companion.

In reply, Angus took a long sip of his drink.

"I love the soda here," he mused. "There's something about it that tastes different."

"It's probably the fifteen years of black mold buildup in the soda fountain," she quipped.

Angus nearly spit his drink out and started coughing.

"You were saying?" Nancy raised one of her eyebrows.

"Sorry, Nance," he spluttered with a grin. "You know I like to tease you." He sat up a little straighter in the booth and pushed his drink away. "Okay, the Benjamin brothers—Theodore and Barron," he paused dramatically. "As I'm sure you've already discovered, they're both very successful businessmen. They're highly educated and run in wealthy circles."

Nancy nodded. These were all things that she had discovered herself.

"As far as anything to do with the law is concerned," Angus continued. "They are both clean. Neither of them has a criminal record."

Nancy let out a breath she hadn't realized she was holding.

That was good news at least. Not that a criminal record or something popping up on a background check would have necessarily meant anything nefarious. A parking ticket hardly constituted shady behaviour—as the recipient of two in the past, Nancy could certainly attest to that. But Angus *had* said that he had found something interesting.

"So, what *did* you find?" she was on the edge of her seat.

"It seems that Theodore has been known to travel in some . . ." Angus paused while searching for the appropriate word. "Questionable circles."

Nancy waited for him to continue. There were a few circles she could think of that would constitute 'questionable'. Mafia, gangs, cartels. Her Tuesday night therapy sessions, if she was being honest. There wouldn't be too many people who could argue with that if they had attended any of their meetings.

"He's a big gambler," her friend continued. "It looks like he got himself into a bit of a bad spot a few years ago with an underground gambling ring run by the Mob."

Now this, *this* was interesting.

As a successful financier, Teddy would have to have been

gambling obscene amounts of money in order for him to end up in a bad spot. Which did put one curious piece into the puzzle. While Barron had an addiction to women, it looked like his twin had an addiction to gambling. Which could spell big trouble if he had found himself in debt, unable to pay it personally, and in control of tens of millions of dollars of investor money.

"How did you find this out?" she questioned. Nancy had done a thorough background check on each of the brothers into the far recesses of the internet. But she hadn't stopped there. She had looked at their university and work records, found photos of them at friends' weddings, had looked at the social media profiles of those friends and colleagues, and dug into their respective backgrounds. In all her hours of research, there was nothing that had indicated that Teddy had Mob connections and a penchant for big-money gambling.

"I, uh . . ." Angus looked a bit abashed.

*Oh no*, she thought to herself. She hoped like hell that Angus hadn't gotten himself mixed up in illegal gambling. *Especially* given his job with the Toronto Police Service.

"Nothing illegal," Angus assured her after seeing her look of concern. "I happen to have some . . ." He paused again, searching for the right word. "Acquaintances who deal in . . . underground activities."

"Underground activities?" Nancy repeated in a skeptical tone.

Angus nodded. His brow had furrowed a bit.

"Less than savoury, but nothing I'm part of. What my acquaintances do on their own time is their business, but . . . ," he trailed off.

"But you figured you would ask around."

He nodded his head indicating that her logic, so far, was sound. "Correct. *But*," he said with emphasis, "I only asked around because, while both brothers had no criminal records, there was something unusual about Theodore." Angus took a sip of his Diet Coke and continued, "There was a report filed by a Theodore Benjamin with the same birthdate and same home address as the one you're investigating."

"And?" she asked eagerly. Angus was really drawing it out on this one.

"One year ago, Theodore Benjamin called in to the police and reported that he was being harassed by two men. He said they were staking out his home and were sending him threatening voicemails and text messages. When he was interviewed they asked him about any illegal dealings or activities he might be involved in but he denied any wrongdoing. It was suspicious because the messages he was getting alluded to him owing money, but Theodore never budged on his story. The police went to his house, saw the two guys in the vehicle and went to talk to them. They denied being the ones sending the messages and denied even knowing Theodore. Said they had pulled over after getting lost and were just trying to figure out how to get to their friend's place.

"In the end, nothing ever came of it because the police couldn't prove those two were leaving the threatening messages. And if Theodore did owe them money, neither of them would cop to what it was for or how much. Hell, they wouldn't even cop to *knowing* Theodore Benjamin or knowing of him."

Nancy sat back in the booth and mulled this over. It was an interesting development and she wasn't sure if it fit into the case and, if so, how.

"The report," Angus continued, "detailed the officer's suspicion that there may have been some illegal activity involved. But without any evidence and without Theodore wanting to press charges, there wasn't anything they could do. Plus," he added as an afterthought, "the police usually don't want to deal with the rich—they can make things difficult. So even if there *was* anything going on, the police would stay far from it even if it was served up on a silver platter on their doorstep."

"How do your acquaintances fit into this?" Nancy asked.

"Well," he said sheepishly. "One of them is a friend of my cousin's, and he let slip a while back that he's part of an underground ring. He said it was mostly men and mostly wealthy, anonymous types whose names I wouldn't recognize. I'd forgotten all about it until you asked me to run a check on Barron and Theodore. I called up Ritchie—that's my cousin's friend—and asked him about the betting ring."

Nancy could see where this was going.

"He's in Mexico right now on vacation and was totally blasted. I asked him if he knew whether Barron or Theodore Benjamin had ever been a part of the illegal gambling. He said, and I quote: 'Shit, yeah, man! Teddy Benjamin's been betting on sports for years.'" Angus paused at the look on Nancy's face. "I know what you're thinking, Nance," he said seriously. "Trust me, Ritchie was so sloshed on Mai Tais, he won't even remember his own name tomorrow."

"Okay," she nodded her head. Angus knew she hated having other people know what she was working on or having them asking around on her behalf, but there was nothing that could be done about it now. And besides, the information that Angus had given her could prove to be invaluable. Illegal sports betting. That *was* interesting.

Was it just Teddy or was Barron involved in it too? If the Mob had been harassing Teddy, then logic dictated that it was only him they were after. Unless Barron had shut down their harassment of him another way. And wouldn't it just be convenient for the playboy financiers to open up a private equity firm that could bring in tens of millions while they were in debt to the Mafioso? But Ritchie hadn't mentioned Barron, so maybe he wasn't part of it. And maybe underground gambling had nothing to do with the case at all.

She was getting ahead of herself. Speculation was fine and it could lead to some useful avenues, but it was still just that. At the end of the day, what she needed was cold, hard evidence. With this bit of information, things definitely felt like they were heating up.

"That's interesting," Nancy murmured, repeating the word that Angus had used when he had first asked her to meet up. "Very interesting."

# CHAPTER 7

This week's Addicts Anonymous meeting consisted of the same group as the week before so they did away with the introductions. In spite of herself, Nancy had dressed up this evening and was wearing a black mini-dress with puff sleeves and a low-cut neckline. Maybe not the best choice when you were meeting with a group of addicts, two of whom had a difficult time keeping it in their pants. For some reason, the sad, cement building that housed their meetings looked particularly dreary today. When Nancy breezed through the faded lilac door, Eric was the first thing that caught her eye.

*Damn.* Surfer boy was looking fine today. His hair draped messily around his shoulders and the long-sleeved blue shirt that he was wearing hugged his muscles in all of the right places.

He gave her a wide, impish grin.

"Hi, Nancy."

Despite herself, she smirked back.

"Hi." She looked around. "Are we early or is everyone else late?"

She took a seat next to him despite her better judgment. There were some people who just oozed sex appeal and Eric was one of them. Sitting next to him was like seating a crack addict next to a stack of their favourite supply.

"So, what's your deal?" he asked casually as she slung her purse on the arm of the chair.

She took a second to remember the rules of AA: No specifics. She had to silently remind herself that they were there to help each other deal with their addiction, not make friends or bedfellows.

"My deal?" she realized that she hadn't told any stories or talked about herself during last week's meeting. Come to think of it, she hadn't talked about herself at *any* of the meetings except for her first one. And even then she hadn't divulged much. Whether it was due to wanting to keep her cards close to her chest or because she still wasn't sold on the whole thing, she didn't know.

Eric raised his eyebrows and tilted his head downwards, encouraging her to continue. Before she could deflect, she heard the door open to their right and they both looked towards it expectantly.

"Hi, guys," Rhys walked into the room with his backpack in tow.

She sent up a silent prayer that Carmella would appear soon and put a stop to, what she anticipated would be, Rhys's pre-meeting brag-fest. What Rhys needed wasn't a weekly meeting where he could indulge in story-telling about his sex-capades—he needed the Betty Ford equivalent for whores.

Nancy knew that referring to Rhys or Theo as 'whores' would be wholly frowned upon by their therapist, but when she was using her internal dialogue, she couldn't help it. And besides, she wasn't going to censor her thoughts just because Carmella would find them offensive. If anything, Carmella should be offended by the revelations the weekly platform she provided Rhys enabled. She was actually surprised that they didn't have a larger audience. If the group wasn't anonymous and if there weren't people there genuinely looking for help and who had kept their addiction a secret from their friends and family, Nancy could see the stories drawing in tens of people each meeting. Why pay to read erotic fiction or *Penthouse* when you could come to the once-a-week equivalent of amateur porn-reading night.

"—story tonight." Lost in her thoughts, she only caught the tail end of what Rhys said and realized he was looking at her.

"Sorry, what was that?"

"I said I've got a great story tonight," he repeated as a bead of sweat rolled down the side of his head from the closely cropped sandy hair that brushed the top of his tanned forehead.

It was a mystery just *how* Rhys managed to bed so many women. She supposed that if you weren't particularly choosy . . . although it baffled the mind to think of just how many not particularly choosy women there apparently were in the city.

Carmella, thankfully, showed up shortly after and cut Rhys's story preview short. Nancy mostly zoned out during the group chat that night, but a few times she was broken out of her trance when she felt Eric's gaze trained on her. Each time, she met him with an answering look and his eyes lingered on hers for a second—twinkling with just a hint of flirtation before he moved his attention back to the pleasure-seeking speaker at hand.

Nancy wasn't sure what it was about him. She didn't find Eric particularly interesting. He had shared a story about himself at the previous meeting and it was a garden-variety sort. The blandest tale-as-old-as-time: his relationship had been less than satisfying, both in the bedroom and out of it, and, instead of dealing with his problems, he had turned to porn. OnlyFans, to be specific.

He wasn't braggadocious like Rhys and he wasn't shy about his addiction like some of the other men. He was matter of fact about what had led him to the group and what he had hoped to get out of it.

"I found the group online and thought that it would be helpful to have people to talk to," he said bluntly. "There's no one in my friend group who knows about this and I haven't told anyone in my family." He shifted in his seat. "I want to deal with this on my own."

When Carmella gently prompted him to tell the group more

about what made him realize he had an addiction, Eric was candid.

"I realized that I wasn't interested in sex with my girlfriend anymore. She could walk around naked and I would be glued to my phone."

The group nodded at him in understanding.

"She finally left me two months ago," he said with a slight nod. "I didn't care at first. I only came to terms with it a couple of weeks ago and realized that I need to do something."

Compared to what Nancy had heard from the rest of the group, Eric's story was pretty tame. Aside from keeping several OnlyFans creators in business and his girlfriend leaving him, all in all, it didn't sound so bad. And she had to admire the fact that he had found his way to the group all on his own. Some of the people there had gone at the urging of their therapist. Some, as an ultimatum from their wives and girlfriends, and in Theo's case, his employer.

She shook herself out of her reverie as she felt Eric's gaze on her once again. This time when she shot him a discreet glance back, she raised one of her eyebrows in question. The side of Eric's mouth twitched in what she was sure was him trying to temper a smirk before he turned his focus back to the speaker at hand.

"All right, thanks everyone!" Carmella smiled in her perky manner a few minutes later. "See you all next week!"

Nancy absent-mindedly grabbed for her purse near the floor when she felt something slip into her hand. Glancing down, she saw the hand that had slipped what appeared to be a card into her palm was tanned and attached to a muscly arm with a dusting of sun-bleached hair.

Eric.

A brief glance at the paper before she clenched her fist around it revealed a business card.

Naughty Eric. That was definitely against the rules and she was going to dispose of the evidence as soon as she left the meeting.

"See you next time, Nancy," said Eric.

She answered with a brief smile and then headed for the door. In her vehicle, she took a closer look at Eric's business card. Real estate. She was surprised that surfer boy had a career. He gave off the air of someone who took on odd jobs and spent his days smoking weed at the beach. The urge to keep the card was strong. Though she had vowed to toss it in the garbage as soon as Eric was out of sight, she found herself sliding it into one of the slots in her wallet.

It was ironic, really, as she thought more about Eric's attempt at getting attention. Going to a meeting meant to curb unhealthy urges and being tempted by another attendee.

She didn't look back as she peeled out of the parking space and headed for home.

*

Back at her condo, she scoured the web searching for any sign of illegal sports betting in Toronto. She wasn't looking for a website and building location, per se, but for any hints from online posters on Reddit, X, and similar sites about where some of these outfits might operate. It was relatively easy to find someone—a person, place, a thing—on the internet. But those rules changed if that person, place, or thing didn't want to be found. There was something almost eerie about it. Odd when she considered that Google had only existed for about twenty-five years. Prior to that, unless someone was in the news, a politician, or in the entertainment industry, anonymity abounded. And for the Mob, quietness and anonymity were key, which meant that all of her internet searches came up empty. She hadn't expected much, but there was still a slim chance that someone would slip up or mention something in passing on one of the social media sites. People were nothing if not infallible.

Defeated on the illegal gambling avenue of inquiry, next she Googled the Canadian Mob families. Background research was always good when you weren't entirely sure what you were getting into—her knowledge of the Canadian Mafia wouldn't even fill half a page. She spent an hour combing through news articles, Wikipedia pages, and X posts, learning more about the Italian families who had made Toronto their playground. It seemed that most of them had similar money-making rackets—drug trafficking, illegal gambling, loan sharking, murder, and extortion. Typical run-of-the-mill activities for a particular set of Sicilians.

Given the way the chips had fallen with Elena's case, illegal gambling and loan sharking was, obviously, what she was most interested in. But, aside from specifics about jail terms, charges, and mugshots, none of the news articles or social media posts *about* the news articles were enlightening. To dig up more dirt, she wanted to get on the inside—go underground and move amongst the mafioso crowd. Unfortunately, it wasn't as easy as picking up a shovel and going to Google Maps for directions. Until, that is, she came across a curious news piece that opened up a whole world of possibilities. It was a little-known oddity in the city, it seemed, what one of the Mafia's biggest money-making schemes happened to be. It sounded strange at first, but made a lot of sense when Nancy thought about it. And it was something easy for her to observe.

She looked at the clock. Quarter to seven. Late, but not too late. And definitely not too late for what she had in mind.

Thirty minutes later she was driving westbound on the Gardiner. A long stretch of empty road in front of her provided the perfect opportunity to execute her plan and she moved over to the right shoulder of the expressway, putting her car in park, and turning on her hazards. Before she left home, she had saved a couple of phone numbers in her mobile. Now she pulled one up and hit 'Call'. A short phone conversation and ten impossibly short minutes later and a gruff but handsome tow-truck driver was on hand.

*AAA Towing* was emblazoned in red letters across the door of his truck. Simple logo, simple company name, and, she was sure, simple way to get some dirt on what was going on.

The white tow truck was parked just ahead of her vehicle, its red brake lights glowing as black clouds of smoke wafted upwards from the exhaust. The driver's door slammed shut as cars on the freeway whizzed past and the driver, sporting a two-day beard, a dusty blue jumpsuit, and sun-kissed skin, made his way back to her vehicle. Despite the proximity of the high-speed vehicles flying past him, the tow-truck driver seemed unfazed as he approached the driver's side door.

She had read about the racket online—whispers of illegal activities in the towing industry prompted a reporter to go undercover for several months to investigate. Essentially, the Mob had their hands in every facet of the road-side assistance industry. They charged upwards of $500 for a tow and then thousands of dollars per day to keep a vehicle in the impound lot . . . of which there were many. A tow-truck driver would drop off the broken-down vehicle in one yard and then they would transfer it to multiple different yards while the owner of the vehicle went on a wild goose chase to try and track it down. When the owner finally tracked down his vehicle, the holding fees for sitting in the tow yard typically approached the double-digit thousands.

It was quite the setup. Typical for the Mob in that it took from the little guy and made the Made Men thousands, but atypical for the Mob in its choice of racket. Tow-truck driving? It seemed absurd. But Nancy also knew that if there was money to be made in absurdity, someone would find it. And sometimes there was genius in the bizarre.

Either way, according to what she had read in the article, tow trucking was working for the criminals. Ballpark estimates had the crime families taking in upwards of $10 million in any given year and the best part? Their enterprise was entirely legal.

Maybe not the murders and money-laundering that was reported to have gone on during trucking industry turf wars, but the business itself was solid.

Nancy rolled down her window when the driver reached her door.

"You called for a tow?" the tow-truck man asked, wiping his brow and shooting Nancy a smile.

"Yes," she nodded with a smile. "Thanks for getting here so quickly."

"No problem," he said watching as a car whizzed closely past. "That's what we're here for. I'll just have to ask you to step out of the vehicle."

Nancy obliged and headed to the shoulder while watching the man hook up her SUV. They exchanged small talk and the man was evasive when she asked which impound yard he was taking her vehicle to.

"Sorry, Miss," he said as he hooked up one of her tires with some sort of pulley. "I won't know until I'm on the road. We radio dispatch and they tell us where there's space. But I'll give you the number to call," he added as an afterthought.

A fake smile bloomed on Nancy's face. She could see right through him. *I'll bet you will, Gary.* She glanced at his nametag. "Thanks."

Standing on the passenger side of the road while the gruff man fiddled with the driver's side tires, Nancy dug around in her purse for a moment before she discreetly pulled out an AirTag. With magnetized accessories, of course. She kept it hidden in her hand and wandered to the front of the truck—a bored and stranded driver ostensibly checking out her mechanical saviour—before finding a perfect spot for the GPS tracker. A quick glance over at the driver showed his head still bent down, fiddling with the tires of her vehicle. In one quick movement she pressed it on the underside of a metal part of the towing platform.

Before she had left home, she had also left an AirTag in her own vehicle. A call to dispatch was something she wouldn't need to make, nor would she have to go on a wild-goose chase to find her car.

After Gary took off she climbed into a waiting Uber and headed home. From the comfort of her couch, she tracked her Range Rover's trek through the city until it reached its final destination—at least until it got moved to another towing yard. It was nearing 10 p.m. and the impound yard didn't open until

7 am., so Nancy headed to bed and set her alarm clock for an ungodly early hour.

*

The next morning, she jumped into an Uber and headed for North York—the location of her vehicle's AirTag. *Of course* her vehicle was in North York—technically part of the city, but a whopping forty-minute drive on a good day. But it was no bother—at least with her hands free from driving it would give her time to go over some of the information she had gleaned about the case. Details were swirling around in her head as she tried to figure out her next move. There was no guarantee that the particular impound lot she was going to had any connections to the Mob. But the tow-truck driver *had* given her the spiel mentioned in the exposé and she *had* watched her vehicle, via the AirTag, travel to two different lots the previous night. It led her to believe that she was on the right track, but just how she was going to parlay getting her vehicle out of impound into getting information about illegal gambling was a bridge she had yet to build—she hadn't even drawn up a blueprint.

She had dressed herself up on a whim that morning—putting on her pushiest of push-up bras, a low-cut spandex tank top, and some daisy dukes. It was a little much for 7 a.m. on any day of the week and she had seen the eyes pop out of her condo concierge's head as she had passed by his desk on her way through the lobby.

The Uber slowed as it turned into an industrial area and drove up to a trailer that sat just in front of a large, chain-link fence. A small white sign with blue letters read 'Tony Romano's Towing'.

*Tony Romano*? she thought to herself. Well, it certainly *sounded* Italian.

"Is here okay?" the driver asked, his Eastern European-accented thick as the car came to a stop.

"Yes, thank you." She unbuckled her seat belt and stepped out of the vehicle.

It was quiet out here in the industrial area. Oddly so. There was the distant, low hum of traffic from the 401 and various muffled bangs and clangs from the building next door, but the busy sounds of a bustling city were fairly muted. The dusty trailer in front of her that served as Tony Romano's Towing's office looked like it had seen better days. The white panels of the wall were caked in a thick layer of dust and a beat-up air-conditioning unit hung in one duct-taped window. The glass door was propped open with a square cement brick and bore the company's name in blue letters across the glass.

Inside the trailer, Nancy was greeted by a wooden desk with a computer and a dark-haired, olive-skinned man sitting behind it. The man had been scrolling on the computer when she walked in and he sat back and rested his arms on the desk as she approached.

"Can I help you?" he asked in a bored, monotone voice.

"Yes," she gave a sweet smile. "My vehicle broke down on the Gardiner last night and I was told I could pick it up here."

The man scratched his chin with one hand, moved the computer mouse and clicked a few times.

"Make and model?" he asked, his eyes fixed on the screen.

Well, this certainly wasn't going to be easy.

"It's a black Range Rover. Current year." She added on her license plate number.

There was silence as the man typed something into the computer.

"Are you Tony?" she asked lightly, trying to make conversation. The man grunted. Nancy couldn't tell if it was a confirmation or a denial.

She tried a different tactic and pulled a wad of cash out of her purse—$4,000 in hundreds—and fumbled with it to catch the man's attention.

He didn't look up.

"Can I pay with cash?" she asked loudly, flourishing the stack of bills absurdly.

The man glanced at her and his eyes widened as he spotted

the mountain of money in her hands.

"Uh, yeah," he said, taken aback. "Cash is good."

"Great," Nancy said with a smile, this time batting her lashes and leaning in slightly When sweetness failed, it was time to try seduction. "Can you also tell me if there are any horse betting tracks nearby?" she asked casually. "I'm not familiar with this part of the city."

That fully grabbed the attention of the man who may-or-may not be named Tony. He peeled his eyes away from the computer and fully looked at Nancy for the first time.

"You into horse betting?" he asked.

"I'm into any kind of betting," she said with a wide smirk. "Cards, sports, horses, slots . . ."

"What did you say your name was?" he asked.

"Laura," she said, ignoring the fact that she hadn't.

"Laura," he repeated slowly, then muttered to himself. "Laura who likes betting."

"Have I met a fellow gambler?" she asked playfully.

The man scratched his head and leaned forward in his chair. "Something like that," he said with a nod. Nancy thought she had struck out until he said casually, "I'm Tony. Your vehicle is in the backyard. It's $700 plus taxes. We'll get your car and then we'll talk business."

Nancy counted out the cash and placed it on the desk. It quickly disappeared into a drawer and was replaced by a few bills and some change. Tony fished a walkie-talkie from the drawer, clicked it on, and radioed for help.

"Gus, come watch the desk," he said into the device. "Got a customer I'm gonna help."

He set the walkie-talkie on the desk and spun around in his chair.

"I'll take you to the back myself." He stood up and opened a cabinet on the far side of the wall. There was a loud jingling and Tony emerged with her Range Rover keys in hand.

Seconds later Gus popped in, gave Tony a nod, and sat down behind the desk.

"I'll be back in ten," he said as he walked past Nancy and beckoned her to follow behind him. A cloud of cologne hung around him and Nancy followed his scent out of the building.

A tall chain-link fence surrounded the perimeter and the chain-link doors stood slightly open. Three oversized padlocks hung off of one door and a heavy-looking steel chain dangled from them. They passed through the gates with Tony leading the way and he made small talk as they walked past the myriad of impounded vehicles—a veritable goldmine for the towing yard.

Which is what made the fee that Tony had charged her all the more curious. She had expected to spend at least $2,000, but he had only charged about one-third of that. She had an inkling that, along with the casual mention of her love of gambling and the thick wad of cash she had produced, the substantially lowered impound fee meant that she was about to be welcomed into the world of illegal betting.

"Where ya from?" Tony asked, meandering along beside her. His shiny black locks glinted in the sun. It was a wonder BP hadn't sourced his hair for oil, Nancy thought to herself—he looked like he combed his hair with a porkchop.

"Edmonton," Nancy replied automatically. Which was true. She stuck relatively close to the truth when people asked about her background. Edmonton was a city large enough to get lost in. As 'Laura Richard', a name as generic as they come, it was easier for her to maintain anonymity. Her real name, Nancy Screw—her classmates had had a field day with that one during her teenage years—was something that stuck out like a sore thumb. It was one of the reasons why she stuck to her disguises and avoided, as much as she could at least, telling anyone her real name. Both of her jobs required her to keep a low profile.

Tony's small-talk questions kept coming and she suddenly realized that he wasn't trying to be kind. He was feeling her out. Making sure she wasn't a cop or, worse, a rat. She had to give Tony credit. He was smooth—like a snake. And, like the smooth-skinned reptile, if he discovered at some point that

Nancy *was* a rat, he would eat her for breakfast.

"So, what do you do for a living, Laura?" he asked as they approached her vehicle, which was parked in the back of the lot.

It was the final test question and she knew that her answer would either open the door to the underground gambling scene—or slam it shut

She gave Tony a coy smile: "I'm a dancer," she said without elaborating. The job would certainly explain why she had so much cash and would help sell her to Tony as someone who was trustworthy.

"Oh yeah?" he appraised her from a new lens although she could tell he was putting together the equation of her vehicle, outfit, wad of cash, and inquiry into gambling. It all added up to one thing. "Which club?"

Nancy's smile widened. "Not a club—an agency."

"Ah," Tony nodded in comprehension.

'Agency' was code for 'escort'. No further explanation needed. It would be another tick in her favour. After all, if she was already engaged in illegal work, she was unlikely to rat on a backroom betting circuit.

"So, Laura," Tony said casually, as if something had just occurred to him. "You said you like gambling. I know of a joint that does some underground betting. Sports, cards, horses—you name it. It's a $5,000 minimum buy-in—you interested?"

Bingo. She was in.

Nancy arranged her features into a feigned look of surprise. "Oh," she said with a nod. "I'd love to join. When and where?"

A few minutes later she drove out of the impound lot with a note in her phone containing Tony's number and instructions on how to part with $5,000 of cold hard cash every Sunday. It was like some twisted version of a church offering plate—Joel Osteen in a track suit with a Tommy gun.

Cards weren't one of Nancy's strengths, but she had several days to brush up on her skills before she stepped into that underworld. But first, she had a busy schedule: a date with

Barron, surveillance of Teddy, stalking two of Clover Capital's analysts, and a roster full of BDSM clients.

# CHAPTER 8

The date with Barron that evening came after a couple of appointments in The Cell and an afternoon filled with administrative work. Barron, who Nancy discovered liked to take charge in and out of the bedroom, had suggested that they meet at One—a swanky Yorkville establishment that hosted high-flying businessmen, ladies who lunch, mistresses, girlfriends, hookers, and everything in between.

She walked into the restaurant's adjoining lounge to find Barron seated at the bar, sipping a Manhattan with his back to the door. Only two other seats were taken—it was early on a Wednesday, but in under two hours the place would be packed. His black mop of loose curls brushed the back of his suit collar, and she could just barely see the outline of his muscles beneath the navy suit that would, undoubtedly, offset his handsome blue eyes.

"Is this seat taken?" she asked innocently, standing just behind him.

Barron turned around with a curious glance that quickly morphed into a sexy smile when he saw who it was.

"It is now," he said as he stood up and pulled out the chair beside him for Nancy to sit on.

Fuck, he was hot. It was almost a shame that he was part of

a case and that she hadn't met him organically. He may not be the relationship type, but with Nancy's job and her heart still broken, the relationship that she was looking for was more up Barron's alley. No strings attached—nothing but fucking and fun.

She ordered a gin martini. When it arrived, they clinked their glasses together and she took a sip. The salty tang of the martini lingered on her tongue.

Barron set his glass down first.

"How is Mrs. Jones?" he asked.

Nancy had almost forgotten that she had enlisted her neighbour's help the night she and Barron had first met. She had rushed away from Barron's place to help Mrs. Jones with an 'emergency'.

"She's doing a lot better," Nancy said gratefully. "I really do apologize for leaving so abruptly—Mrs. Jones fell, but thankfully it wasn't anything serious—just a sprain. I went to the hospital and then brought her home."

Barron looked concerned. "I'm glad that you were able to help. I'm sure she appreciates it."

Handsome, successful, intelligent, and caring? How the hell was this man single? And then she remembered his revolving door of one-night stands. Maybe she should give him the meeting information to her weekly AA sessions. He'd fit right in.

They continued on with pleasantries and small talk until the hostess came over and told them that their table was ready. Barron drained his drink and gestured for Nancy to lead the way.

They were shown to a table in the far back corner—a special request of Barron's. He wanted privacy, he explained. He added there was a good chance he would run into people he knew here. It was something that surprised Nancy. She expected Barron, as a self-styled playboy, to take her somewhere nice, yes—but somewhere nice where there was virtually no possibility of him seeing anyone in his circle. Bachelors like him tended to keep their dating and personal lives apart.

Barron read over the wine list and picked out a bottle—an expensive California cabernet. Their waiter murmured in approval and left with a flourish.

"How are things with work?" Nancy inquired. To her surprise, Barron was animated when it came to talking about his job.

"Things are good. We have six more funds that we're launching in the next year," he said proudly.

"Ambitious." Nancy genuinely admired his ambition. There was nothing hotter than a sharp, driven man who was focused on working his way to the top.

Of course, a rock-hard body didn't hurt things either.

"How do you manage to find investors for so many funds?" She was curious. "If investors don't see returns for several years isn't it a bit of a gamble to give you money?"

"Good questions." Barron took a sip of water and leaned back self-assuredly. "The majority of investors come from relationships I've cultivated over the course of my career. Some of them have trusted me with their money for years, while others come through introductions as a result of those relationships."

Nancy was just about to ask him about his current funds when the waiter reappeared with a bottle of Caymus. A hollow 'pop' accompanied the removal of the cork and the waiter poured out a tester into Nancy's glass.

She took a sip and smiled.

"That's great, thank you."

Glasses poured, Barron switched gears and asked Nancy about her job.

"I do marketing research," she said vaguely. It was her go-to. Common enough that it avoids suspicion, and boring enough to prevent any questions. They traded some back-and-forth 'get-to-know-you' questions until dinner arrived—risotto for her, steak and mushrooms for him—at which point Nancy asked him about his family.

"I'm a twin," he said, watching her face closely.

"A twin!" Her eyebrows shot up and she feigned surprise. She wasn't supposed to know anything about him or his brother, after all. As far as Barron knew, the evening of their first encounter she had just been out for a late-night drink—solo. Nancy had orchestrated the entire thing, but in his mind, their first meeting was purely due to chance.

"Yes," Barron grinned. "The older twin by two minutes. And I never let him forget it. We're identical—most people, even our closest friends, have a hard time telling us apart."

Nancy laughed.

"We grew up upper-middle class," he continued, picking up his glass. "Our dad worked and our mom stayed at home. The two of us were thick as thieves." Barron took a sip of his wine. "We still are, given we work so closely together, but we also lead pretty separate lives."

Nancy took a bite of her risotto; creamy, seasoned to perfection, and slightly chewy—the chefs really knew what they were doing.

"Your own lives, but from what you've told me, you don't sound so different," she observed.

Barron washed down a bite of steak with more wine.

"I guess we're similar with regards to work and our lifestyles . . ." He trailed off. "We're both bachelors, which at our age is a little unusual. But we were both too busy building our careers to date anyone seriously when we were younger."

Nancy raised an eyebrow, a teasing smile playing around her lips.

"Well, if your legion of fans at Louix Louis the other evening is any indication, it doesn't look like you're hurting when it comes to attention from the opposite sex.

He shrugged off the comment.

"Some women like status and wealth. The women you saw the other night—that's what they are after." Barron paused a beat: "You're very observant."

"It's hard not to notice a table full of women throwing

themselves at one man," she said dryly. He laughed and Nancy switched gears. "What about your brother?" she asked. "What's his name?"

"Teddy—Theodore, but everyone calls him Teddy," he cut another piece of steak. "He's quieter than me. More reserved."

"How do you two work together?" she pushed her risotto around with her fork.

"I do most of the fundraising and Teddy does most of the money management. We have weekly meetings so that we both know what one another is doing," he dabbed his mouth with his napkin.

This was an interesting development. If what Barron was saying about the money raising and money management being siloed was true, it could mean that only one of them was involved in what she was increasingly suspecting was something shady.

"It sounds like you two complement each other well. Are there ever any arguments about business?"

Barron broke a piece off of a dinner roll and slathered it with butter.

"Here and there, but nothing major. We have a good relationship. Although Teddy can be a bit of a hot head," he added and then popped the piece of bread into his mouth.

"What about your parents?" Nancy asked—she was curious about the twins' upbringing.

A flicker of sadness crossed over his face.

"My dad passed away twenty years ago, and my mom passed away two years after. It's just Teddy and I left."

"I'm sorry," she said gently. His expression turned somber, and sorrow lingered in the air.

"What about you?" he changed the subject, obviously uncomfortable talking about the deaths of his parents. Even twenty years later, it was clearly still a source of pain.

"My parents were in a car accident when I was nineteen," Nancy said truthfully. "They didn't make it. My older brother, Noah, and I have been close ever since. We have some aunts and uncles and cousins, but I couldn't tell you the last time I saw any of them."

She took a sip of her wine, realizing how much she had just let slip about herself. The bit about her parents wasn't any character backstory that she had concocted. It was the truth.

Well, almost.

For ten years now it had just been her and Noah. Their mom had died in a car accident when Nancy was nineteen. And their dad? He had been absent their entire lives; to Nancy and Noah, he was as good as dead.

Noah was three years older and lived in a different city than his sister. He had cut out of Edmonton as soon as he turned eighteen, and headed east for Toronto. A few years later, after the death of their mother, Nancy had followed him. Now, Noah lived in Ottawa, almost five-hours away. A medical doctor by training, he had moved to Ottawa for his residency and never left.

The siblings chatted on the phone every month and exchanged text messages here and there. As the older brother, Noah felt responsible for Nancy's well-being, but both of their busy work schedules kept them from really being connected. Like Barron and Teddy, Noah and Nancy led very separate lives.

While Nancy kept busy with her detective and dominatrix work, Noah had gone to university to be a surgeon. Somehow, he had found his way into pathology—working with the dead instead of the living. In some ways, it wasn't a surprise. Her brother had always been a bit of a loner and Nancy supposed that dealing with the dead was how he preferred it. Quiet, reserved, polite, and studious—that was Noah. It was surprising that he had remained single, virtually since high school, but she supposed that when your job involved interacting with the deceased, it didn't leave a lot of room for 'getting to know you' conversations and opportunities to ask women out for dinner. Still, she loved her brother, and hoped that he would one day find a partner. He had met Nancy's ex, Jamie, once when he was in Toronto for a conference. They had gone for dinner and she could tell that her brother wasn't impressed. He never came out and said that he didn't like her boyfriend—Noah was too polite for that. But he did tell her to 'be careful' and that he would be there for her no matter what.

It wasn't exactly a winning endorsement of her boyfriend, but it hadn't stopped her from soldiering on. And when Jamie had unceremoniously dumped her, Nancy didn't let on how devastated she really was. Despite that, Noah booked the following weekend off of work and made a surprise visit. Nancy was grateful for the distraction, and they spent a fun-filled few days at the museum, a winery, and out for nice dinners.

That was Noah—she could always count on him. Even when it came to her cases. In her line of work, it was rare to be hired for homicide investigations—those were mostly left up to the police. But there had been a few instances where she had called on her brother for his medical expertise.

One case involved what the police had deemed to be a suicide that had actually turned out to be a murder. The family of the deceased hadn't believed the coroner's ruling and had brought Nancy in to investigate. With several weeks of detective work and the help of her brother looking over the autopsy report, she had discovered that the sudden death, ascribed to 'natural causes' was actually due to a lethal injection administered by the deceased woman's psychotic ex. Nancy's sleuthing and Noah's medical expertise tied the case up into a nice little bow and the police had reopened the case and promptly charged the ex-boyfriend with first-degree murder. She'd sent a big gift basket to her brother's house for his help on that one.

As someone who typically kept her personal life private, she wasn't sure why she had told Barron about her family. Maybe it was because he had opened up to her about his family. Or maybe it was something else.

She felt comfortable with him. Which could be her downfall. His charm was disarming. It was, she imagined, one of the reasons why he was so successful in business and in the business of getting women into bed.

They finished dinner, dessert, and moved onto after-dinner cocktails. Nancy managed to get through it without spilling any more secrets about herself. She also managed to omit the fact that she had snuck into Clover Capital's office two nights before.

After several days of surveillance, she had mapped out which floor the financial firm was on and figured out what times it was empty. To Nancy's advantage, work in the downtown office towers could go on all night depending upon what firms had on the go. If a court case was imminent or there was a big business deal about to break, it wasn't unheard of for bankers and lawyers to pull all-nighters and catch a few hours of in-office sleep before work the next day.

It was also to Nancy's advantage that the building that housed Clover Capital was home to one of the city's best restaurants. Canoe was situated on the fifty-fourth floor of the imposing building and served up expensive drinks and Canadian-centric cuisine for the 9–5 crowd.

With this in mind, she had gone to the building late one night and followed a man into the elevator. His navy suit marked him as a banker or lawyer, and the two delivery bags full of dinner—Italian, if her olfactory senses were correct—marked him as a junior. He looked to be in his mid-to-late twenties and the dark circles under his eyes indicated that this wasn't his first all-nighter at the office. The button for the eighteenth floor lit up, and Nancy reached across and pressed '54' for Canoe. But it wasn't a pre-break-in dinner or cocktail that was on her mind—she was going to leg it down forty-one flights of stairs to the offices of Clover Capital.

When the lift dinged and came to a stop on floor eighteen, the sleep-deprived man stepped off and turned left. The doors closed again and the elevator began its fast ascent to the fifty-fourth floor. When the doors opened into the lobby, she wasted no time in heading towards the women's washroom, but instead of going inside, she diverted to a different door. A red, eye-height warning sign on it indicated that a fire alarm would sound if it was opened.

*We'll see about that,* she mused as she pushed it open and slipped through to the stairs. The promised alarm did not go off, as she had expected. The door clicked shut behind her as she took in the cold, gray interior. She quickly navigated the forty sets of stairs and, ten dizzying minutes later, she was breaking into floor fourteen with her lock-pick.

An audible click sounded; the handle gave way and she swung the door inwards before strolling onto the fourteenth floor. A quick, inconspicuous ceiling scan didn't reveal any cameras and she headed towards Clover Capital's office. Two frosted glass doors with the company's name emblazoned on them stood at the end of the hall. She once again pulled the lock-pick out of her purse and set to work. It took a lot less time to unlock Clover's doors and she quickly found herself inside the darkened office. It really was wild how lax security was for these firms when she really thought about it. Law offices, financial institutions . . . corporations holding secrets and documents that could do hundreds of millions of dollars' worth of damage, and all that stood between them and a determined prying eye was a lobby security guard and a lock-pick.

Although she supposed that nowadays, with the advent of technology, the real security firms needed was online. In present day, there was a dearth of physical files available for the taking. Which was both a blessing and a curse. Wading through mounds of paper documents was time-consuming and, even with an eagle eye, could be rendered fruitless due to human error. On the other hand, paper files provided tangibles and were easy to access.

Computer files, by contrast, were easier to comb through, but they were a lot less accessible. Password or fingerprint requirements aside, they tended to sit on personal laptops or the company's server. And when you were dealing with big money, there was big security, which was usually hard to bypass.

Clover Capital's office was fairly ordinary, which was

something that she hadn't expected. For a firm dealing in such large sums of money, she had envisioned rich wood, high-end furnishings, and high-priced artwork and tapestries. What she found, instead, was a cold, minimalist space with a reception desk, two glass-doored offices, one glass-walled board room, and a table set out in the back with desk space for associates and analysts.

The reception desk had a password-protected computer that Nancy didn't try to get past as the receptionist wouldn't have access to any records. The meat of what she wanted would hopefully be in the brothers' personal spaces.

The glass-doored office closest to her was Barron's, which was made apparent by a thank-you card she found in a desk drawer. She had half expected it to be from a woman, but was surprised to see it was from a family office thanking him for his donation to their scholarship foundation.

She liked that.

Heavy-handed business dealings and serial womanizing aside, it seemed that Barron also had a caring streak. Although Nancy's cynical side didn't rule out the appeal of tax benefits either. One thing that was unquestioningly clear was that the financier was sentimental; there weren't many men in his position who kept family photos on their desk.

A picture of Barron and his brother, his mom, and his dad sat turned towards his chair, for his eyes only. In the photo, the twins looked to be in their mid-thirties. The fact that Barron was now pushing fifty and still kept this photo on his desk spoke volumes.

The rest of his office was sparse—an abstract black-and-white painting on the wall, two plush black chairs for guests, and a desktop monitor and keyboard were perched on his heavy wooden desk. She was surprised to find the drawers unlocked, but reasoned that with such a small office and team, there wasn't much for him to worry about. Which was further confirmed when she saw what was inside. Post-it notes, pens, notepads, stacks of papers with graphs, presentations, financial reports, and projections. Along with a bottle of expensive face lotion, and a half-empty bottle of bourbon. In all, she found nothing of note, but nothing ventured, nothing gained when it came to her line of work.

Teddy's office, like his appearance, mirrored his brother's, right down to the stash of liquor in his desk. But where Barron had a family photo facing towards him, Teddy had none.

She didn't read too much into it. And she also didn't find anything else. The reports, graphs, and documents in Teddy's drawers were much the same as his brother's. All up to snuff, and nothing suspicious or of note.

She rummaged around the rest of Clover Capital for a few more minutes but didn't find what she was looking for. She wasn't even sure what she *was* looking for. But snooping around the space did give her a better sense of the brothers. There hadn't been much to see and so far she had no evidence of any crimes, but it felt like she was on the right track.

Still, she had a long way to go with her investigation and, after infiltrating Barron's life, her next task was to infiltrate Teddy's.

Barron and Nancy parted ways outside of the restaurant that evening and she got into an Uber. They'd shared a smoldering kiss and butterflies had danced in her stomach when she pulled back and looked into his eyes. He'd given her a cheeky grin and pulled away, but not before Nancy felt how much he wanted her.

At first, Barron had insisted on driving her home but Nancy stubbornly refused. The last thing she needed was Barron knowing where she lived. It hadn't been easy for her to decline the invite to go back to his place—she wanted nothing more than to get the deliciously attractive man into bed. But she also knew that it was better to keep him wanting more. Put up a challenge, and Barron would be the first to accept.

When she arrived home she changed out of her dress and into sweatpants, fuzzy socks, and a comfy top. All traces of her makeup were wiped away with cotton balls, and her face shined from the hydrating serum she applied to her skin.

If she was honest with herself, she liked Barron. It was easy to see why he had so many women after him and why he was so successful in his career. Not that Nancy ever imagined anything ever happening between the two of them. Well, not as Nancy, at least. The sensual experience she'd had at his place the previous week was one that, as Larissa, she definitely intended to repeat.

# CHAPTER 9

"This is divine," Mrs. Jones moaned as the caramel macchiato fumes wafted out of her Starbucks lid and invaded her senses. She was seated on the passenger side of Nancy's Range Rover, a silk scarf tied around her head and large aviator sunglasses covering her eyes—shades of Sophia Loren. Nancy, seated next to her, sported a blonde wig and the biggest sunglasses in her arsenal. She took a drink of her Americano. Straight black—she was hardcore when it came to caffeine.

"Just wait until you take a sip," Nancy prompted her neighbour. "It tastes even better than it smells."

Nancy had popped into a nearby Starbucks and ordered up drinks for her and Mrs. Jones. Her neighbour had requested something warm and sweet and Nancy had obliged. It was always a delight when Mrs. Jones joined her for a stakeout. The old lady didn't get out much and it usually turned out to be a treat for them both—Mrs. Jones got to participate in something she considered exciting, and Nancy got to stave off the boredom of her multi-hour surveillance.

The rough polyester pulled through her hands as Nancy buckled her seatbelt and put the car into drive. Their mission that Saturday was simple—to tail Teddy Benjamin from dawn until dusk. Nancy wanted to see where he went, who he saw, and what he did. She had his office schedule down pat. But his personal life was still a mystery. When it came to his twin, Barron, she had a much better lay, pun intended, of the land. And Barron seemed, so far, pretty innocent.

She almost snorted at her own thought. Barron Benjamin—innocent? About as innocent as a dog who's just been caught with the Thanksgiving turkey in his mouth.

She and Mrs. Jones chatted as she navigated the roads to Teddy's house in Yorkville. Her rudimentary background search had provided his home address and when she had looked his property up online, she was a little surprised by what she had found. Unlike his brother, Teddy had the proverbial white picket fence. Minus a wife and 2.5 kids, but with the addition of a dog.

She had inadvertently discovered he had a canine companion while loitering in the lobby of the Clover Capital building one morning. Phone up to her ear while ostensibly listening to a call, she saw Teddy run into a friend—bald-headed and short in stature. The two of them started talking and Nancy, phone still to her ear, had walked by the duo and loitered, while murmuring the odd 'hmm' and 'yes, I agree' into her device. She had caught a snippet of their conversation and the short, bespectacled man asked Teddy how Pietas was. Her ears had perked up at that. Pietas—it was Latin, surely. But it didn't sound like a man or a woman. Maybe it was a company?

She hadn't heard Teddy's reply and had walked out of the building when the bespectacled man glanced her way. The last thing she needed was to attract any attention.

The wind whipped at her hair as she typed 'Pietas' into the Notes function on her phone before stuffing it in her pocket. Across the street she popped into a coffee shop that was bustling with the early morning crowd and took a seat at a corner table. The next few minutes she spent on Google. There weren't any companies she came across that were based in or in any way related to Toronto so she felt sure that a company wasn't what the bespectacled man had been asking about.

She pondered for a moment—Pietas was an odd name for a person, but the monied crowd often took strange liberties when it came to names. Maybe Teddy actually had a girlfriend? Or maybe Pietas was a friend that Teddy and the bald man had in common?

She Googled every which way she could think of to see if there was anyone in the city with Pietas as a first or last name, but she came up empty. Next, she Googled the word itself. It was Latin, she had been right about that, but she hadn't the faintest idea of what it meant. Loyalty, duty, love, devotion—it would be a great name for a company. The only problem was one didn't seem to exist.

She threw in the towel a few minutes later. It was always a disappointment to come up empty on a potential lead, but, in a stroke of good luck, she had discovered just who Pietas was two days later.

In an effort to get a feel for Teddy's neighbourhood, she had driven to his street and parked a few houses down from his place. Then she'd thrown on saucer-sized sunglasses and gone for a slow, leisurely stroll outside to get a better look at his house.

It was one of those hot summer days where the mid-morning temperature was already in the low twenties and brought the promise of a sweat-soaked afternoon. To fit into the 'burbs, Nancy had put on a pair of running shoes, black spandex shorts, and a tank-top.

She had been startled when, having just reached his next-door neighbour's house, she saw movement from Teddy's front door, which swung inward. Seconds later a tall, athletic-looking woman with a messy ponytail, short shorts, a white t-shirt, and a blue leash stepped outside, followed by a large black lab, who wiggled around excitedly on the porch.

"Pietas!" the woman said sharply.

*Ahhh*, Nancy thought to herself. *Of course.* Pietas was Teddy's dog. Why hadn't that possibility occurred to her?

One good reason why it hadn't occurred to her was that Teddy didn't strike her as the type of person to have a pet. His brother Barron seemed to be the more sentimental of the two, and he had the emotional range of a marble statue. That type of stoicism didn't exactly mark the twins as the type of people who would get the warm and fuzzies from an animal friend.

She had watched as Teddy's dog walker and, probable, housekeeper, untangled the leash and set off in the same direction as Nancy. She kept her leisurely pace past the multi-million-dollar houses before turning down a side street and circling the block. With the little mystery of who Pietas was unexpectedly solved, she spent a few minutes checking out Teddy's house from the sidewalk before getting back into her vehicle and heading for home.

This morning, Nancy's Range Rover sat five houses down from Teddy's, with her and Mrs. Jones settled in for what promised to be a long day. The Americano in Nancy's hand was almost empty when she spotted movement from Teddy's house. Like it had the other morning, his front door swung inward. This time, instead of a blonde-haired woman, out walked Teddy himself, clad in a pair of gray sweatpants and a blue t-shirt. He was holding the same blue leash she had seen the other day, which was attached to Pietas, the black lab who seemed to live in a steady state of excitement. The dog enthusiastically danced on the doorstep as he waited for his owner to lock the door. Seconds later, they were walking away from the direction of Nancy's vehicle, presumably on their way to the park.

"Oh, he's a looker!" Mrs. Jones had said in a loud whisper when Teddy first appeared on the porch.

"I told you!" Nancy whispered, keeping her eye trained on the financier. "I almost can't believe that there are two of them."

Once Teddy and his dog were around the corner, Nancy turned on the vehicle and headed towards the park. From her Google Maps sleuthing, she had found several parks in the area, but only one of them had an off-leash area for dogs. She couldn't be sure, but she had a hunch that Teddy would take Pietas there. It stood to reason that the energetic pup had friends at the dog park, and an early-morning play-date would allow the lab to burn off some steam.

Despite Toronto traffic, where someone on crutches usually beats a car to their destination, they arrived at the dog park before Teddy. She parked next to a tree that provided cover, but also provided the opportunity for some inconspicuous stalking, and waited for Teddy to appear. Several minutes later she spotted him trudging down the sidewalk with his exuberant black lab leading the way.

The expanse of dog park, not large by most people's standards, but grand given the property costs in the area, was walled off by a chain-link fence. Teddy entered the gate and let Pietas off his leash. Immediately, the lab took off and ran around full speed, his tail wagging with glee as he bowled into other dogs and played around with his friends. Mrs. Jones giggled as the eighty-pound lab took a particular interest in a pint-sized Chihuahua. Nancy was dismayed to see Teddy stood off to the side the entire time with Pietas's leash in one hand while typing on his phone with the other.

He ran a company and had a lot of responsibilities and investors to answer to, but to Nancy, he was coming across as a shitty pet parent. It was probably a good thing that he had remained a bachelor—sans the wife and 2.5 kids. Terrible taste in names aside, if he couldn't even be present for his dog, how the hell would he have been present for a family?

Although, when she thought about it, absence seemed to be the workaholic way.

Her mind wandered to Jamie. He had also been a workaholic, but Nancy was so busy at the time that she didn't mind. In fact, it made her savour the time that they did spend together even more. When you genuinely missed someone, it made the time that you did get to spend together that much more special.

"I wonder who that gentleman is?"

Mrs. Jones jolted Nancy out of her reverie and her eyes came back into focus. There was a man talking to Teddy. As far as she could see, there was nothing remarkable about him. He was dressed casually enough in blue jeans and a checked button-down shirt. And while she didn't recognize him from the distance, there was something about him that seemed familiar.

The men's conversation seemed comfortable enough, but Nancy was too far away to see any facial expressions. What she could see was that checked-shirt guy didn't have a leash. Nor did he appear to have a dog. Which was curious.

She reached into the cup holder and grabbed her binoculars. The magnified view revealed agitation on the guy's face. Teddy, for his part, had his jaw firmly clenched. Not quite the casual conversation, it seemed.

The other man looked young—early-to-mid-twenties, Nancy guessed. It struck her as odd. What would a twenty-something-year-old have to argue with Teddy about on a Saturday morning? And why were they meeting at a dog park when one of them didn't even have a dog?

She swapped the binoculars with her phone and zoomed in to get a photo of the two of them. She kept snapping pictures as the conversation appeared to get more heated until the checked-shirt man shook his head at Teddy, turned, and walked away.

"I wonder what that was all about?" Mrs. Jones inquired, with the binoculars pressed against her face. Always looking to get in on the action, she had snatched them up as soon as Nancy had put them down.

"Good question." Nancy moved the photos she had just taken into a secure folder on her phone. "It could be personal, but I have a feeling it somehow ties into things."

The duo sat in silence, both contemplating the different possibilities of what the altercation could mean when a lightbulb suddenly went off in Nancy's head. There was something about the man that had seemed familiar to her and the realization of where she had seen him before hit her all at once. His photo was on the 'Meet Our Team' section of Clover Capital's website. He worked for the Benjamin brothers. But what was his name? *Richard? Wayne?*

She unlocked her phone, Googled 'Clover Capital', clicked onto the employee section, and scrolled.

Jackpot.

Her heart pounded as the name caught her eye.

Brian. Brian Innis. Financial Analyst at Clover Capital.

What would one of Barron and Teddy's employees be doing meeting one of the brothers outside of working hours in an out-of-the-way dog park? she pondered. And why would they be having a heated conversation?

*

Later, over tea and chocolate biscuits at Mrs. Jones's place, Nancy gave a brief overview of Ms. Elena Fineberg's case. Of course, she didn't reveal the name of the well-to-do woman who had hired her, she just referred to Ms. Fineberg as her 'client'.

"The more I'm uncovering, the more I think my client was onto something." Nancy, her tea cup held mid-air, continued. "I just can't figure out what the Benjamin brothers' racket is and who is involved."

Mrs. Jones took a quiet sip of tea, then set down her cup. She picked up a biscuit and took a bite.

"Well, Theodore certainly looked suspicious today." Mrs. Jones said through chews. ". . . whatever he was doing."

Nancy nodded in agreement. "And where there's smoke, there's usually fire."

An hour later, Nancy was at her condo prepping for the next day. Two clients had made appointments to avail themselves of her dominatrix services and she needed to get ready. One of her clients, Siraj, was into pain—candles, spikes, whips, and chains. Masochists always served her well when she was in the middle of an investigation. She unleashed her frustration using the tools of her trade and it usually made for a better session—she pushed the pain-seekers right to their limit. The other client,

Oliver, was into feminization. For the uninitiated, this means he enjoyed being forced to wear women's clothing—a wig and pumps included—while Nancy paraded him around on a leash. Although, given how Oliver looked in a dress, Nancy wasn't entirely sure if his proclivities had more to do with a fetish for humiliation.

When she had first taken him on as a client, she had instructed him to buy a wig. Depending upon what a new client was into, Nancy had them buy their own accessories, which stayed at The Cell. Oliver had shown up two years ago with a paper bag in tow and Nancy had barely managed to keep a straight face when she saw what was inside of it. The long fiery-coloured wig with a single braid in the back gave her visions of Princess Fiona from *Shrek*. When he had first put it on, she had had to stop herself from putting on a Scottish accent and blurting out, "What are you doing in my swamp!" With no small amount of effort, she had kept her composure and given Oliver what he had wanted—ordering him to undress, put on a bra, high heels, and a pink dress.

A smile passed her lips as she put her Longchamp bag together for the next day. She had found a new pain product to use on Siraj—steel claws for her fingers that made her feel like some sexy, less-lethal version of Wolverine. For Oliver, she had found a soft-pink tutu. She couldn't think of anything more humiliating to add to his outfit. The layers of tulle stuck out from the opening of the purse and she stuffed the pink netting inside. When zipped closed, the fabric made her bag bulge from all sides—puffed up like a marshmallow in a microwave.

Marshmallows—those reminded her of her neighbour. Mrs. Jones had a major sweet tooth. She knew nothing about Nancy moonlighting with a second career. The old lady was very laissez-faire, yes—especially when it came to Nancy's detective career and her methods. But her dominatrix work was something she kept all to herself. It's not that Nancy didn't think Mrs. Jones would approve—she was sure the elderly lady wouldn't be offended—it was that Nancy didn't want *anybody* knowing about it. Unlike her weekly AA meetings, being a part-time domme wasn't something she was embarrassed about. She just preferred to keep it private.

That evening Nancy laid out the specifics of what she had compiled for Ms. Fineberg's case so far:

1. Teddy had a gambling problem and, from the sounds of it, had run into some trouble with the Mob.

2. Teddy and Barron were running a *very* successful firm, although it was starting to look more like a very successful fraud.

3. The Benjamin brothers were just as delicious in person as they were in print.

4. Barron Benjamin was promising to be dynamite in bed.

Okay, those last two points weren't something she needed to share with her client. But were they pertinent? Oh, yes.

To her, at least.

She didn't have much to go on so far, but hoped the next couple of days would provide some clarity. Just why was Teddy meeting with that Clover Capital analyst outside of business hours? She didn't know, but she intended to find out.

# CHAPTER 10

"Hi, beautiful." Barron's deep baritone voice came from somewhere behind her. Nancy turned around with a teasing grin.

They had opted for Bymark this evening—a restaurant in the downtown core that Nancy chose because of its closeness to Barron's condo. She had been surprised when he had asked her where she wanted to go for dinner. Barron wasn't the type to let others take control when it came to decision making; even when it came to something as simple as a restaurant. He was also, however, shrewd enough to know sometimes you had to give up the reins to get what you want. And what he wanted was Nancy.

She wanted Barron, too. Badly. She had since the moment she saw him. But there was one thing that she wanted even more. Something she hadn't had since the night of their first encounter: access to his home office. Her plan tonight was to kill two birds with one stone. She was finally going to see what was inside of Barron's pants and she was going to get off . . . by stealing his hard drive.

Barron leaned down and placed a gentle kiss on the side of her face before taking his seat. The soft lighting in the caramel-coloured space cast shadows across their faces, silhouetted against gleaming windows, darkened by the night.

"Good to see you, Brock," Barron nodded at the waiter who stopped by their table.

"Barron," Brock gave a little wave. "Haven't seen you in at least twenty-four hours," he joked.

Barron let out a laugh and then directed his attention towards Nancy: "I had a meeting with one of my investors here last night," he explained before introducing her to the waiter.

They shared a bottle of wine over a dinner of pasta, sea bream, bread, and asparagus. When their meal was finished, Nancy excused herself to the washroom to freshen up. She checked out her reflection in the dark-lit room, admiring her outfit from every angle. She had pulled out all stops with her ensemble that evening. A tight, low-cut royal-blue dress with a hem that fell just to her mid-thigh accentuated her ass, breasts, and waist—the Holy Trinity when it came to men.

She had a surprise for Barron that night that had nothing to do with his hard drive. She had a different surprise for him—one she was going to let him in on.

After dinner they headed for a drink at Canoe. At the bar, Nancy shot Barron a mischievous smile and beckoned him to come closer. When he was within whispering distance, she cupped one hand around his ear and purred in a low voice: "I'm naked underneath this dress."

Barron pulled back with a look of surprise; mischief mirrored in his eyes.

"Is that so?"

He grabbed Nancy's chair and pulled it closer. With a playful toss of her hair, she locked eyes with Barron, who discreetly placed one hand between her thighs and gently nudged them apart.

Her pulse quickened at the promise of his touch and her body flooded with desire. *Damn*, she thought to herself. How did he manage to do that to her with just one touch?

In Barron's eyes stirred an intense hunger that would have instantly dampened Nancy's panties—except, of course, for the fact that she wasn't wearing any. The predatory look on Barron's face reminded her of a documentary she had once watched that featured an antelope being stalked by a lion. In the documentary, the antelope had ended up getting eaten. Nancy was hoping for a similar fate this evening. She was Barron's prey and she couldn't wait to be devoured.

Without a glance to the people around them—bartenders, patrons, wait staff, and busboys, Barron slid his hand up her thigh to the wet spot between her legs. She let out a strangled gasp as Barron began gently massaging her while keeping his eyes firmly focused on hers. It was the most Nancy could do to keep it together as his fingers moved in slow circling strokes and then began exploring further. She struggled to keep her face neutral as her pulse quickened and her body began to respond to his motion. She could feel his fingers moving inside of her, in and out in a 'come hither' motion with just the right amount of pressure. *Damn*, he was *so* good at that. Desire burned inside of her and she was almost at the edge when an impish smile spread across Barron's face and he removed his fingers.

Nancy, her breathing heavy, took a second to gather her wits while Barron, his eyes still trained on hers, reached for his glass of wine and knocked it back in a single gulp.

"Bartender," he said with conviction, his eyes locked with Nancy's. "Cheque, please."

Minutes later, their eyes burned with desire as they rode the elevator on the way to the ground floor. They kept a reluctant sense of decorum in the lift, thanks to the other couple—it lasted precisely as long as it took to get to Barron's building.

When the elevator reached his floor, they spilled out onto the foyer, in a chaotic tangle of lust. They barely made it inside of his condo before tearing each other's clothes off. Barron's sport jacket hit the floor by the door, quickly followed by his white button-down shirt. Nancy gasped as Barron's hands found her chest, tugging down the low-cut blue fabric of her dress so her breasts spilled into his palms. He grabbed them hungrily, eyes locked with hers, as her hands slipped down to the sizable bulge in his pants. Still half-dressed, she lowered herself to her knees. With practiced ease she undid his belt, pulling his pants and briefs down with one motion and freeing his hard-as-a-rock member. She wrapped one hand around him, licking up and down his shaft while never breaking eye contact. Then she took him deep into her mouth, eliciting a deep groan from his chest. His fingers tangled in her hair as she moved up and down, switching between deep-throating, licking, and sucking—like he was a delicious lollipop she couldn't get enough of.

Barron's groans deepened, and she tasted a hint of his saltiness before he leaned down, pulled her up from her knees, and brought his mouth to hers. As their lips melted together Nancy felt something stir inside her chest. All at once it was light and heavy—anchored somewhere deep inside of her. A heady mix of butterflies and adrenaline, excitement and arousal. It was chemistry, yes, but it was more than that. It was a raw, unconstrained electricity. A powerful feeling she hadn't experienced since her ex.

Barron slid one hand underneath her dress while the other eased her shoulder straps down her arms. They barely came up for air as she pulled the rest of her dress down her legs, stepped out of it, and kicked off the garment before pressing herself into him. Barron stumbled slightly, tugging off his shoes and pants. Nancy's hands roamed all over his chest, tracing the hard lines of his body, while Barron slid his fingers inside of her again with the same beckoning motion he had at the bar.

At the rate that they were going, Nancy didn't think that they would make it to the bedroom. Barron didn't appear to think so either—he guided her towards his living room.

One of his hands squeezed her bottom, pulling her against him, while the other continued to stroke in and out of her. They just reached the edge of his couch when Barron dropped onto it and pulled her on top of him.

"Sit on me," he growled.

Nancy bit her lip and did as she was told.

A gasp of pleasure escaped from her as she impaled herself onto his throbbing length. She groaned deeply, adjusting to his girth as she sank down, taking him to the hilt. She didn't know if she had ever felt so full. Eyes locked on his, she bit her lip and rode him like a prized, show-winning stallion—fierce and in control.

Barron's head rolled back but his gaze never wavered as she moved hard and fast, fucking him with relentless rhythm.

Nancy's groans built from deep in her chest, raw and urgent and Barron met each one with equal fervor. She could feel her climax gathering, rising, but just as she teetered on the edge, Barron gripped her hips and held her still. Then, with one swift motion, he rolled on top of her.

"Not yet," he commanded.

Still riding the edge of ecstasy, Nancy let out a strangled cry—frustrated that he had pulled her back from the peak.

"Not yet," he repeated, panting.

She bit her lip again and gave him wide, pleading eyes.

"Good girl," he growled pushing her legs apart and into her hands before driving back into her.

She was entirely exposed beneath him as he loomed over top of her, driving himself deep into of her body. His groans took on a deeper, unrestrained edge and Nancy felt herself rushing towards the brink of euphoria. With each thrust she could feel her climax building, her breath hitching as his pace quickened. She held her legs above her head until her back suddenly arched and a cry tore from her lips. Seconds later, Barron followed, groaning as he came deep inside of her. Waves of ecstasy rippled through her as she felt him pulsing inside of her, and with one final thrust, he collapsed onto her—spent and breathless in her arms.

They lay there together, their hearts racing, chests rising and falling like they had just run a marathon.

It took a few minutes for the breathlessness to ease, and Nancy spoke first.

"Will that be all, Mr. Benjamin?" she asked, her voice mock-innocent.

Barron broke out in a fit of laughter and she joined in with some giggles. His head was cradled in the crook of her neck and he placed some feather-light kisses on her skin before resting his head back down on her body.

"Wine pick-me-up?" he asked after a beat.

They had consumed a non-negligible amount of liquor, but Nancy was up for one more. She knew that she was sleeping over tonight, and she was hoping that the alcohol would put Barron into a deep sleep. After the last drink at Canoe, she knew she would be grappling with an unholy hangover the next day, but duty called—if Barron wanted one more, so did she. She didn't want to chance him waking up and ruining her plans for the rest of the evening. When it came to providing customer service for her clients, Nancy really prided herself on going above and beyond. She was wholeheartedly enjoying herself, true, but she was also on the clock for Ms. Fineberg.

Barron rolled off her and threw her a fluffy throw. She wrapped it around herself and watched his tight, bare ass head for the kitchen. He worked out, she knew that, but—*Jesus.* He was great in bed, handsome as hell, whip smart, and unapologetically successful. Was there anything finance boy wasn't top dog at?

She sat back and let out a sigh.

People talked about their work perks all the time, but she doubted any discount gym memberships or free drip coffee could compare to getting your rocks off with a handsome, charismatic millionaire. She'd been looking forward to getting between the sheets with Barron, but she hadn't anticipated it being so mind-blowing. Then again, with his revolving door of women, it wasn't exactly surprising that he knew his way around the bedroom.

Not that that was everything.

There was a connection between them. An electric spark that shot through her every time that they locked eyes. She was lucky this time. It wasn't always that she slept with her target in order to solve the case, but when she did, it was rare for her to feel the kind of chemistry that she and Barron shared.

If she didn't know he was such a playboy and she wasn't investigating him for Ms. Fineberg, she might allow herself to fantasize about them being together. Fortunately, Nancy was always good at keeping a cool head when it came to emotional matters, even when things down below were getting hot. She wasn't sure if Barron felt the same electricity, but something about the way he had ravaged her made her think that he was feeling it, too.

Minutes later Barron returned with two glasses brimming with wine and a bowl of blackberries.

*Such a gentleman*, she thought to herself as she popped a plump berry into her mouth and washed it down with the aromatic red liquid.

*

Barron was snoring like a hibernating bear, having drank his weight in wine. Nancy, on the other hand, hadn't allowed herself to sleep. She had waited until Barron's rhythmic breathing turned into chainsaw snoring and then she made her move.

She slid out of bed and stepped softly towards his bedroom door under the guise of getting her phone from the living room. Which, to be fair, *was* what she was doing. Not for a 4 a.m. email check or Instagram scroll, but if Barron woke up, that's what she would tell him. She crept into the hallway like a cat burglar, taking care to quietly close the door behind her. If Barron somehow rose from his wine slumber and went looking for her, the door would at least give her a few seconds' notice.

The first time she had snuck into Barron's office she had made note of his laptop make—a sleek, gray, MacBook Air—and her mission this morning was to get a copy of it. It could be done quickly, given the advanced technology nowadays, and the high-powered tech that she had in her purse. But, while ten minutes was seconds compared to how long cloning a hard drive would have taken ten years ago, ten minutes left her with a lot of time in which to get caught. It was fortunate that Barron was sleeping soundly—his snoring had practically rattled the bed—Nancy was just hoping that her luck wouldn't run out in the next thirty minutes.

Sneaking down the hallway into the living room, she picked up her purse and pulled out her phone. Opening up the back compartment of her bag, she dug around a bit and pulled out a USB stick, a small converter cord, a mini roll of tape, and her container of loose face powder.

Items in hand, she walked back the same way she had come and stopped just outside of Barron's bedroom door to listen—the deep sound of his snoring couldn't even be muffled by the heavy wood.

She breathed a light sigh of relief and kept walking.

At the first door past Barron's bedroom, she turned the light on and pulled the door shut. On the off chance that Barron woke up and went looking for her, he would think that she was in the washroom—not using the master ensuite because she didn't want to wake him up.

A few seconds later she walked into his office, closed the door behind her, and activated the flashlight on her phone. Even if Barron did seem comfortably ensconced in his cabernet sauvignon slumber, she wasn't taking any chances. If she turned the lights on, it could alert him to her activity.

At his desk she placed her phone between her lips so the flashlight illuminated the wooden surface and she had both hands free to perform her task. First, she unscrewed the top of her face powder and tested the makeup pouf—fluffy, as expected. Then, she opened up Barron's closed MacBook. The laptop immediately sprang to life and gave her the option of a password or fingerprint login. She hadn't the faintest idea what Barron's computer password was and she wasn't about to start guessing. Instead, she lightly dusted the pale face powder over top of the laptop's Touch ID.

Next, she cut off a short length of tape and carefully placed it over top of the powdered button. When she lifted the tape up, she was rewarded with Barron's fingerprint outlined in pale powder. She used her lungs to get rid of the excess powder on the keyboard—her second blow job of the evening—and then dusted the remainder off with the back of her hand. Next, she positioned the tape fingerprint on top of the ID button and gently applied pressure to it using the side of her hand.

Moments later, as if Barron himself had put his finger on the ID button, she was in.

*Makeup*, she smirked to herself triumphantly—it wasn't just for your face.

Now that she was inside his computer, she pulled the tape off the button and folded the sticky sides together. Then, Nancy got down to business. She placed her phone, screen side up, on the desk, connected the USB stick to the adaptor cord and plugged it into the computer; a few short clicks later and the entirety of Barron's laptop was downloading onto her little device. She screwed the top of her face powder back on and pushed it to the side. As the minutes counted down she checked the messages and emails on her phone. There was nothing pressing and she clicked the screen to black as she watched the time estimate on Barron's computer screen tick down.

Finally, ten grueling minutes later, the green progress bar on the screen reached the end and stated 'Complete'. Satisfied, she exited out of the window, removed the USB and cord from the computer, and shut the laptop. She picked up her phone, grabbed up the tape, face powder, USB stick, and cord, and was just about to head for the door when she spotted one of her long black hair strands on the desk.

*Jesus.*

That was all she needed—Barron finding her hair in his office. Sweeping her finger over the desk surface she pulled the strand between her fingers and set off for the door. When she reached it, she put her ear to the heavy wood and listened, but it was impossible. She couldn't hear anything. Which could mean one of two things: either the two-door barrier rendered Barron's snoring inaudible, or Barron was awake.

She hemmed and hawed for a second before making a decision to stand behind the door. She would give it a minute to see if she heard any noises in the hallway. She turned the flashlight off on her phone and stood with her back against the wall.

One minute passed. Then two.

Decision made, she crept to the door and gingerly pulled it open. A cautious glance down the hall and the heavy sound of Barron snoring assured her that the coast was clear. Relieved, she crept to the bathroom and turned off the lights before making her way back to the living room and depositing her detective tools back into her purse. Phone in hand, she was just about to head back to bed when she was startled by a creak behind her. She spun around, clutching her mobile to her chest as her heart beat a million miles a minute.

"Barron!" she let out a surprised yelp when she saw her paramour standing a few feet behind her.

"Everything okay?" he yawned, his black tousled locks giving him a sexy bed head as he squinted through sleep-deprived eyes.

"You scared me," she relaxed her hand and took a deep breath before walking towards him. "All okay," she smiled, putting her arms around his naked torso as she looked up at his sleepy face. "I couldn't sleep so I came out to get my phone," she flashed her mobile.

His arms went around her then, with one of his hands finding its way to her bare bottom.

"Well, now that we're both awake, I can think of a fun way to tire ourselves out again," he squeezed her left cheek and gave her a sleepy smile.

Nancy's heart kept racing, but this time it was for a very different reason. Round two with Barron? She couldn't think of a better way to celebrate her success.

She smirked and then bent her head to one of his nipples, licking all around it, and nipping at his skin with her teeth. Barron drew a sharp intake of air and she guided one of his hands to the space between her legs, which had already moistened in a Pavlovian manner. Like earlier in the evening, their eyes burned into one another's; her carnal desire was mirrored in his. Electricity surged through their bodies—a silent buzzing that was so powerful she was surprised there weren't any sparks. Without breaking eye contact, Barron brought his free hand up, took the phone from her hand and threw it on the couch. Then, he cupped her breast with that hand while stroking her with the other.

Nancy's hands slid up his inner thighs until they found his smooth, hard shaft, growing more excited by the second. She stroked it back and forth with increasing intensity as Barron's fingers found their way deep inside of her. She let out a long, low moan as he stroked her g-spot, then pulled his fingers out and slid them into her mouth.

Nancy moaned, hungrily sucking his fingers as she sank to her knees. Barron, his eyes still locked with hers, pulled his finger out of her mouth as Nancy grabbed a hold of his shaft and sensually licked the length of it. Now it was Barron's turn to moan. She alternated between deep-throating him and twisting her hand back and forth until, minutes later, both were spent and snuggled up on the couch. Nancy grabbed a blanket from the armchair and threw it over them before they both passed out in a blissful sleep.

*

"Pancakes?" came a voice in Nancy's ear.

She took a deep breath and cracked open her sleep-heavy eyes. When she did, she saw Barron's smiling face looking back at her. She returned the smile and nodded in answer.

Barron's grin deepened and he gave her a quick kiss on the forehead before peeling out from under the blanket and heading for the kitchen.

Nancy put her head back on the cushion and took a moment to relax.

She felt good. Better than good—she felt great. The remnants of their late-night wine sat on the sturdy glass table:

two empty glasses and a half-empty bottle.

*Empty? Definitely half-full*, she corrected herself. She had never considered herself to be an optimist, but now seemed like a good time to start.

Eventually, she crawled out from under the blankets and put on her dress, which was more than a little wrinkled from the seven hours it had spent on the floor. Then she went to the washroom to freshen up.

*Not bad*, she thought as she caught a glimpse of herself in the mirror. Her waterproof mascara and eyeliner had done as promised and looked as if she had just applied it. The lower half of her face and her neck, on the other hand, looked ravaged.

No bother.

She headed for the living room and swiped some balm on her chapped lips.

Barron entered moments later wearing a white t-shirt and briefs, with two cups of coffee in his hands.

"It's 6 a.m. and you look like you're ready for a date," he snorted as he handed her a cup of coffee.

Nancy giggled in reply.

It was true. While her sexy short blue dress had done its duty the night before, she felt a little self-conscious that she would be heading home in it. Nothing screamed 'walk of shame' like high heels and a slutty dress at 7 a.m.

Barron offered her a change of clothes but she declined and then they tucked into breakfast. An hour later, Nancy, with large sunglasses perched on her nose, exited the building and stepped into a waiting Uber. She was thankful for Barron's thoughtfulness when it came to breakfast—by the time she walked into her condo, she felt refreshed and ready to face the day. And the first thing on her docket was to go through Barron's hard drive.

She sipped from a glass of sparkling water as she waited for the contents of his laptop to load onto her computer. On his desktop, she could see five files, all with unambiguous labels attached to them. Having seen the state of his home and office, she was unsurprised his computer was so organized.

She clicked on the folder labelled 'Funds' and found five more subfolders inside. Clicking on 'Financials', she was treated to a list of different spreadsheets, the most recent one was dated two days earlier. She clicked it open and found a standard-looking financial statement. Well, it was a little deviant, she supposed. But only because of the heart-stoppingly large numbers on display. There were more zeros than Tinder.

With the crash course in financials she had taken during the divorcee case, a brief glance showed that everything seemed up to par. But appearances could be deceiving. She clicked around through different files but her sleuthing didn't last much longer. It was difficult enough to find something when you knew what you were looking for. Right now, Nancy didn't even know what that was. The haystack was there, but what was the needle?

Discouraged, she snapped her laptop closed and then a thought popped into her head. She opened up her device again. Aaron W.—a name scribbled on a piece of paper on Barron's desk the first night she snuck into his office. A name was something and there was a chance that she might find an Aaron W. mentioned somewhere in Barron's files. Kerry Killen had already been crossed off of her list of people to check out, having determined that she was the head of a family office. But Aaron W. was still a mystery.

She clicked through a folder labelled 'Clients', which contained several sub-folders titled 'Fund 1 Clients' through to 'Fund 8 Clients'. There were eight in all, and one additional file that stood out: 'Potential Investors'.

Meticulous and methodical, as a P.I. had to be, Nancy clicked through each of the files starting with 'Fund 1 Clients'. The search function on each Excel spreadsheet revealed the presence of a few individuals named 'Aaron'. While the investors, typically Limited Liability Partnerships, or LLPs, were listed as the name of their LLP, the names of the individuals involved in them were written in another column along with information pertaining to dollar amounts, contact information, links to agreements, and various other key info.

Narrowing her search to 'Aaron W' brought fewer results. In 'Fund 1', there was just one match: Aaron Winter. She wrote down his name along with his contact information, partners' names, and the name of their LLP. 'Fund 2' through to 'Fund 5' revealed another Aaron W.: Aaron Wachowski. She noted his details as well. It was when she searched through 'Fund 5' that she came across an Aaron of particular interest. 'Aaron Wallace' might have been just another name on the growing list of Aaron W.s, except for one thing. Unlike Aaron Winter and Aaron Wachowski, whose contact information indicated they lived in New York and Toronto, respectively, Aaron Wallace's address placed him in the Cayman Islands.

As Nancy knew, if there was any offshore money-laundering to be done, the Cayman Islands was the place to do it. His residency wasn't damning, but it was curious. Another potential piece of the puzzle. She had yet to find any cold, hard evidence of nefarious dealings by the Benjamin brothers, but she couldn't help but feel that each new 'curious' thing she came across was a breadcrumb that would eventually lead her to the holy grail.

Her suspicions had mostly been focused on Teddy Benjamin up until that point, believing that he was the only one likely to be implicated in whatever fraud Clover Capital was perpetrating—and convinced that Clover Capital was perpetrating fraud, she was. But her suspicions changed with the discovery of Aaron Wallace. The fact that Aaron W.—surely Aaron Wallace—had been scribbled on Barron's desk was concerning. Sure, 'Aaron W.' could have referred to any of the three people whose names she had found in the 'Fund Client' files, but she had a feeling that it wasn't a coincidence. In Nancy's line of work there was no such thing as a coincidence. There was only evidence. And what she had now, however minute, was evidence. Evidence that Barron might be involved in something sketchy.

# CHAPTER 11

Clover Capital's office hadn't been the only thing under Nancy's surveillance the previous week. She had also been keeping tabs on the firm's two analysts, Josh and Brian. Under her watchful eye, she discovered that Hy's, an upscale steakhouse with an oversized lounge, seemed to be their after-work watering hole. It was a few short blocks away from their office, which made sense, and tonight Nancy was going to make her move.

She took a window seat in the pizza parlour across the street to watch people's comings and goings at the storied steakhouse. Her black locks had been stuffed into a plastic cap and hidden beneath a bouncy-blonde, long-haired wig, while her heavily made-up eyes were offset by a pair of bright blue contact lenses. Her lightweight trench coat, buttoned up tight, hid a bright-red crop top and a matching red miniskirt. Beneath it all, she wore one of her fake silicone chest-plates—opting for double Ds—the biggest ones in her arsenal. The silicone breast-plate was sweaty, not to mention heavy, but effective. The few diners who were seated in the pizza parlour had done double takes when Nancy had walked in the door. She didn't think the restaurant was used to heavily made-up women with high heels and pageant hair patronizing the place.

No bother.

She ordered a vodka soda and an appetizer, and saddled herself up to the window to keep an eye on the entrance to Hy's. No sooner had she finished her drink than she spotted the two Clover Capital analysts heading into the restaurant across the street. She fished $40 out of her purse, pulled on her shades, and told the waitress to keep the change. Seconds later she was across the street, having walked through the slow-moving traffic, and into the steakhouse.

A quick scan of the restaurant showed that the analysts—Josh and Brian—were seated at the bar and, fortunately for her, there was an empty seat beside one of them. She peeled off her trench coat as she walked past the hostess.

"Good afternoon." The black-clad hostess shot her a dazzling smile—her short brown hair fell to just beneath her chin. On the surface she sounded friendly, but Nancy could see right through it. The woman's thoughts were written all over her face, and they all said one thing—*hooker*.

She would definitely remember seeing Nancy again. Not that it mattered with her expert disguise. Nancy smiled back and kept walking: "I'm going to take a seat at the bar," she said over her shoulder.

As she made her way towards the Clover Capital employees, she could feel the eyes of other people on her—she couldn't blame them, really, given her getup. But she didn't pay them any mind—she was in character. She hadn't exactly gone for the hooker look, but it seemed that her 'big-tit bimbo' disguise had landed close enough.

"Excuse me," she spoke in a faux French accent to Josh, the analyst, who had an empty chair beside him. He turned away from his conversation with Brian and a look of surprise flickered on his face.

"Is this seat taken?" she inquired with a smile.

Stunned, Josh shook his head back and forth in slow, jerky movements while his mouth wordlessly opened and closed. His workmate, Brian, quickly jumped in.

"Please." He put his arm across the bar in front of his friend. "Take a seat. Don't mind my friend. He gets tongue-tied around beautiful women," he grinned at her.

*Smooth for a twenty-three-year-old*, she thought to herself.

"Merci beaucoup," she responded in perfect French and slid into the bar chair, taking care to toss her hair back seductively and cross her legs in an exaggerated manner. Josh, she was pleased to see, had yet to regain control of his motor functions; he was now staring at her gape-mouthed. She smiled sweetly and then turned her attention towards the bartender.

"Hello, Miss," he smiled through his chin-length, ruddy beard. "Can I get you anything to drink?" he gestured at the drink menu.

"Vodka soda, please," she said in her French accent. From the corner of her eyes, she saw Brian subtly smack Josh in the ribs. Josh shook his head briefly and then collected himself and took a big gulp of his drink—it looked like an Old Fashioned.

Nancy smiled. Josh's Old Fashioned screamed insecurity. He was trying to look seasoned, mimicking the older power players. An amateur might see him as an easy mark—someone who would spill his secrets to an attractive lady. But she knew better. Brian, self-assured, confident, and, she suspected, boastful—he was the one to crack. She hadn't expected that it would be easy, but with the way Brian was coming across, if she got him alone for ten minutes, she was confident she could get the information out of him in less than five.

They introduced themselves, with Nancy giving her name as 'Laura', and the three of them engaged in small talk about the bar. They were regulars, Brian bragged, talking about the various deals he had cut while doing business at the restaurant. Internally, Nancy rolled her eyes. As a financial analyst, the only deals Brian was cutting was on drink specials during happy hour. Still, she found his willingness to talk encouraging. She was certain that he could help her, inadvertently, navigate the case. Additionally, she had seen him at the dog park in a strained conversation with Teddy. That had to mean something. And whatever that something was, Brian was also clearly embroiled in it. Josh, on the other hand, she needed to get rid of. She just had to figure out how to shake him.

While Brian droned on about his academic achievements, Nancy thought through different options in her head. Should she fire up her fake Tinder account and swipe until she, inevitably, found Josh? Pay someone to hit on him as a distraction? She didn't know yet, but Josh had to go.

Brian was still talking and Nancy was coming up empty. None of the options seemed like a viable way of getting rid of Josh, which she needed to do if she was going to get any dirt from his friend. It was unlikely that Brian would jeopardize his job by talking shop in front of his colleague, but risking it in hopes of getting in a hot girl's pants? One only had to look at the myriad wealthy and powerful men who had been brought down by thinking with the wrong head to know how tempting that could be.

"Pardon me," she smiled at Brian, slid out of her chair, and grabbed her purse. "I have to make a call. I'll be right back."

In the short time since she had arrived the bar had become packed. It was a popular after-work watering hole for lawyers, bankers, and assorted businessmen who spent their Monday to Fridays in the downtown core. With the variety of suits and business-casual men and women milling around, today didn't seem to be any different.

She headed back to the entrance of the restaurant where the brown-haired hostess sniffed and gave Nancy a look of disdain. Nancy shot her a fake, sweet smile, then pulled out her phone, searched through her contacts and hit 'Call'.

The phone rang twice before her neighbour answered.

"Hello, Nancy!" Mrs. Jones sounded delighted—the old lady loved nothing more than to participate in investigations, which was usually what a phone call from Nancy meant. For most other matters, the two of them stuck to texting.

"Hi, Mrs. Jones," she turned towards the double-door

entrance and stepped into an alcove. The hostess appeared to be busying herself with tidying up the menus but Nancy could see her head tilt ever so slightly in an effort to hear her conversation.

She kind of got it. If she suspected someone was an escort, she would be interested in hearing what kind of phone conversation they were having in the lobby of a restaurant, too.

"Would you be able to stay on the phone with me for a few minutes?" Nancy asked.

Mrs. Jones was more than happy to oblige.

"Is there anything you need me to talk about or ask you?" the older lady inquired.

That was one of the myriad of things Nancy loved about her neighbour. Not only was she kind, great company, and a hoot to have along during a stakeout, but Mrs. Jones really 'got it'. Without any explanations, she understood the nuance of things Nancy asked of her.

"You're always so sharp," Nancy laughed appreciatively. "Nothing in particular this time. I just need to buy a few minutes to get rid of a guy."

"Lucky for you," Nancy could hear the sparkle of laughter in Mrs. Jones's voice. "When it comes to repelling men, that's where I do my best work."

The two of them shared a laugh and then Mrs. Jones took the lead by launching into a story about her day.

Smart old lady. It enabled Nancy to half pay attention while she navigated her way back inside of the bar. Josh and Brian were still keeping her seat and there was a crowd of suited men milling about just behind them. The group closest to the analysts consisted of five guys in a spectrum of black suits, each of them with a different drink in hand. Red wine, vodka, beer, martini, and some amber liquid that denoted hard liquor of the bourbon, scotch, or whisky variety.

"Mmm," she murmured as she zeroed into the red-wine drinker. He was facing away from her and was boisterous, gesticulating wildly with his glass, which looked to be at least ten to twelve ounces full. It was a good indication that the man was a repeat customer. Bartenders were known to be generous with the drinks when it came to their regulars.

She laughed at a quip that Mrs. Jones made about one of their neighbours as she positioned herself closer to Mr. Red Wine. When he made a wide gesture with his wine glass—usually a solid piece of proof that someone had been overserved—she took her cue and fake fell into him, pushing hard against his back as she 'tried' to steady herself.

Three things happened simultaneously—the man yelled "What the fuck!", the contents of his wine glass went flying, and Josh took a cabernet sauvignon shower.

"I have to go," she whispered into the phone to Mrs. Jones. "I will call you later." She ended the call and staggered upright, apologizing profusely to the man whose wine she had intentionally spilled.

"I am so sorry," she said in her French accent, giving him the most innocent, doe-eyed look she could muster.

His initial anger melted away as he saw the blonde bombshell who had bumped into him. From the corner of her eye, she watched Josh stand up and reach for a napkin. It was no use, really—she could see where the liquid had stained his white dress shirt and drenched the top of his head. His navy suit would do a lot to mask the vino, but nothing except for a shower could stop him from smelling like sour grapes. She mouthed "I'm sorry" to him apologetically as she righted herself and readjusted her clothes. Josh mouthed "It's okay" back to her and then gathered up his bag. He said something to Brian, who was laughing at his coworker's misfortune, and then turned to leave. The only thing Josh would be attracting that evening was fruit flies so Nancy wasn't surprised to see him heading home.

Exactly as she had hoped.

She watched him go, a flicker of triumph tightening her smile.

The man who she had 'tripped' into was gracious. He turned

down her offer to buy him another drink and instead he offered to buy her one.

"Thank you, I appreciate the offer, but I am occupied," she said apologetically and went back to her seat.

Brian, for his part, looked unphased. She was sure that he liked his coworker, but being down one friend made it a hell of a lot easier for him to put the moves on the blonde woman whom he thought he might have a shot at getting with.

"I feel so terrible that I caused your friend to go home," Nancy said, sounding sincere. "I would have at least liked to have paid for his dry cleaning."

"It's okay." Brian did a quick scan of his missing friend's chair to ensure there were no traces of wine and slid into the seat beside her. "Why don't you give me your number? I'll make sure he gets it."

Nancy demurred, saying that she would do so before she left, and then changed the subject to what she was really interested in talking about—well, listening to, at least—Brian's job.

"So, what do you do for work?" she asked innocently.

Brian's eyes lit up—it was his time to shine.

"I work with the Benjamin brothers," he said proudly.

A quizzical look crossed Nancy's face. "Benjamin brothers?" she feigned stupidity. "Is that like the Ringling brothers?"

Brian looked a little crestfallen—he had expected her to be impressed by his work credentials, not ignorant.

"You haven't heard of them?"

He immediately launched into a two-minute elevator pitch about Barron and Teddy Benjamin. By the end of it, she could understand why Clover Capital had snatched him up—Brian could sell ice in a snowstorm.

"Wow." Nancy arranged her face in some semblance of being impressed. "Do you work directly with them?"

"Oh, yeah," said Brian. "We're a boutique PE firm so I work with Barron and Teddy every day."

"That's so cool," Nancy gushed.

It didn't take much encouragement from her for Brian to start bragging about the work he did for the brothers. Before she knew it he was telling her how he had been hired on with them—"they were looking for the best, and that was me"—to the projects they were currently working on. A few well-timed gasps and compliments were all it took to keep him talking.

"That's so impressive," she looked at him with amazement. "Your first job out of school and you're working for two of the industry's most successful men."

"Working *with*," Brian corrected her.

"Of course," Nancy corrected herself. "Working with. They must see so much talent in you to give you such important projects."

Brian paused for a second—calculating, Nancy knew, the odds of him being able to get her into bed. She seemed impressed so far, yes. But he was thinking about what else he could he do to tip the scales in his favor.

"Let me tell you something," he boasted with a conspiratorial smirk. "I'm working on some side stuff with Teddy. We work together very closely."

"Oh?" she raised her eyebrows innocently. She appreciated Brian's game—talking up Barron and Teddy's success and then inserting himself into it.

"Yes." He paused for dramatic effect and took a sip of his drink. "He trusts me to get things done and be discreet."

"What kind of things?" Nancy played up the dumb blonde persona.

Brian sat back for a second, with one hand grasping onto his glass.

"It's a secret project with some of our accounts. Let's just say we're dealing with large sums."

"What kind of accounts?" she asked innocently, tossing her hair before taking a sip of her drink.

"Investment accounts," he leaned in closely. "Between our funds we have around $750 million of investments. When one fund matures, the investors get back their money plus the percentage that they were promised, and then we get to split the rest."

"Sounds like an easy way to make money," she prodded him in her faux French accent. "What's the catch?"

"No catch. We just have to ensure that the funds do what they say and actually make the money."

"Then what are you working on with Teddy?" she scrunched her brow in curiosity.

"That's a secret," he said with a smirk.

Nancy gave him a flirtatious grin back: "How about a hint?"

Brian's smirk widened and he said one word: "Wires."

It was a vague answer, but in conjunction with the records she had swiped from Barron's computer, she was starting to put the puzzle together.

For the next twenty minutes, she pretended to warm to Brian's advances as what he told her roiled around in her head. When Brian began to get a little too familiar, his hand brushing the tops of her thighs, she excused herself to the washroom and slid out the back door. She hadn't given him her number. A clingy analyst was not a complication she needed with this case.

And besides, she was fucking his boss.

Later, at home, she sat pondering what Brian had told her. It sounded like Teddy was doing something without his brother's knowledge. And typically, when you're in a partnership, it's like a marriage—you don't keep secrets. Secrets could sink the ship.

She might have to set up another 'chance' run-in with Brian, she reflected—the analyst's information could prove to be invaluable. If she needed more intel, Nancy knew where to find him—saddled up to the bar at Hy's waiting to impress a pretty face.

# CHAPTER 12

The next day she had blocked off to prevent any bookings in The Cell. Her dominatrix clients needed their fantasies fulfilled, but she was on a roll with Barron and Teddy. She wanted to spend the day working on the case.

Teddy was starting to look dirty at this point, but she was secretly hoping that Barron was clean. She liked him. Then again, what woman with a pulse didn't? His revolving door of hookups was a testament to that. Not that Nancy's feelings for him mattered either way. One of the rules she had for herself was to never get involved with clients or the people she was investigating—emotionally, that is. Getting them into bed? Well, that was just another handy tool in her arsenal. If sex appeal got her get closer to the truth, she wouldn't hesitate to use it.

Her mission that morning was to do some digging into the construction company that was renovating Clover Capital's buildings. She didn't know who she would run into, but she planned to dig up as much dirt as she could. With the list of buildings that Clover Capital owned, courtesy of Ms. Elena Fineberg, Nancy zeroed in on the apartment that had initially put her client on alert.

Orchard Estates was in a rough neighbourhood, near a school that Ms. Fineberg's foundation worked with. As far as infiltrations went, the apartment building would be a lot easier for her to access than Barron's laptop and Clover Capital's offices. And as for disguises, it didn't take her long to put one together.

In her hallway mirror she took in her long legs and tight red dress. She planned on posing as a real estate agent who was looking to cash in on new clients. With the addition of a long, brunette wig, square rimmed glasses, and the highest heels in her closet, Nancy was sure she looked the part. She was going for sexy librarian and, if the image in the mirror was any indication, she had nailed it.

She had whipped up some fake flyers for her fake real estate work in under thirty minutes—quick, dirty, and just convincing enough. She wasn't sure if she would actually have to use them, but it was always good to come prepared. Which was one of the reasons why she had chosen her current outfit. If there was one thing she knew about where she was heading, it was that men who worked manual jobs in male-dominated industries would appreciate an attractive, scantily clad woman in pumps. What they *wouldn't* realize was that her sex appeal was meant to disarm them before she used her brain to get the dirt.

A swipe of candy apple–coloured lipstick topped off her ensemble and she headed for her car. Minutes later she was hightailing it onto the Gardiner Expressway. Traffic was light, which was a surprise for a weekday. Probably the summer lull that had people on vacation and working reduced hours. Still, it took her a good twenty minutes to drive to her destination. She could see why Elena Fineberg's foundation did charity work in the area—the neighbourhood definitely looked like it needed it.

Spray paint littered every vertical surface in sight, and rusted out gates and garbage cans dotted the streets and back alleys. Unkempt houses were overrun with junk and overgrown weeds while air conditioning units balanced precariously in their upper-floor windows.

Nancy's eyes caught on a rusted tricycle lying on its side. She exhaled slowly—no kid should have to grow up like this.

In a word, it was bleak; the children who lived there were put at a disadvantage from the minute they were welcomed into the world. Which, of course, was why Ms. Fineberg worked with the neighbourhood school. Trying to give disadvantaged youth a shot at success that would be more elusive for them due to circumstances beyond their control.

It was admirable, really. Not everyone who accumulated wealth wanted to give back. Some of them spent their time cooking up tax-avoidance schemes, lunching, shopping, wining, dining, and one-upping. But there *were* others who put their hard work and good fortune to philanthropic use. And Ms. Fineberg's altruism was one of the reasons why Nancy was so focused on figuring out this case. Her investment with Clover Capital was meant to generate returns that would enable her foundation to support more underprivileged youth. Nancy couldn't think of a more worthy cause.

Her vehicle bounced around the gravel parking lot of Orchard Estates—the run-down building just ahead. The name gave off visions of abundance and grandeur, but the reality of it was much less luxe. Orchard Estates was a low-rise building with about ten floors in total. Which, Nancy was given to understand, was typical for this type of neighbourhood.

*Funny*, she thought to herself. She was starting to think like a real estate agent. Which was fitting given that, in a few minutes, she would have to start playing the part.

It was maybe a surprise that Nancy had had no formal training in acting. Instead, she found she came by it naturally; it was easy for her to morph in and out of personas. She was like a chameleon. And once she put on a disguise, she was in character until the camouflage came off.

She put her vehicle in 'P' and stepped out onto the dusty, gravel-littered pavement—it was the hallmark of any construction site; they would need a backhoe-sized broom to get rid of the mess. High heels probably weren't the smartest choice when going to a renovation site, she reflected.

Aside from her SUV, which she had parked closer to the street than to the building, there were only three other vehicles in the parking lot—all of them situated near the entrance of the apartment. Just as Ms. Fineberg had described, the trucks were dated, dusty, and rusty. 'The Reno Crew' was emblazoned on the side of the vehicles in a red-and-white logo. Elena hadn't remembered the name of the construction company when she came to see Nancy so she hadn't been able to run any background checks on it. She pulled out her phone and ran a search. Time to see what The Reno Crew was really up to.

The Reno Crew's 'About Us' revealed a ten-year-old construction firm that specialized in new builds and renovations. Company size wasn't mentioned, but the totality of three vehicles for a ten-story building and lack of any notable names on the website that the company had done work for led her to believe it was a small outfit. Which made sense—the smaller your workforce, the smaller the costs. And from everything that she could see, the Benjamin brothers were looking to cut costs any way they could. The rest of the The Reno Crew's website revealed the founder's name, Michael Butterfield, but no photo. Disappointing but unsurprising. Trades typically weren't concerned with posting photos of themselves online like they were in business, law, and finance. But she *was* hoping that Michael would be at the building, and she felt that the odds were in her favour, given that it seemed to be a small company. It made sense that the owner would be working alongside his employees to get the job done.

The workers hadn't razed the building from the ground up, instead it looked like they were gutting each unit—tearing them down to their wooden bones. She dodged rocks, dust, and potholes as she teetered over to the building, and double-checked to make sure she had stuffed her fake realtor pamphlets in her purse. She had kept the pamphlets simple with her name, contact information (a burner number and email, of course), and photos of houses that Katarina Kusnetsova ostensibly had up for sale.

A couple of 'Caution, Men at Work' signs outside of the building signified to visitors to tread carefully. Nancy, in her sky-high heels, braced herself for dust, dirt, and grime, and walked through the set of propped-open glass doors.

The lobby of the building was bland and carpeted in a grime-darkened floral pattern that had clearly seen better days. Boot marks from the construction crew left a trail towards the elevators, and the white walls were covered in scuff marks and water stains. A large grid of mailboxes was embedded in the west-facing wall while the other contained a glass-encased bulletin board. The lobby, she assumed, would also be getting a makeover and she was curious to see what it would look like when it was done. With the current state it was in, a lit match would be an improvement. Which was hardly a surprise. There was a reason why the Benjamin brothers sought out buildings like this—they could be spruced up with a reasonable amount of time and money. When you were dealing with dirt, beat-to-hell appliances, gross carpeting, walls, and doors, it only took a bit to make it look better. And with the amount of money Barron and Teddy had raised to invest in the buildings, they could do a lot more than a little. She assumed the apartment's structure was sound—the brothers were focused on unit facelifts, not foundations—and hoped the remodeling wasn't merely a case of putting a little lipstick on a pig.

While the state of the building's disrepair didn't surprise her, what *did* surprise her was the deafening silence. Renovation work wasn't quiet, and the work being done on Orchard Estates wasn't confined to one unit—it was a full-building makeover. The crew had to be there somewhere, the work vehicles indicating as such. It was just a matter of her finding out exactly where. Which would be a lot easier if she had the sound of heavy machinery to go by. Instead, it looked like Nancy would just have to check it out floor by floor. She headed towards the elevators and was thankful to find that they were working. It wasn't a guarantee when an entire building was being gutted.

On some construction sites the elevators were programmed to only respond if someone inserted a special key.

The 'up' button illuminated and several seconds later, the elevator doors opened. She stepped inside and hit '10'. At each floor, when the lift's doors would open, Nancy would take a step onto the floor and listen. On the top three floors, she was met with silence. It wasn't until she made it to the seventh floor that she struck audible gold. She smoothed down the sides of her tight red dress before heading down the hallway.

On the seventh floor she finally heard something—chatter, the thud of a hammer, and, briefly, the whine of a saw. Building materials, two-by-fours, large orange pails, tools with electrical cords attached to them, and plastic drop-cloths littered the hallway, and she maneuvered around it all until she reached the unit with people inside—714.

She poked her head around the corner, her wig itching slightly, and saw the men a split second before they noticed her.

"Hi!!" she enthused as five sets of surprised eyes turned to meet hers.

There was a collective look of confusion on the faces of the five men who, seconds before, had been diligently working away.

"Can I help you?" inquired a silver-haired man with lightly toasted skin and a lined face. He carried a clipboard in one hand and his gray, sweat-stained t-shirt and blue jeans were covered in a thin film of dust.

"I'm sorry." She smiled as she stepped into the room and took a brief glance around her. When Clover Capital said that they would renovate each apartment unit, they weren't kidding. Suite 714 was completely gutted—a wooden skeleton whose meat and skin would be added on in increments.

"I'm a real estate agent and I'm new to the neighbourhood," she said in a friendly manner. "I saw that this building was being worked on and I thought I would come and say 'hi' and introduce myself. I'm Katarina," she added as she looked around at the eyes still trained on her.

The group said nothing. Despite her explanation, they still seemed confused as to why she was there. Obviously real estate agents weren't popping in every day to have conversations with their crew.

"Nice to meet you, Katarina." The silver-haired man finally spoke. He walked forward, wiped his hand on his blue jeans to brush off some of the dust and then stuck it out in greeting. "I'm Michael."

*Michael—Michael Butterfield.* The exact man she was looking for.

The rest of the men, realizing that Michael was going to take care of the intruder, turned and got back to work. Nancy engaged The Reno Crew's owner in friendly chit-chat and she was pleased to find that Michael was genial, down-to-earth, and a bit of an open book.

She steered the conversation towards the company they were doing renovation work for.

"Between you and me," he said pointedly, "we didn't get the Clover Capital contract at first. I was disappointed but that's business," he lamented over the background sound of his crew hammering away. "But two weeks after they told us another company had won the bid, Clover Capital contacted me and said they'd like to hire us."

Nancy nodded along.

"It's a huge contract. Great for our small business," he said with pride. "It keeps us going and really gives us the chance to show what our guys can do. We're working hard to stay on time and on budget."

"Congratulations," she said sincerely. "I'm sure Clover Capital will be impressed with your team. They look like hard workers," she gestured to the men who were busying themselves with the renovations. "Did Clover Capital pick out all of the materials for the furnishings?" she asked casually.

"Well, see," said Michael, "that's another thing that changed." He rubbed his stubbled jaw with one hand while holding the clipboard in the other. "The materials were all changed at the last minute. Appliances, countertops, toilets—the whole shebang." He gestured at the apartment unit.

"Interesting." She smiled. It really was. "What would be the reason for doing that? I suppose to save some money?" she asked innocently.

Michael nodded. "Likely. In this economy, with interest rates as high as they are, it makes sense that they would cut back on costs. But it was pretty abrupt. And surprising that they were able to source all new material in such a short time frame."

It was Nancy's turn to nod, but privately, she didn't find it so strange. If her intuition was correct, the cheaper materials had been sourced long before the abrupt switch. And it had been done in secret. The question was—just who from Clover Capital had made the decision? And who from Clover Capital was in on it?

After giving Michael her fake realtor spiel, she stuffed some leaflets into his hand, thanked him for his time, and headed back to the parking lot. She was just about back to her vehicle when she noticed her SUV was leaning to one side.

Odd. She squinted her eyes in confusion before realizing the problem—a flat tire. Fantastic. Just what she needed.

"Everything okay?" a muscly construction worker who had just emerged from one of The Reno Crew's trucks yelled over.

She paused for a moment and shook her head 'no'.

"Flat tire," she yelled back. "Slashed tire," she corrected herself more quietly. She had parked far away from the building to avoid dust, dirt, and dings. But in doing so, she had created another problem. In the short time she had been inside, someone had taken the liberty of slicing open one of her tires.

*Better a slashed tire than a keyed car*, she mused, but a flat *definitely* did not fit into her schedule today. And while she was a self-sufficient, independent woman, changing a tire was not something that was in her skill set.

Muscles suddenly appeared beside her like a shirtless mirage. He eyed the slash and let out a whistle.

"That's a shame." He turned to Nancy. "You got a spare?"

The sun glinted off the slight sheen of sweat that covered the man's face. His hair was slightly tousled, slick with sweat, and a five o'clock shadow covered his jaw. A Greek God in construction clothes—blue jeans, steel-toed boots, and a sweaty white shirt.

"I do," Nancy smiled at her slashed-tire savior. The familiar longing sent a jolt through her body as she pictured what was underneath his sweaty shirt—washboard abs tanned to perfection, she imagined. Most of the time she could take care of herself, but there were those rare instances where she required a muscled man in vizzy-vest armor to rescue her.

Unfortunately, back-seat 'thanks' wasn't something she had time for. Not that she couldn't fit it into her schedule if she tried. She smirked at the thought. She had been working hard to avoid impulsive choices lately. Maybe the weekly AA meetings were doing something to help her after all. Or maybe the case had just taken priority over pleasure today. Either way, muscles wouldn't be getting his rocks off this afternoon. At least, not with Katarina.

She popped open the trunk and stepped back as muscles took over. He grunted and groaned while working the tire over like it was a piece of dough. She found herself wishing she was the spare tire. What she wouldn't give to have those rough mitts all over her body.

"All done, Miss." Muscles stood up from the pavement and dusted himself off.

"Thank you," She paused, not knowing his name.

"Rocky." He held out his hand.

"Rocky." She smiled back. "Katarina. Thank you, I don't know how to repay you."

Okay, that was a lie. She knew exactly how to repay him. Rocky wasn't wearing a wedding ring and by the way that he was eyeing her up, he was undoubtedly single.

"No need to repay me, Katarina." He wiped sweat from the top of his brow and pushed his hair off his forehead. "Just pay it forward," he said with a grin.

"Done." She smiled before Rocky turned and headed back towards the building.

Crisis averted, she was soon en route to her office. The information that she had learned from Michael was forefront of her mind as she made the now forty-minute trek back downtown. It had been as Ms. Fineberg has suspected—her eye for interior design, and high-end appliances and materials had not led her wrong. The builder had confirmed that they were using materials that were several thousand dollars cheaper than the ones that they had been shown at the start of the project.

Michael had been told that Clover Capital was trying to cut down on costs and that the investors were in the loop. Only it seemed that none of the investors *had* actually been made aware of it. Not that the builders would care—it wasn't their money. They were just being paid to install it.

She had also found out, due to the chatty builder, that The Reno Crew hadn't initially won the construction bid. Oddly, Clover Capital had initially chosen a rival construction company—one Michael heard was charging nearly two-and-a-half times what The Reno Crew had bid. If Nancy had to guess, that was no accident. A higher price tag gave them cover for where all of the money was going. Then, right before the documents had been signed but after the monthly update to the investors had been sent out, Clover Capital had pulled out of the agreement and contacted The Reno Crew instead. It had been entirely unexpected for Michael, but it was a huge get—they were going to be refurbishing all of the buildings for one of Clover Capital's funds. Seven buildings in all. A massive and lucrative contract for the company. And because there had been nothing binding with regards to the builders' bids, Clover Capital had easily been able to switch companies without the original contractors giving any blowback. The Benjamin brothers' firm needed no reason and she imagined that no reason was given.

Another piece of the puzzle clicked into place. Things were starting to take shape now in Nancy's mind. By telling investors

they were going with a construction company that would charge sky-high prices, it would justify where a large portion of the money was going, in addition to the high-end finishes and appliances. And when they switched out the materials and the builders for much more economical, low-cost ones, that left them with a large surplus of money.

What was or would be done with that money was a different question. But if Nancy was a betting woman, and she was, she would bet that some of that money was being skimmed off of the top.

Teddy, from what she knew, had a bit of a gambling problem. Barron, she still wasn't sure of. But her discovery last night that had led her to Aaron Wallace, one resident and investor based in the Cayman Islands, made her suspicious that he was in on it, too. Additionally, it was nearly impossible for her to believe that one hand of Clover Capital didn't know what the other was doing. *Especially* given the two partners were twin brothers. It would make sense if both of them were in on it. It would be pretty ballsy if Teddy had gone it alone and was trying to pull the wool over his brother's eyes.

She needed a closer look at the company's financials. And *not* the ones that they shared with investors. Everyone knew that those could be doctored. A piece of paper stating that you had millions in the bank meant nothing. Look at Bernie Madoff. Nancy needed the originals, which she was sure she would find on Barron's hard drive.

Her plan for that night was to spend some serious time doing a deep dive into Clover Capital's financials. Now she felt more confident in scouring the spreadsheets. She still didn't know exactly what she was looking for, but she had a better idea of it now. That was how cases went—one day you didn't know what you were doing, but one conversation could turn into a lead. She had that now, and was hoping it would lead her to the culprit. Or culprits, as she was starting to suspect. Still, she mused, her conversation with Brian, the Clover Capital analyst, had made her aware that Teddy and he had been keeping their 'special' project a secret from Barron.

There was the chance the Aaron W. whose name Barron had written down on his desk *had* actually been in reference to another of the Aaron W.'s invested in their funds. Or maybe, just *maybe*, Barron had some suspicions of his own.

She mulled the thought over. It did have merit. She was usually pretty good when it came to judging a person's character. And with the exception of him being a hard-partying playboy, she didn't get any bad vibes from Barron. His brother? She really couldn't say, but from what she had seen of him so far, there was something about him she just didn't trust.

The secrets and interplay between the brothers and their employee Brian were another piece of the puzzle. She was trying to figure out how it fit into the bigger picture but that picture was still too blurry for her to see. Spreadsheets danced in her head as Nancy fidgeted about in bed, her mind too wired to sleep. She had spent several hours going through the financial records that evening, but she hadn't found what she was looking for.

It was typical for an investigation. Aside from the cheating-spouse cases, which were usually easy to solve, mysteries didn't come together as quickly as they did in books and movies. Oftentimes, especially if she was dealing with financial crimes or a complicated case, it could involve several days of slogging through computer files and email accounts. Bloodshot eyes and a massive migraine were the usual end result along with, most importantly, what it was she was looking for. Sometimes it was a name, sometimes it was an admission, sometimes it was an obscure reference that sparked an idea in her head. It wasn't always the case, but her labour, typically, bore fruit.

# CHAPTER 13

She woke up in a puddle of cold sweat, her heart pounding like a drummer on speed.

*Jamie.*

The image of her blond-haired, green-eyed ex-boyfriend had popped up in her dream. They had been skating at The Bentway—exchanging laughs, knowing grins, and teasing touches. In her dream, her heart had swelled. She had skated over and nudged him playfully, but dream Jamie had turned to her with a look of disgust. Hurt and confused, Nancy had asked him what was wrong, but he just stood there, staring at her like she was roadkill while people skated merrily around them.

He hadn't been on her mind before bed and it had been nearly four months since Jamie had last shown up in her dreams. She shook her head as she reached for the glass of water on her nightstand. The liquid caught in her throat and she let out a spluttered cough, which fully woke her up.

Would she ever get over him?

Still coughing, she took a few deep breaths, successfully downed some more water, and then settled back into the fluffy confines of her down comforter. Mentally, she washed away the image of her ex. The Benjamin brothers took his place at the forefront of her mind.

Maybe one day she would deal with the damage that Jamie had done to her, but today was not that day. For now, she would box his memory firmly away and shelve it as best as she could. Unfortunately, it was much easier to do when she was awake. The subconscious played by different rules. She could only hope that one day, when memories resurfaced, it would no longer elicit the feeling of being punched in the gut or of the floor giving away beneath her.

Before she started attending the AA meetings, she would have consoled herself with a stiff drink. Or seven. Which probably would have ended in a one-night stand with the first guy who glanced her way. But this morning? That didn't even cross her mind.

That had to count for something, didn't it?

Privately, she had a theory about why thoughts of Jamie had resurfaced. Aside from him, it had been six months since she had really connected with anyone. Sure, Barron was handsome, intelligent, charming, and fun. But more than that, there was something else—the two of them had a spark. A connection. Even if she knew that it wouldn't go anywhere. *Couldn't* go anywhere.

He was at the center of Ms. Fineberg's case, and no matter how tempting it was to imagine something more than an orchestrated fling, she had to keep her head on straight and keep her emotions out of it. Still, she was enjoying his company. While certainly helping to move the case forward, he was also a welcome distraction. She just had to make sure that she kept her wits about her.

With a reluctant sigh, she slid out of bed and made herself an espresso. The strong scent of coffee filled the kitchen and, mug in hand, she headed to her laptop and fired it up.

The spreadsheets stared back at her, just as they had the previous evening. The more she looked at them, the less they revealed. It was like being faced with an impenetrable wall—she needed to see what was on the other side, but she had no ladder, no chisel, and no way through.

One thing she knew was that if the Benjamin brothers were hiding something, it wouldn't be easy to find. With the advent of technology, if someone *were* to get ahold of their records, the last thing they would want was an easily combed-through document that readily revealed evidence of fraud. What Nancy had going for her was her access. She had all of the records, every document, file, and financial statement, thanks to Barron's computer. Because of that, she could at least see the wall, which was better than feeling her way around in the dark. All she needed now was to find a crack.

In an inspired moment the night before, she had run several spreadsheets through some forensic accounting software—FraudFindr, SpreadsheetSoftware, and Ocrolus. It was a long shot and, as she had anticipated, they had turned up nothing. But that didn't discourage her. She would have been shocked if it had been that easy.

Espresso in hand, she spent the next two hours in spreadsheet hell. It was overwhelming at first as she poured over the records, but the deeper she dove, the more she began to understand the size and scope of Clover Capital's business. Their balance sheets were squeaky clean, and three of the four funds had north of $80 million in investments—some of which Nancy knew came from Ms. Fineberg's foundation.

Financial institutions had strict reporting requirements, but private equity firms played by looser standards. They only had to report to their investors, which gave them a lot of leeway. And, unlike mutual funds, individual stocks, and ETFs, many PE clients were locked in for years. Which was the case with Clover Capital. The funds that their clients were invested in disallowed them from taking their money out for three years.

From everything that Nancy could see, the numbers lined up. In their first fund, the investment was even outperforming projections. Which certainly explained why Clover Capital seemed to have such an easy time obtaining capital. Yields like those would have investors lining up with briefcases full of cash.

Yet, Clover Capital wasn't that well-known. It was crazy to think of the vast amounts of wealth out there—so much that a firm with almost a billion dollars under management was just another blip in the financial landscape.

She spent another hour combing through the various records of wire transfers—there were a lot of them. It would have taken her years to go through them manually, but thanks to the fraud-detecting software, she simply uploaded the files and watched each spreadsheet clear the scan within seconds.

Still, it didn't make any sense. Her Hy's encounter with Brian, the young Clover Capital analyst, had her convinced that whatever was going on, the key to it was the wire transfers. But maybe she was wrong. If there was something in the wire transfers, surely the fraud-detecting software would have caught it?

By late morning, Nancy's eyes felt like sandpaper. Knowing the sheer number of records she still had to slog through, she thought that if she never saw another spreadsheet again, it would be too soon. After she solved this case, she wasn't taking on another financial investigation for a while. She would be happy to chase cheating partners for a bit if it gave her brain a bit of a reprieve.

She sat back for a moment and took a sip of her sparkling water. Lemon—her favourite. On a whim, she clicked the 'Properties' of the spreadsheet she currently had open, and skimmed the details.

Created by Theodore Barron. That checked out. Last edited? That checked out, too. Next, she clicked on 'File', 'Info', then 'Version History'.

Two previous versions of the spreadsheet popped up. She clicked on the first one and, what appeared to be, an identical version of the spreadsheet she had been looking at popped up, too. She minimized the two sheets so that she could view them side by side and started doing a quick scan.

She was only a few rows down the sheet when she spotted a discrepancy.

Curious.

In the previous version of the spreadsheet, the one that she had just opened, it showed wire transfers going to a numbered company. The version that had been saved on Barron's laptop, however, showed the wire transfers going to a different numbered company.

That couldn't be right.

Unless . . . one of the spreadsheets was fraudulent. Intentionally doctored to make it appear as if the wire transfers had gone somewhere else.

This was it. This was the key. She was sure of it.

But which brother was involved? Barron, Theodore—or both of them?

She meticulously scrolled through the two spreadsheets side by side, checking each wire and highlighting the differences. Two hours later there were ninety-four teal-highlighted rows. Ninety-four transactions that were actually wired to a different account than what the official records showed. The doctored spreadsheet had various amounts ostensibly being wired into two of the firm's different funds—account numbers of which she had obtained from the banking records on Barron's hard drive. The original spreadsheet, the un-doctored one, showed that the money—some sums in the millions, others in the hundreds of thousands—was being wired to two different account numbers. Ones that hadn't shown up anywhere in Barron's banking records.

In total, it appeared that more than $120 million that was supposed to go to two accounts for Clover Capital had actually been wired to two accounts that appeared not to have any connection to the company. There was certainly the possibility that the brothers had other numbered companies that operated in and around the firm. But if that *was* the case, Nancy reasoned, she should have been able to find records of those account numbers somewhere. The fact that she hadn't found any led her to believe that the $120 million had gone to personal accounts. Holding companies were likely, but not ones that were affiliated with Clover Capital. Whoever had transferred the money, it looked like, was taking it for themselves. Why else would they have gone through the effort to doctor the 'official' wire records?

Next she clicked onto the financial statements for the two funds that had, ostensibly, received the $120 million wires. Just as Nancy thought, their balance sheets showed that $60 million had been wired to each fund account. Only, Nancy had the evidence proving that they hadn't. Which meant that Clover Capital had been sending out fraudulent financial statements to their investors. But how, she wondered, were they managing to cover the costs for the real estate that the funds purchased? The money that they raised was used to buy apartment buildings, which were then refurbished and rented out for a higher price. Apartment buildings weren't cheap and each fund purchased anywhere from ten to twelve buildings. At $5 million on average per building, there was a reason that the brothers needed to raise such a large amount of money. But they would also have to actually *purchase* each of the buildings and get mortgages on them. And the banks certainly wouldn't give them any money if they knew that there was fraudulent activity going on. Nor would they give them any money if they knew that the firm didn't actually have the amount of capital they purported to.

Well.

They actually *did* have the money at one point, Nancy reasoned. It had just been wired *after* they had shown their financials to the bank and obtained a mortgage.

Smart. Fraudulent but smart.

She pondered what to do with the information and realized that she needed more evidence. She needed to find out more about the numbered accounts where the money had been diverted to. Who did they belong to? Where were they based? And, perhaps the biggest question of all: who knew about them?

If Nancy's instincts were correct, Teddy was the dirty twin, and he had done all of this behind his brother's back. Of course, speculation and instincts were all well and good, but it wouldn't hold up in a court of law. Nor did she think it would be enough evidence to bring to Barron. Blood was thicker than water, and she needed to ensure that she had all of her records in a row in order to take down one half of Clover Capital. Ms. Fineberg's money was supposed to be tied up in one of the two funds that had been robbed by way of several secretive wires. If Teddy got wind that she was sniffing around, there was a good chance that he would bolt. It was just a hunch, but everything that Nancy knew about money laundering told her that, with that massive sum of money, Teddy had more than likely wired it offshore to render it untouchable by the tax-man and any feds who came after him. He would have been smart enough to put the accounts either under a different name or in two holding companies that had a convoluted, barely discernable paper trail that ended at him. Was that where the Cayman Islands resident Aaron Wallace came in?

The whirring of the Xerox printer went off at full blast as it began spitting out papers. She made copies of all of the records she had found that showed fraudulent transfers. After she had compiled all of the info she would bring it to Barron to confront him about his brother, and then bring it to the police.

But before she did any of that, she had to make absolutely sure that Barron wasn't in on any of it. It wouldn't do any good to fuck up her case if she warned the handsome financier about his brother only to find out he was also involved. It also wouldn't be good for her health. When that kind of money was involved, people were expendable. And while she could hold her own when it came to physical combat, she would rather not have to be concerned about being taken out by either of the brothers or any hired henchmen. After all, $120 million could buy you a lot in terms of personal protection. Nancy had watched enough *20/20* episodes to know that sometimes you could get someone to off your spouse for as little as $10,000—mere pocket change to someone who had almost $120 million sitting in the bank.

If she was lucky, she felt that she would have this case tied up in a bow by next week. When it came to investigations, as soon as you had the key, things were smooth sailing. Teddy, she was certain, would be behind bars soon or, if he was lucky, out on bail. Barron would hopefully be able to get out ahead. And Ms. Fineberg—Nancy was sure that she would get her investment back given the paper trail that she had found. The investment wouldn't come with the returns that the brothers had initially promised her, but at least she would be made whole.

Nancy hoped that the foundation's Board would take it easy on the old lady. The Benjamin brothers' real estate model was actually pretty promising, and had Teddy, alone she assumed, not decided to enrich himself to the tune of $120 million, Ms. Fineberg's investment would have boosted her foundation's bottom line.

Where Barron was concerned, she was fairly convinced of his innocence and consequently felt badly for him. It wasn't his fault that his brother had made moves that would take down Clover Capital, but he would certainly reap the consequences of his brother's actions. How Barron would ever be trusted in finance again was unfathomable. She couldn't see anyone wanting him at their company or, if he decided to set up his own company, wanting to invest with him. He may not have been the one who committed the crime, as far as she could tell, but because of his close proximity, and the family name, the stench of fraud would rub off on him. If there was anything she knew about the Toronto social scene, Barron would be persona non grata.

She briefly wondered how it would affect his sex life.

Probably not much. He still had a large amount of money in his personal accounts and he was, after all, a financial whiz. Unless he was sued by investors, for which he could claim complete ignorance and innocence, Barron would never want for anything. In fact, such a fall from grace might just give him the kick he needed to settle down his wild, bad-boy partying and womanizing ways.

She had slept with Barron several more times over the past

little while and genuinely enjoyed his company. But she wouldn't let her mind wander too far. He was a great catch, sure. But she knew better than to start daydreaming.

A glance at the clock told her she needed to get herself in gear and head to The Cell. Aside from her next objective that afternoon, which was to research the numbered companies that the wires had gone to, she had some domme clients to attend to.

*

The black latex squeaked with every step Nancy took around the room as she checked to ensure that everything was ready for her client. Barry, a sixty-year-old partner at one of Bay Street's top firms, was known as a pit bull in the courtroom. His name was regularly in the papers, boasting about the companies that he had gotten off the hook. A top-tier litigator, he argued cases for companies the likes of Coca-Cola, Boeing, Rogers, and Concord. The billable hours he brought the firm were astronomical, and, even in his day-to-day work life, he made associates and partners alike tremble with fear. Barry's aura of no bullshit, no nonsense straight-shooting and inability to suffer fools gladly had made more than one administrative assistant quake in her shoes. The short tenure of Barry's new hires had become a bit of a joke in legal circles.

But what the tabloids, various associates, companies who retained him, friends, family, and colleagues *didn't* know about Barry, was that in the bedroom, or at least in the confines of Nancy's not-so-safe space, the high-flying litigator liked to be humiliated.

He had submitted an inquiry about her services two years ago via her website, and Nancy had discovered information about his law career while doing her routine due diligence on the potential client.

It wasn't a surprise to her, really, what the lawyer was into. It seemed like most of the powerful men whom she counted as clients enjoyed being dominated and fully at her mercy. At least for the odd hour here and there. She supposed it had something to do with always being in control and the desire to give it to someone else, however briefly.

She always found it entertaining when she encountered men who craved humiliation. It was an ironic fetish for people who enjoyed dressing down their foes. But maybe it was a way of getting a taste of their own medicine. And maybe it was why people like Barry enjoyed their work so much. If humiliation was his fetish, he inflicted enough of it on his courtroom adversaries to keep himself satisfied for centuries. Or maybe that sort of humiliation only served to satiate his ego. Because, goodness knew, being on the receiving end of it was what satiated him sexually.

She always looked forward to sessions with Barry. His greatest pleasure was derived from the denigration of his manhood. She had put together scripts when she first started, and had practiced them in front of the mirror. It wouldn't have suited to have her clam up and not know what to say or come off sounding meek during a session. As she had gotten more clients she sharpened her verbal shaming skills, and was now a pro at dressing down undressed men.

Sometimes the insults that flew out of her mouth left even Nancy feeling surprised, but the one thing she could always count on was that they would usually make their intended mark.

She glanced at the clock—quarter to the hour. Barry would be here any minute and she was ready for him.

Unlike most middle-aged men, Barry kept himself in tip-top shape. He was the typical type A personality. He ran five days per week, played squash the other two, lifted weights regularly, and meditated every day. Her mind boggled at how the man managed to fit it all into twenty-four hours. And despite having a packed daily schedule, he always made time to fit in a bi-weekly session with Nancy.

Most of her prep work for Barry involved loading up her verbal arsenal with insults and humiliating phrases. It was kind of fun. Their sessions made her feel a bit like a dirty poet—the Bard of Bawd.

As the door to The Cell swung inwards, Nancy greeted Barry with a smile.

"Oh, look," she mocked, "it's shrimp dick."

# CHAPTER 14

She was close to solving the mystery. So close, she could almost taste it. Or maybe that was the expired almond milk she'd taken a chance on this morning.

*Here's hoping that one doesn't come back to haunt me*, she glanced at the half-drunk glass on her coffee table.

Her sessions in The Cell the previous day had left her exhausted; she hadn't made it home until around 9 p.m. But that was always how it was when she was working on a case. As the investigation heated up, she had to dedicate more time to her detective work. And that meant cramming more domme clients into fewer days.

She reflected on everything she knew so far about Ms. Fineberg's case. While everything wasn't quite tied up with a nice little bow, she knew that evidence of the wire transfers was one of the ribbons. The only thing she needed now was the transfer records. And she suspected that Brian, the Clover Capital analyst she had met the other evening, would have those records in his possession. His bragging about the secret work he was doing with Teddy all but sealed it. It was too bad she had left him high and dry during their first encounter and hadn't taken down his number.

She berated herself silently.

Sometimes, when it came to solving cases, she wasn't blocked by obstacles that were put there by others, but by barriers she accidentally created for herself. She had violated one of the prime directives of her detective work: always ensure you get contact information for any suspects or side-characters who could be useful in solving the mystery. With Brian, she had legged it out of the restaurant as soon as the twenty-three-year-old had gotten handsy. Sure, she'd gotten some information out of him, but now she would have to try and track him down the old-fashioned way. No phone, no AirTag, no social media . . . she would have to go full stalker, vintage style.

Frustration started building in her chest and an overwhelming urge—one she hadn't felt for almost eight weeks—suddenly reared its ugly head. It hadn't always been like this, but since Jamie, urges to drink and act impulsively took over any time she felt she had screwed up.

She paused for a second and considered, very briefly, how bad a road that would be to go down. Attending her weekly AA meetings had so far been keeping her self-destructive tendencies in check, and she didn't want to give up the progress she had made.

A game of tug-o-war started playing in her mind. She had two choices: one, distract herself until she overcame the urges, or two, give in, get drunk, and get laid.

Seconds later, her fellow AA member Eric's business card was in her hands and she was typing his number into her phone.

*Hi. It's Nancy*, she typed out and paused.

She shouldn't be doing this. She *really* should not be doing this.

She pressed 'Send'.

A few minutes passed with no response. Maybe she would get lucky and he would ignore her message?

Two minutes later a text popped up in reply.

*Nancy! Great to hear from you. Glad you reached out. What are you doing tonight? Do you want to go for drinks?*

She hesitated. She did want to go for a drink. But she knew exactly where it would lead her in her current state of mind

She was playing with fire and felt conflicted. But no small part of her was shamefacedly enjoying it. Like a pyromaniac with a flame in her hand and two conflicting consciences on her shoulder.

*Absolutely* she texted Eric back.

To tamp down Eric's expectations, she kept her outfit neutral. Black slacks, kitten heels, and a light, long-sleeve sweater with a crew neck. Before she could say "bad idea" she was headed in an Uber to King West. The Wheat Sheaf was Eric's place of choice, which fit with his surfer-boy persona. It was a low-brow establishment with cheap drinks and live entertainment.

She spotted him sitting at the bar as soon as she walked in. His hair, his crowning glory, was recognizable at any distance.

"Hi," she slid into the seat next to him.

He turned to her and smiled: "Glad you could come."

She smiled back and the bartender came over to take her order.

"Gin martini. Extra dirty."

"Extra dirty?" Eric's voice was imbued with a hint of flirtation. "Is that also how you like your men? Because if so, I happen to know someone who might fit that bill."

*Oh god.* She *really* should not be doing this.

Eric's eyes flickered with desire and as she gazed at them, she felt a familiar rush of excitement well up inside. This was her high. The thrill of the chase and the rush of success. It was pure predation. Impulsivity running wild.

"So, what do you get up to when you're not attending Addicts Anonymous meetings?" Eric said coyly.

Nancy leaned back in her chair.

"Meeting up with not-so-anonymous addicts at the bar," she teased back.

This was wrong. So wrong.

Eric let out an involuntary laugh as the bartender placed a

gin martini in front of her.

"Cheers," Nancy clinked her glass against Eric's vodka on the rocks and took a drink. The first sip cracked open the floodgates. Her frustration at the case was immediately forgotten and her attention focused on surrendering to her impulses, no matter the cost.

They bantered back and forth for nearly forty minutes as the alcohol coursed through their bloodstreams. Nancy's first martini disappeared quickly and, just as quickly, she ordered up another. It was liquid courage, but a different form. She was using one addictive substance to push her into another.

Two martinis later and Eric was leaning in close. He brushed Nancy's hair behind her ear and stared at her with hungry eyes.

Well, the 'hungry eyes' part was mutual. The two addicts shared a heated glance. How no one around them seemed to notice the energy they were giving off was unfathomable. It crackled—dangerous and electric.

*This is wrong*, she thought to herself again. *So wrong.*

There was a reason that she had been going to her weekly AA meetings. Getting blitzed and seducing men wasn't going to fill the empty hole in her heart and it wasn't going to allay her work frustrations. It helped her to feel better in the moment, but like addicts are wont to do, when it was over, the high would transform to a low, leaving her with a moral hangover in addition to an actual hangover, too.

Minutes later, the bill was signed for and Nancy was ready to tear off Eric's clothes. The heady rush of adrenaline mixed with the alcohol in her body and lit a fire in her veins. The guilt she had been feeling minutes before disappeared—pushed to the back of her mind while her inner addict took over.

Eric looked like he was similarly affected.

"Your place or mine?" his voice had taken on a deeper tone.

"Yours," Nancy blurted out quickly.

In the Uber, they were all over each other. Nancy caught a glimpse of their tangle of limbs in the rearview mirror. Eric's mouth was on her neck as he passionately kissed up and down her skin and she gasped in pleasure.

*Wrong*, she thought to herself again. The alarm bells were going off in her head, but instead of 'panic!', the alarm had transformed into strobe lights and was giving 'Panic! At the Disco'.

She was practically sitting on top of Eric now. Her hands running through his hair and down his hard-muscled body. He grabbed her ass and continued ravaging her neck, his fingers wandering to the heated place down below.

Pity she had worn pants. She'd meant well at least. But she didn't know who she thought she was fooling.

When the car pulled up to Eric's condo, they spilled out into the street, their hands still desperately groping. They rode the elevator up to the penthouse, barely managing to keep their clothes on. Eric's hands went up her sweater and grasped at her breasts in her balconette bra.

It all happened so fast she didn't even register what his home looked like. They were like a couple of crack addicts—each of them looking to get their fix. Their clothes lay strewn across every surface just inside of Eric's condo—they had practically torn them off the second they stepped through the door. Then they had stumbled, like some four-legged abomination of nature, into Eric's bedroom.

Before Nancy knew it, she had gotten her fix.

Eric's eyes were closed next to her as they lay there beside each other, both breathing heavily and lost in their own thoughts.

She stared at the ceiling. The high that she had been chasing had abated and was replaced with a fast-creeping, inebriated shame. The reality of what she had done hit her like a ton of bricks. She had just hooked up with a fellow Addicts Anonymous member. This was a new low. Anxiety began gnawing at her brain and co-mingled with the overwhelming sense of shame.

She had to get out of there.

Nancy flung the navy duvet off the bed and headed for the

door. In the flurry of her and Eric wanting to satiate their individual needs, she hadn't registered where all of her clothes had landed. All Nancy knew was that when they had entered his bedroom, she'd been fully naked.

She found her pants crumpled up against the foyer wall and she shook them out before stepping into them. Her bra, which had been the last to go, lay on top of the kitchen counter, having obviously gone airborne in their haste. A mirror that stood just inside of his front door had her black sweater hanging from the edge. She cringed as she reached for the knit and caught a glimpse of herself in the mirror.

She didn't just feel like an addict—she *looked* like one. There was a red flush to her skin that complemented her bloodshot eyes. Scratch marks left angry red welts across her body and there was a black smudge of mascara under one of her eyes. Tangles of her black hair stood up in every direction, looking like she had somehow gotten caught up in a hurricane. She recoiled at the sight of herself—her appearance was the literal embodiment of her addiction. She snatched up her sweater and threw it on.

Eric, she noticed, hadn't moved from the bed. Not that she had expected him to. Or wanted him to for that matter. The two of them had crossed a line. She shuddered to think what Carmella would say if she happened to get wind of what two of her therapy attendees had engaged in. Not that she would be telling anyone about this.

Her purse lay on the floor with all the contents, somehow, miraculously intact. She gathered up her things and slunk, ashamed and silent, out the door.

At home, she took a long, hot shower and washed her hair and her makeup off her face. The water couldn't get rid of the scratch marks or the shame, but it did make her feel a bit better. She wondered what it would take to exorcise her addiction demon. She would have to try showering with holy water next time.

Eric didn't text her that evening and she didn't text him

either. She resolved to compartmentalize the experience and push it far into the back of her brain.

There wouldn't be a next time. She was resolute. Frustration with herself be damned. The impulsive action with Eric was her last slipup. She couldn't keep being self-destructive every time she felt down on herself or was facing an obstacle.

She realized that, until now, she had been deluding herself about her addiction—thinking it wasn't *that* bad. But anything that drives a person to take unhealthy actions that leave them feeling guilt and shame is not something to take lightly.

To feel better about her transgression, her solution would have been to really focus on her weekly therapy sessions. But how could she even show her face to the group next Tuesday? Especially given Eric would be there.

If she was lucky, she reflected, he wouldn't show up.

Before bed that evening she drank two glasses of red wine. Two large glasses. It was the opposite of self-care—it was self-neglect. But she needed it in order to fall asleep; the anxiety and guilt she was feeling would keep her up all night otherwise.

That evening she went to bed with wine-stained lips and a heavy heart full of shame.

# CHAPTER 15

Soft beams of light peeked through the edges of her curtains the next morning as she pulled herself out of her groggy haze. She had slept through the night, yes, but it was the shallow, unsatisfying kind of sleep that usually accompanied liquor. As she stretched out in bed she was dismayed to find that, instead of abating, her shame and anxiety from the night before had increased. It wasn't good, but it was a good reminder for her to never go down that road again.

Not just with Eric. With anyone.

A carb-loaded breakfast and some coffee did something to perk her up, but she was still feeling down in the dumps. Not that it would keep her from her investigation. That afternoon, she was planning on another 'chance' encounter with Brian, the analyst from Clover Capital.

Last time, she had excused herself to the washroom before sneaking away when he started to get handsy. Tonight, however, she was going to let him take her home. But she wasn't going to sleep with him—no, no. Nancy knew that she could get what she wanted without dragging him into bed.

It was one of the parts of her job that she loved: strategizing and using different ways and wiles to get what she needed. And what did she need tonight? To break into Brian's computer . . . while Brian was there in the room with her. But first, she had a long day's worth of administrative slogging to get through.

*

A mid-afternoon walk to her local sandwich shop broke up the monotony of the day and she enjoyed the basil, tomato, mozzarella melt on a park bench across the street.

A high pitched bird-song pierced the air as the sounds of traffic played a symphony around her. People talking, dogs walking, and a warm breeze did nothing to cut through the sweltering heat. At her condo a few hours later, she closed her laptop and headed for her bedroom. It was time for her to get into disguise for the mission she had planned for that evening.

The getup that she had donned the first time she ran into Brian was a bitch to get on. The hair usually never took too long owing to her myriad of ready-to-go cut-and-styled wigs. The one she had worn last time and would put on again was voluminous and blonde with big, bouncy, blown-out curls. It was the makeup that was time consuming. She popped in the bright-blue contact lenses that she had worn the first time she saw Brian, before she started on the war paint. *Someone should invent the wig equivalent of makeup*, she thought to herself. Goodness knew that it would cut back on the amount of time she spent getting into disguise.

An hour later and she was in her dark, smoky-eyed face paint with bright red lips, and her double D prosthetic chest. Flipping through her outfits, she hemmed and hawed between a tight, black mini-dress with a scoop-neck that would show off her faux cleavage, and a silky, short, red slip dress.

Given her painted lips, she opted for the black. Besides, it wasn't a bad thing to have a cleavage distraction. Even if it really was just a silicone breastplate. Aside from looking realistic, the dim lighting would lend a hand. She just had to make sure that Brian didn't attempt to get too familiar en route to his place. Although, with the popularity of breast implants nowadays, he probably wouldn't think twice.

She brought a hand up and squeezed one of her silicone boobs. Firm, but not too firm, and just the right amount of softness. With the help of a push-up bra, which was a necessity when you had a chest of this size, no man would be any the wiser.

She squeezed into the black minidress and then pulled on the piece de resistance—the blonde wig—and inspected the results. She only bought the highest quality human-hair wigs, so there was never any risk of looking like she was wearing a cheap rug.

Some spiky black stilettos completed the look. She grabbed a small, black purse and filled it with night out essentials: lipstick, blotting paper, powder, gum, credit cards, and a flask.

The warm, humid weather meant there was no need for a jacket, so she slid on an oversized pair of black Chanel sunglasses and headed for the door. She debated walking but ultimately chose an Uber. That, at least, would prevent people from ogling her on the street. She wanted attention tonight, yes. But she only wanted it from one person.

Minutes later she was in the back seat of a car. The last time she had seen Brian, she had been lucky enough to catch him at the steakhouse. She was hoping that the second time would be just as lucky as the gray Honda Civic wove through traffic towards Hy's.

It was a beautiful summer afternoon—the sun was shining with nary a cloud in the sky. The warm breeze didn't exactly bring much relief from the heat, but it kept the air from feeling too heavy. Nancy thanked her lucky stars that Mother Nature was on her side that day. If the humidex was too high her makeup would be sliding off her face. Not to mention she would be sweating underneath her silicone chest. Given the temperature, she was just hoping she wouldn't develop heat stroke and pass out on the street. What a surprise the EMTs would have when they went out to *that* call—cutting open her dress to find a massive pair of detachable silicone knockers. Knowing Toronto, someone would take a photo and she would end up on the front page of BlogTO with her cover blown.

"Welcome back." The same hostess as last time eyed Nancy as she breezed into the restaurant.

"Taking a seat at the bar again?"

"Yes, thank you." Nancy barely glanced at the girl before heading in. She picked a seat strategically—choosing one with empty chairs on either side. A quick, surreptitious glance around the room told her that Brian was not here. Yet, at least.

She ordered a vodka soda, remembering just in time to put on her faux French accent.

That was the thing about playing different characters during an investigation—there was a lot that you had to keep straight if you didn't want to get caught. She couldn't very well go from French accent to none and expect her target to believe her. She was a good detective for a reason. Whether it was due to the stress of what she had done with Eric the previous evening or the thrill of the chase, her nerves were dancing all over the place.

She always got like this when she was close to solving a case and she thought she had finally figured out what was going on with Clover Capital.

The restaurant was brimming with activity. It was only late afternoon, but leftovers from boozy business lunches lingered, identifiable by ruddy cheeks, boisterous conversations, and empty bottles on their tables. More people streamed in off the street and from the office building above. Nearly ninety minutes passed and all of the seats at the bar were occupied.

But no Brian.

On her second vodka soda, Nancy finally accepted that it was time to pack it in. While she hadn't expected the analyst to show up at 4 p.m., she was certain that he would come by. From her surveillance, it seemed like there was hardly an evening that Josh and Brian didn't go out for at least one drink.

She cursed herself for not giving Brian her number. There were worse things than having a lust-filled twenty-three-year-old chasing you. She took a long sip of her drink and debated what to do. Her disguise had taken no small effort to get into and she certainly wasn't going to waste it by going home.

On the off chance that Brian was still at work, she decided to stake out the lobby of Clover Capital's building from a restaurant just across the street.

She paid with her phone and left Hy's without a backwards glance at the hostess. Clover Capital was just three blocks away, and Cactus Club would give her the perfect view of the firm's lobby.

Unfortunately, everyone else seemed to have the same idea with regards to sitting on the restaurant's patio and for the second time that day, Nancy's plan was thwarted.

Resigned, she stepped back onto the street. She didn't know what to do now. Not wanting to look too conspicuous—not that her slutty getup and overdone makeup were out of place in that part of town—she stepped away from the door and pulled out her phone, trying to figure out her next move.

Moments later she was shaken out of her detective reverie by a voice.

"Can I buy you a drink?"

A turn of her head revealed a brown-haired banker in a gray suit, unbuttoned dress shirt, and a winning smile.

She hesitated before smiling back. After all, tonight didn't have to be a *total* failure.

"So?" he asked again, now that he had her attention. "Can I?"

Nancy cocked her head in feigned curiosity: "I don't know—can you?"

He let out a short laugh. "Yes. I can."

"How about I buy you a drink instead?" Nancy asked in her faux French accent.

The suit looked intrigued.

"Deal—how about Earl's?"

They fell into playful conversation as they walked the two short blocks. It took until they were almost at the restaurant before they formally introduced themselves. Nancy introduced herself as 'Laura', the buxom, French alter-ego whose skin she was currently in. The banker—she had profiled him correctly—introduced himself as Johnny.

The patio at Earl's, as expected on a sweltering summer afternoon, was packed tighter than a can of sardines. Fortunately, that meant that there was space inside. And air conditioning. The breeze had helped to keep her makeup from melting, but it wasn't doing anything to allay the sweat that was starting to pool on various parts of her body.

The dark-green bar was dotted with drinks, cell phones, and plates as the downtown crowd ramped up after work. She slid into a seat beside Johnny and menus were pushed in front of them seconds later.

"I'll have a vodka soda," Nancy asked the bartender before Johnny ordered up a negroni.

"So, Laura," Johnny leaned back, his arm casually resting on the bar. "What do you do?"

Internally, Nancy rolled her eyes. Johnny might look like a scrumptious piece of rib-eye, but his conversation skills were lacking.

"I'm in marketing," she replied with a practiced smile.

"Oh?" Johnny perked up. "Which firm?"

*Lord*, she thought to herself. Of course she would end up out for a drink with the one man in the city who was actually interested in her made-up marketing career.

She smiled sweetly: "It's a large firm out of the U.S."

Johnny contemplated that for a second.

"No specifics," he said flatly.

Nancy kept her smile tight and let it hang there.

"Interesting," he squinted at her.

"I have to run to the washroom," she said in her fake French accent, then slid off her stool.

Johnny was going to strike out tonight, and it looked like she was, too. While he had offered a pleasant enough distraction, she wasn't interested in getting to know him or in getting him into bed. His personality had been a disappointment, but maybe that was for the best. She really felt like she was making progress with her unhealthy patterns, her dalliance with Eric the other night notwithstanding, and she didn't want to sabotage her momentum now.

After taking the maximum reasonable amount of time in the bathroom without it seeming like she had ghosted, she stepped out and glanced around the restaurant.

At a bar on the opposite side of the room, a familiar silhouette caught her eye. A slow smile slid across Nancy's face.

*Well, well, well,* she thought to herself.

What were the odds? Out of all of the watering holes in the downtown core, Brian had ended up at the same one as her. Nancy didn't believe in luck, but she was happy to pretend it was on her side tonight.

Now, she just had to get rid of Johnny.

For better or worse, there was typically little conversation between her and the men she casually hooked up with. Better because she didn't have to endure terrible and boring small talk. Worse because if she *had* actually talked to most of the men beforehand, she likely would have never hooked up with them at all. Like many things in her life, it was a double-edged sword.

Johnny had proven the rule: hot face, empty head. Which just went to show why you shouldn't judge a book by its cover. Sure, she'd had felt a stir of attraction when he first approached, but a few minutes of conversation had been enough to convince her that he was not someone who she wanted to spend more time with.

"Well," she said, interrupting him mid-ramble once she returned to her seat. "Thank you for the drink, Johnny."

"Thank you for the . . . ?" Johnny looked confused, eyeing her still mostly-full glass.

She offered the same sweet smile she had disarmed him with when dodging his earlier questions before she picked up her glass and drained it in one go.

Johnny's open-mouthed stare almost made her laugh. He was starting to comprehend: 'Laura', as it were, was moving on.

"It was lovely to meet you." She said, rising from her seat.

"But I see someone I need to talk to."

Johnny blinked, then turned back to the bar without a word.

Not her most graceful exit, but she was on a mission. And besides, the restaurant was ripe with women just waiting for a man like Johnny to buy them a drink; given how forward Johnny was, she figured that the seat beside him wouldn't be empty for very long. She hadn't particularly enjoyed his company, but she also had to admit: if it wasn't for Johnny, she wouldn't have found her target this evening.

She made her way to the restaurant's other bar. There weren't any open seats beside Brian, but that wasn't going to stop her. Luckily, despite the seats next to him being occupied, he appeared to be there by himself. It was a good bet that he was either flying solo in hopes of picking someone up or he was nursing a drink before meeting up with friends.

Either way, it would work to her advantage.

The way she had left Brian the first night wasn't going to earn her any points. But she also knew that someone like Brian would jump at the opportunity to try again. Especially when that second change was the beautiful and big-chested 'Laura'. She was betting that this ego would take it as a sign and double-down on his attempt to woo her.

The restaurant pulsed with music; loud enough to drown out the raised voices and laughter. Brian sat hunched over his phone, his mop of brown hair slightly dampened from the outside air despite the air conditioning in Earl's, which was running at full blast.

Nancy approached him from the right and gently laid her hand on his arm.

"Brian?" She asked, feigning surprise in her faux French accent.

Brian turned to look at her and surprise lit up his face.

"Laura!" he exclaimed, dropping his phone to the bar with a soft thud.

"I thought that was you." She said with a smile as a drop of sweat trickled down her back.

*Damn silicone tits.*

"Are you here with someone?" His tone was casual, but the eager gleam in his eye gave him away.

*Perfect*, she thought. He was still interested. Probably thinking that fate had intervened and was giving him a second shot at the blonde bombshell.

"I had a drink with an acquaintance," she said. "I was just on my way out when I thought I saw you from across the room."

It wasn't technically a lie.

"Do you have to leave," he asked, "or can you stay for one more?"

Brian played it cool, but Nancy could see tell he was hopeful.

"Well," she pretended to think about it. "I suppose I could stay for one more . . ." she trailed off. "And I'm terribly sorry about the other night." She left out the part about pretending to be going to the washroom before slipping out of Hy's and leaving Brian all alone. "I realized in the bathroom that I was very tipsy and I was concerned that I wouldn't make it home."

"Don't worry about it," Brian grinned. "And don't worry about not making it home tonight. I'll make sure you get home safely."

"That's so sweet of you," she beamed.

He smiled in reply: "Let's get you a seat."

Brian turned to the man next to him and asked if he would shift down two chairs so that they could sit together. The man and his companion happily obliged. Two suits. Obviously happy to help a fellow man on his quest to conquer Nancy.

"Vodka soda, right?" he asked as Nancy got herself settled.

"Good memory," she nodded. Tonight was going to be a piece of cake.

An hour later they were on their second drinks, although she could tell it had been many, *many* more than that for the analyst. She was ready for anything that evening, but if things went well, she wouldn't even have to bring out her flask. Drugging was never her first choice of action, but sometimes it couldn't be helped. Not that what she had in her purse would technically be considered drugs. What it could be considered, however, was some form of gasoline.

Not literally, of course.

It was something that her father had often referred to as 'legal moonshine'. Everclear—the 190-proof clear liquor, the taste of which some had likened to drinking nail polish remover and others had described as a drink so potent that it would "peel the paint off of a wall." All Nancy knew was that when she needed to get someone slur-speech drunk, it did the job.

More people packed into the restaurant as Brian spouted off about himself like he had the first night they had met. He was telling her about the time he had worked on a $10 million deal when he was interrupted by an angry voice behind him.

"Slut!"

Nancy turned to see Johnny, her two-hour old acquaintance. She was taken aback but kept her composure—Johnny was going to be the one who came out looking bad in this situation.

"Who the fuck are you and why the fuck are you yelling at my date?" Brian stood up, posturing like a prize-fighting rooster.

Johnny's hair was out of sorts and his eyes were red and glassy. "None of your fucking business who I am, but I was with this skank," he gestured to Nancy with an upturned chin, "an hour ago." His voice, amplified by multiple negronis, attracted the attention of the people around them and Nancy felt several sets of eyes on them. She saw Brian's hand twitch—she could tell that he wanted to punch Johnny. Nancy didn't blame him. She wanted to punch him, too.

"You need to apologize to this woman and then get the fuck out of here," Brian said aggressively.

It wasn't a challenge; it was a demand. Brian wasn't particularly attractive to Nancy, but his sudden posturing had her reconsidering. There was something about a man who was willing to stand up for a woman that was a total turn on. Probably something that harkened back to the days of the caveman, she pondered. She could more than take care of herself, but Brian's knight-in-shining-armor performance was appealing. And while she wasn't sure which one would win in a fight, she knew that a fight was the last thing she wanted. Having two men fighting over you might be some women's fantasy, but Nancy was more focused on the case.

For a split second, she thought Johnny was going to swing at Brian but he seemed to think better of it and drew himself up with a sneer.

"Enjoy your slut." He turned and slunk off. "Marketing. Hah!" she could hear him yell. "The only thing that bitch is marketing is herself!"

Johnny was an obnoxious asshole. But he wasn't wrong. He had the big picture—sort of. She was marketing herself, yes. But not in hopes of getting paid or laid—just in hopes of obtaining intel.

She was pleased to hear that the people in the restaurant whose conversations had died down at Johnny's outburst had amped back up to their previous level of loud. That was the way she wanted it. As a detective, it was never good to make a scene. Flying under the radar was how things worked in her world. She needed to stay anonymous; just another face in the crowd.

"Sorry about that asshole." Brian turned towards her—there was a tender look in his eyes.

*Fuck*, she thought to herself. She really should have gotten Johnny's number. She wanted to send him a fruit basket. He had tried to embarrass her in front of Brian by calling her a slut. Which she found a bit funny. When it came to embarrassing her, many had tried but few had succeeded. And from the look on Brian's face, it appeared that all Johnny had succeeded in doing was bringing out Brian's caring side. Which perfectly suited Nancy's needs.

One bottle of wine later Nancy had discovered that Brian's tenderness was actually a double-edged sword. It had endeared 'Laura' to him, yes. But it also looked like he was going to end the night by being a total gentleman and not trying to get her into bed.

Which just wouldn't do.

She didn't want Brian to start thinking that she was a woman he could bring home to his family. And, frankly, his tender talk and heartfelt oversharing was a total turnoff. Finally, she could take the fawning no longer and ordered up two shots of tequila.

"To your beauty."

Nancy suppressed a grimace at his toast as they clinked their shot glasses together.

She set down the empty glass and turned to the analyst.

"Brian?" she paused as if about to ask him a serious question.

"Yes?" he asked attentively, probably thinking that she was about to pour her heart out to him like he had been doing for the past forty minutes.

"Let's skip the sweet talk and get to the part where you take me back to your place."

His eyes widened and he looked taken aback.

But still interested.

Nancy may have accidentally just given him a new playbook for his pickup game, she reflected. Although she could guarantee if he tried it on another woman it would be a one-way ticket to loner-ville.

"I just have to go to the bathroom." He pushed his chair back from the bar.

"Actually," Nancy feigned having second thoughts. "How about we stay for one more drink and then get out of here? I'll order for us."

"You're so sweet, Laura," Brian rubbed her shoulder as he made off for the bar.

Nancy grimaced, then waved the bartender over.

"One water-cran and one Aunt Roberta," she ordered.

The bartender's dark eyebrows drew down.

"Aunt Roberta—you're sure?"

"Oh, I'm sure," she smiled.

Aunt Roberta was one of her secret weapons. A heady

mixture of absinthe, gin, vodka, and brandy; it was 100 percent alcohol, and had been described as "less of a cocktail and more of a cry for help."

She didn't have an Aunt Roberta, but the moniker felt fitting. And in a few minutes, she was going to introduce Aunt Roberta to Brian.

The burgundy-coloured drink was waiting for him when he came back from the bathroom and he sniffed it curiously before recoiling at the smell.

"What is this?" he asked, his face screwed up in a look of revulsion.

"It's one of my favourite drinks," she said sincerely and took a sip of her watered-down cranberry juice. "It's called 'Aunt Roberta'."

He shot the drink a dubious look.

"Aunt Roberta must have been a drunk."

Still, he wasn't going to let a glass of turpentine insult his strength. The liquid left a red stain on his lips—similar to the one his hangover was going to leave tomorrow on his soul—and the taste brought out a slight scowl. It was only slight, Nancy knew, because he was making a serious effort to mask it.

She had tried an Aunt Roberta once. And only once—the memory of it still sent shivers down her spine.

Brian set down his glass.

"What do you think?" she asked eagerly.

He coughed as the alcohol worked its way down his esophagus. "It's good," he wheezed.

Nancy smiled. She knew he was full of shit. From her own experience she knew the drink felt like a high-grade acid was eating away at your insides.

As she had hoped, by the time Brian was halfway done his drink, he was slurring. It was really amazing how hard Aunt Roberta hit.

"What do you say we get out of here and go back to your place?" she said with a mischievous grin.

Brian's brown eyes filled with lust and he signaled to the

bartender for the cheque.

"Finish your drink," she encouraged when he made a move to push the glass away. "In memory of my Aunty Anne who loved that cocktail."

Nancy's fake aunt was all the encouragement Brian needed and he chugged the remainder of it down.

Which was perfect. The full weight of the Aunt Roberta would be hitting him by the time they made it to his place and Nancy hadn't even had to drug him. He may not have ordered the glass of gasoline, but he sure as shit drank it freely.

Minutes later the bill was placed in front of them and Brian was swiping his card. Not a corporate card—his own, she noticed. Which made sense. As an analyst who was just starting out in the industry, he was the lowest man on the totem pole. Company credit cards wouldn't be in his grasp for several years. Maybe never, if Brian was caught up in Teddy's dirty dealings.

"Let's go to your place," Brian slurred as he led her by the hand and wobbled out of the restaurant.

*Not a hope in hell*, she thought to herself. His angle was obvious and she found it amusing. Even though Brian had the hots for her and wanted nothing more than to get her into bed, he didn't want to head to his place and chance her spending the night. Much easier to go to Nancy's and then slip out once the deed was done.

"I can't," she tossed off in her fake accent. "I live with my sister and my nephew."

Brian, more interested in getting laid than worrying about waking up tomorrow with a houseguest, quickly replied.

"Okay, let's go to mine."

He pulled out his phone and, with some drunk-eyed squinting, ordered an Uber. The car was two minutes away and Brian decided that it was time to make his move. He pulled Nancy towards him and leaned down to give her a kiss.

Nancy moved her head away and whispered in his ear: "Not here, not yet. Wait until we get to your place," she said in a breathy voice. "Then I'm going to take your pants off and blow you until your knees buckle."

Lust filled his eyes and he took a step back as he looked her up and down. His mouth was gaping open, but she wasn't sure if it was due to drink or desire.

"Laura," he slurred. "I am going to take you to pound town."

It was all Nancy could do to keep it together. *Pound town?* Was Ponyboy fucking serious?

Brian kept his hands mostly to himself during the six-minute drive to his condo, during which time he was hit by the full force of the Aunt Roberta. By the time they got to his building, his face was red and he had a deer-in-headlights look about him that featured in every DUI episode of *COPS*.

As she had predicted, he lived in one of the standard newish condos where the units were doll-sized and the buildings contained every amenity known to man. The vertical communities tended to house people in their twenties and early thirties; the party crowd, the people who were just figuring things out. The crowd who were establishing themselves in both their careers and the bars on King Street.

In the elevator she detected a faint smell of vomit—typical for these types of buildings. Brian swayed on the elevator ride up and it came to a stop on the thirty-eighth floor.

Brian, it appeared, lived in a one-bedroom unit alone. Which wasn't bad for someone in their early twenties. The Benjamin brothers were clearly paying him handsomely. She wondered if he would still be on their staff roster if the brothers knew how loose Brian's lips were—and not *just* when he was drinking. She thought back to the first night they had met and how Brian had talked about his work with Teddy after only knowing her for an hour. Then she thought back to the heated conversation the analyst had had with Teddy in the dog park.

She didn't know what the conversation was about, but it did look like trusting Brian was another bad decision in Teddy's long list of them.

Brian's living room was two steps from the front door and she helped him onto his navy sectional and then went back to the door to remove her shoes. The heels that she had worn that night were some of the highest that she owned and her feet were aching because of it.

"Laura—" Brian started to slur from the couch.

"One second," she said, buying more time. "I have to use the washroom."

She strode past Brian's nearly lifeless body and into the bathroom. The toilet seat was up—*quelle surprise*, she thought in half French before pulling it down with her foot and taking a seat. She allowed herself to relax for a minute and took her phone out of her purse. She had time to kill. Brian certainly wasn't going anywhere. At least, not under his own power.

There were a few text messages, one WhatsApp message, and some emails. The emails, mostly bills and vendors she subscribed to, could be dealt with later. So could the text messages. But the WhatsApp message is what caught her eye.

*I know you didn't ask me to, but I found something that might be relevant to your case.* It was a message from Angus.

*What is it?* she sent back. *Actually, don't text it*, she typed. *Can you meet me at Fran's tomorrow at 9 a.m.?*

*Fran's—9 a.m. tomorrow*, Angus sent back.

She could see that he was still typing.

*What kind of shape are you going to be in? It's almost 1 a.m.!*

She paused for a moment. It was Angus's way of digging into what she was doing. The two of them were friends, but there was a barely concealed jealousy on Angus's side that occasionally crept into things.

Usually, it was when he had been drinking.

*Working on the case*, she sent back without further explanation. From past experience she knew that in the bright light of a sober morning all of his feelings would be forgotten.

*Got it*, he sent back.

The mobile went back in her purse and she rolled her neck around in search of relief. The silicone chest was a heavy burden to bear. She couldn't wait for some relief, but that wouldn't come until she was back at her place. She couldn't very well walk out of Brian's condo holding a giant pair of silicone knockers.

A dramatic sigh escaped her lips as she leaned back on the toilet tank for a few seconds.

*One one-thousand, two one-thousand*, she counted before turning on the water and rinsing off her hands. A look in the mirror showed her looking not too worse for wear. Which was surprising given the makeup she had troweled on her face and the silicone heat-suit she'd been sweating in for the past few hours.

Alas, it was all going to be worth it if she got what she was looking for tonight.

The faucet turned off with a barely perceptible squeak and she put her ear to the bathroom door to listen.

Silence.

No snoring. Just silence.

Which could mean one of two things: Brian had managed to fight off the alcoholic aunty or he was sleeping, just without the deep alcohol snore. If it was the former, she still had the flask of Everclear and could pour him one more drink. If it was the latter, well—she would just have to give it a bit until he fell into a deeper sleep.

She cracked the door open and peered at the couch. Brian's eyes were closed. He was sleeping but not soundly. Which presented her with a problem. If he awoke when she was going about her mission, how would she play it off? She stood there for a second, trying to formulate a plan.

*Fuck it*, she thought and headed for his desk, which was situated just behind the sectional. His closed MacBook sat there plugged in and waiting.

She dropped her purse on the desk and picked up the metal device. Obviously she hadn't known what type of computer the financial analyst would own, but, dimes to donuts, if he was in finance and in his twenties, there was a better than good chance it was an Apple.

The last time she broke into a computer to copy its hard drive she had used her makeup to get inside. This time, she had no need for such theatrical methods. For this break-in she was going for crude, quick, and effective.

Brian let out a snort and she froze for a moment before his in-and-out breathing rhythm resumed. She opened his laptop and the screen came to life—a beach-scene background with a single username waiting for a password or fingerprint ID. Taking the laptop in one hand she crept over to where Brian was lying. The lower half of his body was on the floor and his head was resting on a pillow at one end of the sectional. His left hand was on his stomach and his right hand was wedged between the back and bottom cushions of the couch. Slowly, she lifted the back couch cushion off his hand and maneuvered the laptop toward it. It was an awkward angle and she prayed to the detective gods that Brian wouldn't wake up. With a gentle touch she turned the laptop so that the fingerprint scanner was right beside his hand before she pressed down hard on the bottom cushion with her other hand and slid the laptop underneath his fingers.

She let out the breath she had been holding and waited for a finger twitch or other reactions from Brian's unconscious body, but none came. Next, she slid the fingerprint ID scanner ever so slowly under his index finger.

Immediately, the laptop came to life and Brian's desktop appeared.

*Voila.* She was in.

Using the same technique that had just afforded her success, she removed the device and lightly placed the cushion back on top of Brian's hand. She moved quickly, set the device back on his desk, then inserted the USB stick into the dongle and started downloading the contents of his computer.

The progress bar showed three minutes remaining on the download when Brian started snoring. She knew he was going to be in for a world of hell tomorrow and wondered what his work would bring. Despite Barron and Teddy being hard partiers, they always made it to the office first thing in the morning. It really was some kind of miracle that they could function after a night out and just a few hours of sleep. And not just function, but flourish.

When the green bar indicated that the download was complete, she packed the flash-drive away safely and then headed for the door. The last thing she wanted to do was put on her sky-high heels, but she couldn't very well walk out in bare feet.

With one last glance at Brian, passed out and disheveled on the couch behind her, she slipped on her shoes, gently closed his door, and headed home. Who knew if he would even remember Nancy going home with him? The effect of the drink was so strong that she didn't doubt that it had the ability to retroactively erase memories.

The exhaustion hit her during her Uber ride home, but the tantalizing mystery of what might lie on Brian's hard drive hit much harder. The silicone chest, blonde wig, and cake-batter-like makeup came off the moment she walked in the door. One minute she was Laura, French marketing bimbo. The next minute she was Nancy, determined, if sleepy, detective.

She poured herself a Perrier and Gatorade, a trick learned from her brother, Noah, during his university days. That was before he had matured and entered into medical school.

Bubbles fizzed and popped inside the crystal glass, punctuating the silence as she scrolled through Brian's computer. She discovered that he was tidy and organized—at least when it came to his desktop. He labelled everything in a manner that made it perfectly clear what exactly was in each of the folders. She had half expected to come across one labelled 'Top Secret Stuff I'm Working on with Teddy Benjamin', but alas, it wasn't that easy.

Adrenaline buoyed her through an hour of searching, but in the end, she came up empty. She yawned, finally crashing from the surge of natural speed that had coursed through her body after her heist. She clicked her laptop off and crawled into bed, set her alarm, and fell into a deep sleep.

# CHAPTER 16

"Good morning!" Nancy slid into the booth across from Angus. He looked none the worse for wear despite her suspicions that he had been out last night drinking.

"Morning," he replied.

While his appearance didn't indicate that he had had a late night, the gravel in his voice gave him away.

"Late night?" she asked out of curiosity as much as for plain old conversation, his 1 a.m. text notwithstanding.

"I had a couple," Angus said with a shrug.

No small talk this morning.

Nancy changed the subject.

"So, what did you find?" she asked, getting down to business before the waitress had even taken their drink order. She was tempted to order a pick-me-up this morning. The multiple drinks, the dehydration owing to sweating so profusely from the silicone chest, and the surge of adrenaline as a result of the heist—none of it had been helped by Perrier, Gatorade, and five hours of sleep. But a beer? That probably wouldn't be amiss.

"What would you like to drink?" the twenty-something waitress with a curly brown bob interrupted.

"I'll have a coffee," Nancy requested. "And two shots of

Baileys." It wasn't beer and she considered it to be more of a coffee flavouring than actual alcohol.

"I'll have a coffee, too," said Angus.

The waitress took their breakfast orders before she went off to get their drinks and Angus leaned across the table.

"Teddy Benjamin opened an account in the Caymans two months after the brothers launched Clover Capital."

Nancy thought about it for a second. Opening up an account in the Caymans wasn't necessarily a smoking-gun. After all, thousands of people opened up companies in the tax-haven country. Still, the timing of it, coinciding with the launch of their private equity firm was, if nothing else, suspicious. Not to mention the doctored records of the wire transfers to two numbered companies that she had found on Barron's computer.

"I wasn't able to find anything else out about it," Angus continued. "The bank security down there is tighter than Fort Knox."

"How did you discover this?" Nancy inquired.

"I think you mean 'Thank you, Angus'." Her IT friend grinned.

Nancy laughed. "Thank you. And?"

Angus sat back in the booth, clasped his hands together and rested them on the table. The diner's lights lit up the soft blond hair on his arms.

"Well, that's a bit of a long story," he said with a scrunch of his face. "Let's just say I had some free time on my hands and did a bit of digging." His hand went to his front pants pocket and he pulled out a large folded piece of paper before sliding it across the table.

She unfolded it and gave it a quick read. As she neared the end of the document, her heart rate sped up. She wanted to jump across the table and squeeze Angus in a death-grip hug.

The paper he had pushed across to her was a record from Cayman National Bank. It showed one Theodore Benjamin had opened an account exactly two months after the inception of

Clover Capital. It wasn't a smoking gun, but it was another piece of evidence—a big piece—that would help her build her case.

It showed intent on the part of Teddy. Intent to move money. Why else would he be opening a bank account in the Caymans?

She didn't have evidence yet, but she had a sneaking suspicion that the money from the two accounts that Clover Capital had fraudulently transferred money to would end up in Teddy's Caymans account. If it hadn't already.

She was just hoping she could find the original records of the wire transfers on Brian's computer. That would go a way towards strengthening her case. She wasn't sure what she would be able to find that would prove that the money wired to the two accounts actually ended up in Teddy's Caymans account, but evidence was what she needed. Conjecture could be helpful, but she needed cold, hard proof.

If she could find physical records that tied the two numbered companies back to Teddy, her evidence against him would be as good as gold.

*

She had one client on her roster that afternoon and, for the first time in a long time, she was dreading getting into costume. The mystery surrounding the Benjamin brothers had her glued to her computer. She didn't want to let up until she had solved it.

It was always like this when she was in the midst of an investigation. The closer she got to solving it, the more focused she became. The thrill of the challenge almost gave her a high. She imagined it was much the same for adventurers. She had never climbed Mount Everest, in terms of a case, but this one ranked among the Seven Summits.

An hour before her domme session, she clicked off her laptop, stuffed her black latex into her Longchamp and headed for her office. The back door.

A few dark swipes of black eye shadow and one coat of mascara finished off her look. She was going to turn the lights off for this session, partly because she hadn't put much effort into her makeup, and partly because she knew that her next client was afraid of the dark. In fact, she was going for full sensory deprivation for him. She was looking forward to it in a sadistic way—a chance to vent her frustration at being pulled away from the Benjamin brothers' case.

Today's client, Vince, was a cutthroat criminal defense attorney. And he was good at his job. He had represented some of the country's most notorious criminals, which meant he was hated by a sizeable portion of the population. Nancy understood it—it was repugnant to see someone sentenced to a miniscule amount of jail time when they so clearly deserved to rot there for life. But that was the way the justice system had to work—even the most evil of offenders needed competent representation and a fair trial. But at the same time, should they get to benefit from an expert attorney?

She had done her research on the man when an inquiry from him asking about her domme services had first popped up in her inbox. The email used the word 'hypothetically' several times—a dead giveaway, from her experience, that he was a lawyer. Who else spoke in hypotheticals?

Nancy's latex outfit squeaked as she laid out the tools she would be using for Vince's session. The outfit she was wearing was mostly for the end of the session. After she had driven him mad with sensory deprivation and pleasure, and exactly fifty-five minutes after the session had started, she would pull off his noise-cancelling headphones, remove his eye mask and mitts, and then stand back so he could place his payment at her feet.

Then she would take off the outfit, wash off the makeup, and get back to the case.

She was yearning to get back to her laptop to keep digging into Brian's hard drive, but she couldn't let it throw her off her dominatrix game. There was a reason why she could command such high rates and be picky when it came to her clients—she was considered one of the best dommes in the city. Not that there was any official Top 10 list for dominatrix services. She couldn't imagine what *that* award would be.

When Vince arrived, Nancy was ready. The lights were off, the room was silent, and she had both the eye-mask and headphones in her hand. She stood behind the door and three minutes before the start of his session, the door swung open and Vince stepped inside.

"Vince," she drawled when the door closed behind him.

"Yes, Mistress," he stood there without moving.

"Take your clothes off."

With the lack of light in the room, she couldn't see him obeying her command but she could certainly hear him. It would present a problem for most people, the dark—a person couldn't very well feel their way around the room to get their job done. But Nancy wasn't 'most people'.

She couldn't see her outstretched arm in front of her but Nancy had a trick up her sleeve. One that had come in handy with both of her jobs. With her free hand she reached on top of her head and pulled her set of night vision goggles down over her eyes; Buffalo Bill in a latex onesie. She could now see Vince perfectly, albeit with a green tinge.

He stood there in his underwear with his clothes discarded beside him and a look of excitement on his face. It was always interesting to Nancy what her clients did with their clothes. Some of them were very particular and organized when they got undressed. They folded their clothes up nicely, paired their socks together, and hung their suit jacket on the rack. Other men tore off their clothes with wild abandon and uncaringly cast them to the side.

Vince, the criminal defense lawyer, was one of the latter. Which was all the more surprising given the cost of his clothes. The word 'Canali' practically lit up like the bat symbol on his suit jacket. But then she guessed that, as a criminal defense attorney, he was used to his suits getting down and dirty. When you were dealing with criminals, you were also dealing with their environments. Which was, usually, jail.

"Underwear, off," she commanded.

For some reason the fabric crotch covering was the one bit of modesty he always tried to retain. As a top-notch domme, however, it wasn't one Nancy ever accepted. She saw the grimace on his face as he bent down to remove his drawers and discarded them in the same manner as his other clothes.

He stood there, fully naked, and looked around in the dark. Only then did Nancy step forward and slip the blindfold over his eyes. He startled a bit at that—which made sense because he couldn't see her approaching. Headphones over his ears followed the blindfold and then Nancy reached for the piece de resistance: bondage mittens.

The black leather hand coverings resembled boxing gloves—except the kinky kind fit like baby mittens with no separation for the thumb. And instead of enabling a wearer to defend themselves, bondage gloves were used to render the wearer defenseless.

She grabbed Vince's right hand, stuffed it into the glove, and pulled the metal buckle tight against his wrist. She secured it with an audible 'click', and then did the same to his other hand. A shiver went through Vince—blind, deaf, and helpless—as she guided him by the gloves to the middle of the room.

Over the ensuing forty minutes Nancy used several tools of her trade to prod, poke, and tease her sensory-deprived client. In the last ten minutes, she took things up a notch for the finale. Using a candle, ice cubes, and a feather, she took Vince to places he had only been in his wildest dreams. He writhed, cried out in surprise, and his heart rate quickened. Sweat broke out all over his body and he jerked each time she put the fire, ice, and feather on his skin.

At one point he begged her to stop but Nancy kept going. She had a safe word with all of her clients and would only stop if they used it. To keep things simple, they all used the same word—it wouldn't do for her to have to consult a record book in the middle of a session to double check if a client had uttered their safe word. The word they all used was 'vanilla'. Except for Vince.

The persuasive attorney had insisted on using his own safe word, and Nancy had relented. She had yet to hear him use it during one of their sessions, but her ears were always alert and listening for a "Not guilty!" verdict.

After Vince peeled out of the parking lot in his undoubtedly expensive sportscar, Nancy peeled off her costume, cleaned The Cell, locked everything up, and then headed to her P.I. office around the corner.

She had brought her laptop with her and got to work combing through the rest of Brian's computer. He was a meticulous record keeper, which was good. It stood to reason that he had to be smart if he was working for Clover Capital, but Nancy was floored when she came across an Excel spreadsheet that contained a list of all of his passwords. Login information for his Gmail, bank accounts, and Clover Capital email amongst others. The man even listed the password for the company's main bank account that was used for wire transfers.

*Risky*, she thought. But no more risky, really, than keeping a paper copy on hand. And when she really thought about it, she supposed that it wasn't every day that someone had to worry about their hard drive being cloned.

Her manual search turned up nothing, but a targeted query brought up several interesting records. As she suspected, Brian's spreadsheets showed several wire transfers to the numbered companies that the original un-doctored copies of the spreadsheets that had been on Barron's computer revealed.

Bingo.

The proof that she had been looking for. The doctored spreadsheet which could be reconciled with the original record. Her evidence could only have been stronger if she had computer print-outs of the actual accounts.

It was crafty of Theodore to have the lowly analyst completing the wire transfers. She was sure he felt that it would give himself some plausible deniability if the police came a-knocking. But she imagined, by the time that happened, Teddy planned to be long gone—sipping margaritas on a beach and enjoying the stolen fruits of his and his brother's labor.

But who exactly did the numbered companies belong to? Figuring that out would take some more digging. She had a feeling that Aaron Wallace, the Cayman Islands man whose name she had found on Barron's desk, just might be the key. But did that mean that Barron was in on the ruse? Or did he have suspicions of his own? Or maybe both accounts belonged to Teddy? Possibilities swirled through her head. She knew that since Brian was involved, he had to be getting something out of the scheme. But she doubted that one of the $60 million accounts would be allocated to the pigeon.

She didn't have any answers yet, but she still had one more avenue to explore. Sunday was a day away and she was going to try her hand at cards.

# CHAPTER 17

Tony, from Tony Romano's Towing, had told Nancy that the illegal gambling group met every Sunday night at the docks. She didn't know why, but she had expected it to be in some sort of clandestine warehouse in the outskirts of the city. It just went to show that even detectives could be taken in by T.V. shows and movies.

She had chosen her outfit carefully that evening. She didn't want to show too much skin, but she also didn't want to come off too casual or frumpy. The result?

A tasteful but tight miniskirt paired with a tight, long-sleeve, scoop-neck black top. Cleavage was always a good bet when she was going to be around men. Especially when they were in competition mode or connected to crime—both of which seemed to be fueled by testosterone. Spike heels and a clutch finished off her outfit and she curled her tresses into a messy, voluminous look. Sexy hair to go with a sexy outfit.

She took an Uber to the docks in order to avoid bringing her vehicle. She was a woman of many disguises, but her Range Rover was registered under her real name. The Mafia had their tentacles everywhere and the last thing she needed was for them to take down her license plate and start looking into her. She wasn't investigating them, per se, but she knew that nothing good could come of them finding out that she was a detective.

It would be a good way to find herself sleeping with the fishes in Lake Ontario. Thinking about it, she wasn't sure which part scared her more—death or the sewage-strewn body of water.

The parking lot of the strip mall was almost empty, and when Nancy arrived she went straight to the dry-cleaning store just as Tony had instructed. Classy Cleaners was sandwiched between a sub shop and a waxing studio. A real 'one-stop shop' if she'd ever seen one—get waxed, drop off your clothes, grab a snack, and hire a hitman all within five feet.

Classy Cleaners' storefront was dusty, and inside it looked like every other dry-cleaning store she had ever seen. An empty space up front with a counter that ran nearly the length of the room, a cash register on one side, and racks of clothes in the back. The man behind the counter was the only thing that seemed out of place. He was tall and hulking, covered in tattoos, and completely uninterested in a potential dry-cleaning customer.

"Hi," Nancy greeted the man.

He grunted in reply and didn't bother to even look up at her, continuing instead to flip through a car magazine.

*What is it with these people?* she thought to herself, recalling how Tony had treated her at his towing yard.

She stepped up to the counter and said a little louder: "Hi."

The man looked up from the till and stared at her for a second.

"Can I help you?"

She did away with the pseudo sweetness this time, reasoning that she had tried it on Tony and it had gone over like a lead balloon. She only had a small sample size with which to draw on, but it seemed like the only thing that piqued these peoples' interest was money.

"Yes," she nodded. "I'm Laura and I'm looking for some meat gum."

It was a weird sort of password but Tony had assured her that asking it would gain her entrance to the card game.

The man threw back his head and started laughing.

Nancy tried to not let her confusion show on her face. Had she missed something?

"Meat gum!" the man said through laughter, pausing to wipe away a tear from his eye. "Meat. Gum."

Baffled, she stood there and watched while the man's exuberant laughs turned into intermittent guffaws. Finally, as he wiped away another tear, he looked at Nancy.

"Ahh, Tony," he shook his head. "He really comes up with some good ones."

Nancy breathed a sigh of relief.

"What's your name?" the ostensible dry-cleaner suddenly switched gears.

"Laura," she lied.

"Can I see some ID, Laura?"

She pulled Laura's ID out of her purse and handed it over. Driver's license, credit card, health card—Laura had it all.

He asked her much of the same questions as Tony—occupation, where she lived—and she gave him the same answers.

Satisfied, the man stepped out from behind the desk and instructed her to hand over her purse and stand with her legs apart and her arms out to the sides.

He dumped the contents of her clutch onto the counter and went through it. Then, he turned to Nancy and gave her a pat-down. Checking for weapons and wires, of course. It wouldn't do to let an informant into their gambling group.

Finally, when the man was satisfied, he gave her an "okay" and gestured for her to follow him back behind the dry-cleaning counter.

Racks of plastic-covered clothes filled the centre of the room, but she could see a heavy metal door at the back of the room. When they reached it, he pounded on it three times and the door cracked open.

She couldn't hear what he whispered to the person inside, but the door swung open and he motioned for her to go through it.

Behind her, the heavy metal door slammed shut and she found herself in a darkened room.

"It's a $200 buy-in fee," said a low voice to her right. She squinted a bit while her eyes adjusted to the lighting and then she saw the outline of a man come into full focus.

He was sitting on a stool in the corner and it was too dark for her to make out any of his facial features. She could hear the muffled sound of raised voices and laughter coming from a door just down from where she was standing.

Nancy pulled a wad of cash out of her purse and started counting out the bills.

"You need some help?" the man switched on a flashlight and pointed it at her hands.

"Thanks," Nancy said dryly before handing over the money.

"Drinks are extra and you can ask Angelo for the chips," he stuffed the money into a cash bag and pointed to the other door. "It's a $5,000 minimum buy-in. Through there."

"Thanks," Nancy said again and headed for the door.

She hadn't known what to expect from the other players, but the people seated around the poker table weren't anything like the mafiosos portrayed in movies. There were no Italian-speaking wise-guys, no suited men with bodyguards who were Glocked to the nines. In all, for a fan of Martin Scorsese movies, Nancy was surprised to find she was a little disappointed. She just hoped she wouldn't be disappointed when it came to digging around for information about Teddy.

She was surprised to see she wasn't the only woman there and took a seat at the makeshift poker table. Alongside Nancy, two other women sat at the table. One was clearly a mistress or a girlfriend. She had a bored look on her face and was overly attentive to the overweight, balding man with a Rolex that cost more than a car on his wrist. The other woman, though—she was dealt in. There was also a cocktail waitress wearing a short black skirt.

Far from the silent space she had expected, the atmosphere was loud and relaxed. Vape smoke filled the room, and conversations were punctuated by laughter, the flipping of cards, and the clack of chips hitting the table. It wasn't the serious place she had been expecting. In fact, it seemed more like a local hangout. Albeit one that had a $200 cover charge.

After the hand was over, with Mr. Rolex taking the win, the dealer nodded to Nancy and she pulled out a stack of cash from her purse.

"Angelo," the dealer looked in the opposite direction and then pointed to her with his chin.

A broad-shouldered man wearing all white brought over a briefcase and exchanged $5,000 of Nancy's money for chips. Then the waitress came around and took her drink order. Before being dealt in, she sat back and watched for a few hands and was surprised to see how often Mr. Rolex won.

"I'm Ricky," the man next to her stuck out his hand after he folded for the second time in as many hands. He was short, lean, and had a buzz-cut.

"Laura," Nancy shook his hand and took a sip of her vodka.

The rest of the table continued to talk and play.

"Nice to meet you, Laura." Ricky clinked his beer against her glass. He saw her watching Mr. Rolex who had pushed a fat stack of chips onto the table.

"Louis 'the Wizard of Odds' Garavano," Ricky nodded to the overweight man with the Rolex across the table. "He's a card shark," Ricky added unnecessarily. "Odds are always in his favor."

The next hand, the dealer nodded at her and Nancy pushed some of her chips onto the table.

She wasn't even close to being a poker expert. But she knew the rules of the game. She also knew that the hand she had just been dealt was shit. But losing, and losing badly, might just endear her to those around the table. Shades of the Underdog Effect. If likeability was correlated with losing, she would be top dog in no time.

Thirty minutes into the game and Nancy was down by several hundred dollars. She had a feeling the Wizard of Odds would be taking most of her money.

Gambling, evidently, wasn't her thing, and she normally wouldn't be throwing around thousands of dollars so carelessly. But she was hoping that it would help her learn more about the tight spot Teddy Benjamin had gotten into with the Mob. And the cash that she was throwing around wasn't her own money—it was something she would be billing Ms. Fineberg for at the conclusion of the case.

When the dealer started shuffling the cards for the next round, Ricky, who was seated beside her, announced that he was going for a cigarette. Nancy, although she wasn't a smoker, took the opportunity to join him outside.

The alley behind the building was dark and dingy. Cigarette butts littered the ground and a bench and beat-up chair were perched against the building.

Ricky leaned against the wall and Nancy took a seat on the wooden bench and rested her back against the wall. Ricky lit his cigarette and the tip of it glowed red as Ricky inhaled.

"Smoke?" Ricky offered her through an exhaled cloud of tobacco.

"Thanks," Nancy smiled. "But I'm trying to quit. I just came out to get some fresh . . ."—she paused with a wry grin—". . . air."

Ricky snorted and took another drag.

"Fresh as ten-day-old fish," he said before blowing out another cloud of smoke. "I've never seen you here before. How did you find your way here?"

"I had the misfortune of breaking down on the Gardiner," she explained. "My vehicle, not myself," she added with a smirk which earned a laugh from Ricky. "My vehicle was towed, one thing led to another, and 'boom', here I am."

Ricky nodded as he flicked ash onto the pavement.

"I've been coming here for a few years," he said

conversationally. "It's mostly regulars."

Nancy badly wanted to ask about any well-known patrons—Teddy Benjamin to be exact—but she might as well stamp 'cop' across her forehead if that was the way she was going to go about it.

"How did you get involved?" Nancy was curious. She had gained entry through a mix of orchestration and dumb luck. But what about the other players?

"I know a guy," Ricky said vaguely. He tilted his head against the wall and smoke from the end of his cigarette rose up into the air.

"'A guy'." Nancy let out a barely audible snort and Ricky cracked a smile.

"My brother-in-law." He swatted away an errant fly before taking another drag of his cigarette. "He's, you know—connected."

She nodded in understanding. She was happy to stay curious when it came to his brother-in-law. Curiosity, after all, killed the cat.

There was sudden movement at the back door and both of their heads swung towards it. The other woman who had been dealt into the game walked through the door and stood beside them.

"Mind if I join you?" She pulled a pack of cigarettes out of her purse and took a seat next to Nancy. "Not often I see other women here," she said as she searched around in her purse for a lighter.

"Here," Ricky stepped forward and offered her a blue Bic.

"Thanks, Rick," she flicked the flame on and touched it to the end of the smoke. Her blonde hair hung limply around her head—another victim of the humidity.

"We were just talking about how we ended up here," Ricky said, nodding towards Nancy.

The blonde took a drag, held it in for a second and then blew out a cloud of smoke.

"I've been coming here for years." She flicked ash onto the

ground. "I started coming here with my ex. Total low-life," she added.

"Sorry," Nancy empathized. "I've been there."

"Haven't we all," the blonde lamented as she leaned back and adjusted her dress.

"Oh fuck, not the ex-boyfriend talk." Ricky rolled his eyes. "I'm out." He moved to head back inside before turning to Nancy and adding: "But Maria's right—her ex is a twat." He threw the remainder of the cigarette on the pavement and ground it down with his shoe.

"So, what do you think?" Maria asked Nancy as the door slammed shut behind Ricky.

It was a vague, open-ended question that she wasn't sure how to interpret.

"I've never been to one of these things before, but I like it," she said honestly.

A sour look crossed Maria's face: "If our goddamned city council would let us have casinos, I wouldn't have to go underground."

Nancy murmured in agreement. Maria sounded like she took her gambling seriously.

"Does your ex-boyfriend still hang out here?" Nancy changed the subject. "Do you ever run into him at poker games?"

It was obvious that there was no love lost between Maria and her ex, but it was also apparent that Maria wanted to talk about him. Nancy knew how it was—sometimes you couldn't stop talking about them; other times, you bottled it up. While Nancy was the latter, her poker companion appeared to be the former.

"Hah!" Maria snorted with derision. "No. He's persona non grata around these parts."

That piqued Nancy's curiosity. If a criminal organization wouldn't even associate with you, that sure said a lot about your character.

"What did he do?" Nancy prodded.

"He got caught cheating." Maria took a drag of her smoke. "On me."

Now *that* was strange. As loyal as the Mob could be, Nancy didn't think they would banish someone for cheating on his fellow poker-playing girlfriend. Especially if he was bringing in money.

". . . with Fat Jimmy's wife," Maria continued

Ah. That explained it. You didn't want to fuck with the Mob and you *definitely* didn't want to fuck with their wives.

"I could've kept it a secret and punished him myself." A slight smirk crossed Maria's face. "But I didn't want to end up on murder charges. Better to let the boys take care of it."

She thought Maria had a point, but Nancy didn't know what to say to that and changed the subject again.

"Do you ever get any decent single guys in?"

"Some," Maria blew out a cloud of smoke. "We've also had some high-rollers around here before."

A soft breeze blew through the alley and mingled the acrid smell of smoke with the smell of Lake Ontario.

Delightful.

"A couple of politicians." Maria's eyes were closed. "But no one high up. The Deputy Mayor came in twice. Yes—" her head nodded as though Nancy had expressed surprise or horror. "The *same* Deputy Mayor who has lobbied against casinos within city limits."

*Holy shit, this woman is serious about her gambling,* Nancy thought to herself.

"Some businessmen, CEOs, a Maple Leaf . . ." Maria trailed off. "Not any of the Argonauts or FC Players. They don't make enough."

Nancy wasn't sure how she felt about Maria. Her bluntness was both off-putting and oddly endearing. She couldn't imagine her ex-boyfriend cheating on her. She thought Maria might be even scarier to have after you than the Mob. When it came down to it, neither one would show any signs of mercy, but with the Mafia, it was business. With Maria, it seemed like it might be pleasure. She came across as a total psycho.

"Sounds like Sunday poker games are prime ground for finding a date," Nancy chimed in.

"If only," the woman lamented. "Most of the men are married. Not that that would stop them from trying to get a bit of action on the side." A slight sneer crossed her face. "The single ones that *do* come in look like Louis Garavano. It isn't often an attractive single man comes in."

She paused a beat.

"We actually had one of the Benjamin brothers playing every Sunday for a few years."

Nancy's heartbeat quickened. This was what she had been hoping for. Nothing like a bit of gossip about bad boyfriends and dating. It was prime bonding time for people and, in this instance, it might be crucial for solving her case.

"But fat chance of anything ever happening with one of them," Maria said with disdain.

"I've heard about the Benjamin brothers," Nancy said offhandedly. "Identical twins, right?"

As if she didn't know.

Maria nodded. "I've never met Barron, but Teddy used to come here."

Nancy's heart rate shot up even faster: "I've heard the twins are pretty hot," she said casually. Wasn't that the understatement of the year. "I wonder why he doesn't come here anymore?"

Maria, her eyes still closed, twisted her mouth for a second as if deciding on whether to say something.

"Well—," she shifted a bit on the bench. "Rumor has it he overextended himself . . . financially."

Yes. This was exactly what Nancy needed.

"Like playing on credit kind of thing?" She kept her tone light and her facial expression neutral.

"Like betting more than his bank account could cover and then borrowing from the house to try and recover his losses. We're talking high seven figures. Maybe more." Maria opened one of her eyes and trained it on Nancy. "They play with big numbers around here sometimes. I've seen people lose their house."

Nancy didn't know if Teddy had a gambling problem, but his long-term participation in illegal card games confirmed what Angus had told her about his ties to underground gambling. It also fit with what he had told her about how two men had reportedly been keeping tabs on the financier. If he owed big money to the Mob, it would stand to reason that they would have some of their henchmen watching him. The last thing they would want is for him to flee the country before he made them whole. The intimidation factor wouldn't be amiss either. A silent message: 'we're watching you' from two hired men who, literally, were.

"I don't know how much Teddy was in for and I don't know how he managed to get them to back off," she said pensively. "These guys are mean. They'll slit your throat over twenty bucks."

Nancy didn't doubt that for a second. Society collectively operated a certain way—there was an unspoken agreement about how to treat one another in polite society and known consequences if someone ran afoul. It was the same way with the Mafia. People in their world operated a certain way and there were also unspoken agreements about how to treat one another and known consequences if someone ran afoul. Although, if you ran afoul of agreements with the Mob, it was too late for you anyway—those consequences were deadly.

"Anyway," Maria brushed it off, "Teddy's wealthy, so he probably closed a deal, paid it off, and then wised up and realized that his gambling could be a problem. The Mob always gets their cut," she leaned in conspiratorially. "Or—." She made a slicing motion across her neck.

Nancy nodded in agreement. "You don't fuck with those guys."

"Exactly." Maria sighed and then started to get up from the bench. "Should we head back in?"

"Definitely." Nancy followed the woman's lead. "I still have some chips for the Wizard of Odds to take."

As she followed Maria back into the building, Nancy's mind was whirring. She would play a few more hands and then she would get the hell out of there. She wasn't uncomfortable there by any means. She just wanted to get home to go over all of her findings.

So far she had evidence that Teddy was wiring Clover Capital investors' money into two offshore numbered accounts. She also had evidence that Teddy was, or had been, at least, involved in illegal betting and racked up a huge debt with the Mafia. According to Maria, the Mafia had actually backed off on the debt that he owed. Which was more than a little unusual. Unless, as Maria said, Teddy found a way to pay them back.

She had done some background investigative work on Teddy when she had first started on the case, but there was one thing Nancy hadn't thought to do. Right now, she was itching to get home and get to it.

*

She was two vodkas deep and $3,000 lighter when she walked out the front door of Classy Cleaners. The two vodkas had left her with a mild buzz, but the alcohol was tempered by the adrenaline that was coursing through her body.

The Uber driver had asked her what she was doing at the docks in a parking lot alone and Nancy told him she had gotten lost. By the time she had arrived home it was late into the evening.

She opened up her laptop and searched. If her hunch turned out to be correct, she would have more than enough evidence to go to the police with. A few quickly typed words, some clicks, some more typing, and finally, she had it. Mortgage records.

Specifically, remortgaging records. For Teddy.

According to the document, Teddy had remortgaged his house—all $4.7 million worth—and had taken out a home equity line of credit. And yet, *yet*, he still seemed to be living the high life. He had made no moves to tamp down on his spending, and no moves to sell his house and downsize. This despite having a rumored Mob debt into the high seven figures.

Combined with the evidence of the fraudulent wires, the change in construction companies, decreased quality of the renovation materials, and a bank account in the Cayman Islands, it all pointed to one thing—Teddy Benjamin was up to his eyeballs in debt and was skimming from his company's investors to make himself and the Mafia whole again.

She couldn't be 100 percent certain without knowing who really was behind the two numbered accounts, but if she was a betting woman, she would bet that one account was for Teddy, and one account was for his Italian creditors.

Crafty.

Did *Toronto Life* include criminal prowess in their Top Forty lists? She could picture it now: *Theodore Benjamin—handsome, haughty, and positively criminal.*

To Nancy, Teddy's behaviour meant one thing and she was going to take him down.

She wasn't sure if his theft had stemmed from greed or if it had spiraled from his apparent inability to control himself when it came to cards. But when it came down to it, it really didn't matter either way. What mattered was that he had, as far as she could tell, committed the crime. And as a result, he would have to pay.

Nancy knew that if her hypothesis was correct, she would now have to tread lightly. Now that she suspected the Mob had a part to play in this, she would really have to watch her back.

Millionaires, they could be bought—reasoned with, even. But there was no reasoning with people who negotiated with guns.

The whir of her printer broke through the silence and she grabbed up the papers showing Teddy's outstanding mortgage.

Each piece of evidence had been laid out on her kitchen table; it was a mosaic that grew as she had progressed with the case. The real and doctored wire transfer records with the discrepancies highlighted sat side by side; the notes she had taken from her conversation with the owner of the construction company; the holding company numbers; the photos she had taken of Teddy and Brian meeting in a park; notes about her discussion with the blonde woman at the poker game. Now, she covered up another empty portion of the table as she set down the evidence of Teddy's remortgaging.

# CHAPTER 18

She was purposely late for her AA meeting that week. The door closed behind her with a soft click and she slid into the empty seat beside Seth. As per usual, Rhys was talking—she had missed the first part of his story, but it ended, as most of Rhys's stories did, with a bang.

While she kept her eyes firmly trained on Rhys, in her peripheral vision, she could see Eric. His expression gave away nothing, but she felt his eyes on her as Rhys droned on.

"I had to fight her off," her fellow addict boasted. "Do you know how strong strippers are?" He looked around incredulously. "All that upper body strength."

Nancy could barely stop herself from rolling her eyes.

"And at the same time, the other one insulted my manhood," he said indignantly. "How do you think that makes me feel?"

There was a long silence until Carmella, their therapist, finally chimed in.

"And how did that make you feel?"

Rhys sat back and pondered for a few seconds.

"Like a piece of meat," he said pensively.

*Holy shit*, Nancy thought to herself, *is Rhys actually having a breakthrough? Has Carmella accomplished the impossible?*

Her disbelief was shattered moments later.

"Like a grade A Kobe beef strip loin," he said smugly.

*Jesus.*

She wondered what would happen first—Carmella having a breakthrough with one of her clients or Carmella quitting. Either way, Nancy was looking forward to reading her dissertation. If the university didn't accept it, Nancy was sure she could sell it to a publishing house as erotica for a decent price. Lord knew Nancy had considered moonlighting as an erotic fiction writer with the inspiration she had gleaned from her Tuesday sessions.

"Oooookay," Carmella said awkwardly. "Thank you for sharing that with us, Rhys." She looked around the room. "Who wants to go next?"

Still avoiding eye contact with the man whom she had engaged in illicit sex with the week before, Nancy was startled to see him raise his hand.

"Eric," Carmella smiled. "Thank you. What do you have to share with us this week?"

Nancy was still trying to avoid eye contact but couldn't hold back any longer. She didn't want to give any hints that she might be doing something untoward with a fellow group member. It was her first slipup and she was determined to also make it her last.

Eric ran a hand through his tousled blond locks and looked around the room.

"Last week," he started, "I gave my business card to a smoking hot woman."

*No.* Nancy froze. He wouldn't do this to her. Would he?

"I shouldn't have," he said with a hint of a smirk. "She's connected to me in a way that could make things in my life difficult . . . I guess you could call it a bit of wanting to taste the forbidden fruit."

Nancy was adept at keeping her composure but a swift rage ignited inside of her. It was bad enough that they had broken one of the cardinal rules of group therapy. She felt horrendous about what they had done—caught up in a moment of weakness, gotten obliterated, and given into her urges. Now her partner in crime was going to humiliate her in front of the entire group?

Rhys chimed in: "What did she look like?"

Typical Rhys. Just looking for more material to put in his wank bank.

Eric turned to Rhys.

"Black hair. Body you could bounce a quarter off of," he said matter-of-factly.

She was almost offended at how detached he sounded.

"If we weren't in this room, I would high-five you," Rhys said conspiratorially.

Nancy looked at Carmella. Surely, *surely*, she wasn't going to let this one fly.

"Rhys!" their therapist snapped. "That is inappropriate!"

He had the sense to look ashamed. But Nancy was reflecting on the irony of the circle being a safe space where addicts could talk about their nastiest sex-capades in revolting detail, but where high-fives regarding those stories were considered inappropriate. Jerking yourself off, metaphorically speaking, as Rhys did when he was bragging about his conquests, was acceptable, but it seemed that a circle jerk was where Carmella drew the line.

"Does anyone else have anything to share tonight?" Carmella looked around the room expectantly, but everyone stayed silent. "Okay, everyone. Thank you for sharing your stories and I will see you all next week."

People started gathering their things and headed out the door. Eric was in front of the pack and Nancy snatched up her purse, determined to catch up to him in the parking lot.

When she got there, she saw the men had splintered off in various directions and she saw Eric walking towards a silver Audi.

"Eric!" she called out while hurrying towards him.

He turned towards her with a look of ambivalence on his features

"What can I do for you?"

She gave him a steely glare: "You can shut the fuck up about me or I will shut you the fuck up," she said in a deadly voice. "If you ever, and I meant *ever*, so much as mention me in passing, in code, in anything—I will ensure that you are incapable of performing sexually ever again. And yes," she continued, seeing his open-mouthed look of shock. "That is a threat." She gave him one last steely-eyed glare, turned on her heel and headed for her Range Rover.

Thoughts of Eric were at the forefront of her mind as she wove through the early-evening traffic. It wasn't often that someone was able to get under her skin, but Eric, the proverbial 'forbidden fruit' had done so.

Although when she thought about it, she supposed that it wasn't really Eric she was angry at—she was angry at herself. Sure, she loathed that the devoid-of-morals real estate agent had shamed her during this evening's meeting, but most of the loathing was reserved for herself.

She hated that she had given into her urges and reached out to Eric in a moment of weakness. She had always prided herself on staying in control. It didn't matter what it came to. Impulsivity did not exist in her life. At least, it hadn't before Jamie dumped her like a bad habit and sent her straight into the arms of vodka and questionable decisions.

If there was anyone she should be mad at she supposed it really should be him. No one goes from a long-term relationship to a Mykonos vacation with another woman in the span of a month unless they've been *with* that other woman during their long-term relationship.

She cursed Jamie in her head for what felt like at least the thousandth time.

Realistically, she couldn't blame Jamie for her actions. But she could blame him for his actions revealing just how weak she could be. Nancy had always believed that she was strong, independent, and in control. But she also knew that wasn't entirely true.

# CHAPTER 19

Nancy was still riled up from the AA meeting, annoyed that it had gotten under her skin. Eric's bullshit had struck a nerve. Which, she suspected, was exactly as he had intended.

Between seeing a few domme clients, she had spent the last couple of days getting all of her proverbial ducks in a row to deliver the information to the police, and strategizing on how best to tell Barron. She felt it was only fair that she tell him before turning his brother in, but so far she hadn't figured out how. It would be awkward at best, confusing as hell, and would definitely not endear her to him. Along with dropping the bomb that his brother was stealing money, she would have to confess that their entire time together had been a ruse.

She had never told someone she was investigating that their family member had double-crossed them and she couldn't imagine it going over well.

She dropped her Range Rover in her condo parking lot and went upstairs to put on her running gear. Sneakers, shorts, a tank top, and a hat—she grabbed her sunglasses and headed outside for a quick run. The combination of cardio and fresh air would cool her head and help her consider, once again, the best way to approach Barron.

As far as the evidence showed, Barron was completely in the clear. His brother was the dirty one. She had grown fond of Barron, but that wasn't the only reason she wanted to tell him about his brother. Despite all the evidence she had compiled of Teddy's fraud, she would also need Barron to give a statement to the police.

It was a gamble on her part—ironic given that gambling was one of the catalysts for this case. Blood was, after all, thicker than water. And that meant there was no small chance that Barron would actually warn his younger, by two minutes, brother.

For Nancy, it was a chance she was willing to take. She couldn't be certain, but she had a feeling that the odds were in her favour. Barron was a smart man. He would likely have feelings of hostility and disbelief towards his brother after finding out what he had done. At the same time, he may also want to intervene to try and save him. If he examined the situation objectively, Nancy knew he would cooperate and turn his brother in. It would be the key to escaping the worst of the blowback and Barron was calculating enough to make whatever decision would be in his best interest.

Dealing with Elena Fineberg, however, was a different story. Nancy had kept her updated throughout the case, but hadn't yet told her about her findings. Nancy's updates never included any specifics—a rule she followed to keep clients from inadvertently sabotaging her case. She had made that mistake once—giving into the prodding of a needy client—and it was not a mistake she would ever make again. That particular case had blown up in her face and had been a hard lesson for the detective. For Nancy, there was nothing more unsatisfying than being unable to complete her investigation and, subsequently, unable to close a case.

The few times she had contacted Elena—something Nancy always did to make sure clients knew she was working hard on her investigation—Nancy had told her things were moving along slowly and she was making progress. The last time she had reached out to the woman had been a couple of days ago when Nancy had let her know that she would be wrapping up her investigation soon.

She would tell Ms. Fineberg what she had found, but not before first going to Barron and then to the police.

*

Six kilometers later and Nancy was sweaty and spent. Her head felt clear, her anger at Eric had abated, and she had a new energy surging through her body.

As she had run, options had flitted through her brain about how best to approach Barron.

A phone call was out of the question as was telling him in public. What she had uncovered about his brother was personal and would cut him to his core. It required a gentle and tactical touch that could only be delivered in person.

Her run had ended a few blocks from her place and she headed to her condo to freshen up.

By the time she stepped out of the shower, she had made up her mind about what she was going to do and started getting ready for the evening.

*

The stars were out by the time she was put together—not that you could see any of them because of the bright city lights. She had gone for a more casual look this evening, which included her makeup. In a weird way, it almost felt like she was preparing herself for a breakup.

This time, she would be the dumper as opposed to the dumpee.

She pulled a medium-sized boy bag out of her closet and stuffed as much evidence inside as she could. Teddy's mortgage record, the record of his Caymans bank account, the set of doctored spreadsheets, and the original records. It was a fair amount of paper, but folded up it didn't take up too much space.

From the outside, her bag looked like just another purse. But what was inside had the ability to take down a financial firm that was worth, on paper at least, almost a billion dollars.

Nancy threw on a comfortable pair of pumps, picked up her purse, and headed out the door.

Her plan was to surprise Barron at home that evening; odds were that he would be out having drinks and dinner, but she could wait in the lobby of his building until he came home.

But first, she detoured to an upscale lounge a few blocks away from her place. A drink beforehand, she reasoned, would not come amiss.

She found an empty seat at the bar and ordered a glass of pinot noir. The bar buzzed with conversation, laughter, and clinking glasses just barely audible above the restaurant's lounge music. The medium-bodied red lit a warmth inside of her as she sat there and steeled herself for what she was going to do. She had decided that she was going to come clean to Barron—let him know she had been investigating him, but she wouldn't give him her real name or tell him that she had been hired by one of his investors.

An hour later she signed for the bill and headed outside. It was one of those rare Toronto evenings where traffic was scarce, and only a handful of people were out in the streets. The downtown core bustled with activity during the day, but after the work dinners and after-work drinks with friends, the area quickly emptied out.

Thoughts raced through her head as she walked several blocks in the direction of Barron's condo. Lost in thought, she hadn't noticed she was nearing the Clover Capital building. And just there, to her shock, she saw the tall, dark-haired figure of Barron Benjamin walking out of the lobby.

"Barron!" she called out, her heart racing with a sudden surge of adrenaline.

She hadn't expected to run into him like this and felt a little off-guard.

She took a deep breath as Barron turned towards her.

The light from the building's lobby cast a soft light over his features and he squinted to see Nancy in the dark. She quickly stepped towards him and, as she drew closer, surprise flickered across his face.

"Hey!" He even sounded surprised.

"Barron!" she said again. "Thank god I ran into you," her heart felt like it was pounding out of her chest. "I have to talk to you."

His eyes looked questioning. "About what?"

"Not here," Nancy shook her head. "I need somewhere private. Can we go to your place?"

"Of course," he said before wrapping one arm around her. "Is everything okay?"

"No," she shook her head. "And I don't want to discuss it here." She looked at the people on the street surrounding them. "Let's wait until we get to your place."

"Okay." He grabbed her hand and led her towards one of the taxis waiting outside of the Clover Capital building. He slid into the back seat and Nancy sent off a quick text before getting in beside him. Seconds later they were off to his condo building.

There was a grim silence between them, which seemed odd given that Barron didn't know what she wanted to talk to him about. She studied his face out of the corner of her eye. He looked concerned, but that was understandable. She had unintentionally ambushed him, told him that they needed to talk and that everything wasn't okay. It was usually never anything good when someone pulled out the 'we have to talk' line. *Any* human being would be concerned at that point. Some might just do a better job of hiding it than others.

At Barron's condo they greeted his doorman and when they stepped into the elevator, Barron looked at her expectantly.

"So—" he started. "What's going on?"

"Not here. Wait until we're inside."

The lift pinged on his floor and he unlocked his front door with his phone.

She took her shoes off at the front door and took a seat on

the couch.

Barron followed suit and sat down beside her.

"What is it?" His brows were knit together.

Nancy felt pained. She was, after all, about to ruin the poor man's life. She had grown to care about him, despite the fact that their relationship was purely a part of her work. The fact that he wasn't tangled up in any of this was also a part of it. He was totally unaware of what his brother had been up to. And telling him that his twin had betrayed him and was planning on leaving him high and dry would turn his world upside down.

"Barron," Nancy said seriously. "I don't know how to tell you this, but . . ."

"What is it?" Barron urged.

"It's your brother. Theodore."

Barron looked at her questioningly.

She took a deep breath and let out an audible sigh.

"I don't know how to tell you this, but he's committing fraud."

There was an immediate mix of confusion and alarm written all across his face.

"What are you talking about?" he asked.

"He's stealing money from your investment funds, to the tune of $120 million."

Barron looked at her in disbelief.

"He wired it to two offshore accounts that are registered to someone named Aaron Wallace in the Cayman Islands. He also opened up a bank account in the Cayman Islands two months after you launched your company."

Barron looked like he was having a hard time processing these revelations.

"What are you talking about?" He sounded confused. "How do you know this? How did you find this out?"

"I ran into one of your analysts and he let slip that he was working on something secretive with Teddy. It sounded suspicious so I did some investigating and discovered what they were up to. I wanted to verify what he told me before I approached you about it. I didn't want to falsely accuse your brother of something if it wasn't true."

Barron shook his head. "I don't understand."

Nancy put her hand on his shoulder. "I'm so sorry. I can't imagine what a shock it must be to you."

"I can't believe this. I don't believe this." His brows were once again drawn down. "What evidence do you have?" he asked.

"I have a lot."

Nancy turned to her purse and pulled out the paper copies she had made of the wire records, Teddy's Cayman Islands bank account, and his mortgage records.

"Here," she handed him the doctored spreadsheet and the original copy that had the wire discrepancies highlighted on them. "The one on the left is the original record and the one on the right has been altered."

Barron grabbed them and slowly read down the paper. He paused at the bottom of the first page on each spreadsheet before flipping to the next one. While his concern and confusion had been apparent in the minutes leading up to Nancy's revelation, as he looked through the spreadsheets, his expression was unreadable. She imagined that he was probably having a hard time taking it all in.

Not that she blamed him—it was a lot to take in.

When he flipped to the last page, Nancy broke the silence. "If you look at the highlighted cells on the original record, there are two different numbers. Each of them is an offshore numbered account that isn't connected to your company. And if you look at the doctored spreadsheet," she pointed to the paper in Barron's left hand, "those same cells have been doctored to show the wires going to Clover Capital's accounts."

He put the papers down and looked at Nancy.

"How did you get these?"

Ah, yes. One of the many questions she had been dreading.

"It's a long story, but let's just say I'm very crafty and persistent when I set my mind to something."

It wasn't really a lie and it was as close to the truth as she was going to give him.

"Can I keep these?" he stared at the spreadsheets.

"Of course," she said graciously. "I have the other copy on my computer. I just printed these out to show you."

"What else do you have?" he asked.

It was a fair question and she supposed he would want all of the information before he accepted that his brother had seriously screwed him over.

"I have evidence he got involved with illegal gambling and owed a lot of money to the Mob." She handed him another piece of paper. "This is a record of the bank account he opened in the Cayman Islands. I also have a document showing he remortgaged his house and took out a home equity line of credit."

Torment, confusion, and a dawning acceptance flitted across Barron's face and he stared at the sheets in his hand. His obvious turmoil tugged at Nancy—she felt a rare moment of tenderness. It was an emotion she rarely displayed; tenderness wasn't good for her and definitely wasn't good for her business.

"Hey," Nancy said softly, moving closer to him. Her arm went to his back and she rubbed it in a gentle, soothing manner.

Barron put his head in his hands and closed his eyes.

"I can't believe he would do this to me," he said, sounding pained. "My own brother. I have to turn him in."

"I'm so sorry," Nancy said again as she kept up the circular motions on his back. "And I'm so sorry I had to be the one to tell you."

Barron let out a painful sigh.

"This will destroy our firm," he said, a sudden hard edge to his voice. "Everything we've built. My reputation. I'll never be able to work in finance ever again."

Nancy was at a loss for words. His evaluation of how his brother's activities were going to impact him were right on the mark. And nothing she could say would change that.

She moved her hand to his arm and stroked his skin with her

thumb.

Barron reached for her then, seeking comfort in her arms, and before she knew it, they were in a passionate embrace. His lips met hers and they started off with slow, gentle kisses that quickly morphed into deeper, more urgent ones. His hands were all over her body and he kissed up and down her neck.

There was an aggressiveness to him tonight that Nancy had never seen before. But she could understand it, given the circumstances. Everybody dealt with trauma differently. And finding out that your twin brother, your business partner, the only family you had left in the world was double-crossing you? That could cause some serious PTSD.

Barron suddenly broke free from their embrace, stood up and grabbed Nancy's hand. He helped her to her feet and led her to his bedroom. She took a seat on the bed and started taking off her earrings. Getting laid was the last thing she had expected tonight—she had half expected Barron to kick her out. There was no small part of her that realized her investigating him could come off as sounding creepy.

She set her earrings on the nightstand before joining Barron on the bed. He was already shirtless and he reached for the back zipper of her dress. She pulled the garment over her head and Barron's hands reached for her breasts. He grabbed them over her bra, squeezing so hard she cried out in pain.

It was something he had done before, yes, but he had never used such force. She supposed her revelations had brought out his raw aggression. She was more than happy to let him take it out on her

His lips were on her again and her hands were all over his body.

Unexpectedly, he pulled away for a moment and went to the nightstand on his side of the bed. Curious, Nancy watched him rummage around for a second before he emerged with a multi-tasseled leather flogger in hand. She had seen these online before, of course, given her line of work. But she had never seen one in person. It *was* a leather tassel flogger, but with one addition—instead of a handle, a metal butt plug was attached to the end.

In terms of what she hadn't expected this evening, the emergence of the toy ranked up near number one and she nearly burst out laughing. The thing was absurd. It looked like a gothic pom-pom—a black leather flogger that pulled double duty. *Or should that be double* booty? she thought, suppressing a snort. It was giving Wednesday Addams meets Dallas Cowboys Cheerleader.

She was relieved when Barron ordered her to turn around and smacked her with it, hard, across the ass. It was an enjoyable type of pain and she was thankful he hadn't had it in his mind to use it the other way. The thought of having a multi-tasseled leather tail was not one that turned her on.

He flipped Nancy over then and got on top of her while his hands rubbed and grabbed her body in all of the right places. His head was just above hers and she nuzzled her nose in the crook of his neck and placed kisses on his skin. His tousled black curls tickled her face and she pulled back slightly when she noticed a dark mark near his ear.

Confusion flooded her.

*What is that?* she thought to herself. *A hickey?*

She kept her body relaxed but she was now on high alert and focused more intently on the mark. It definitely wasn't a hickey. It was a round and unmistakable two-inch birth mark. And it definitely hadn't been there the last time she had snuggled up to Barron.

Her body tensed in spite of herself, and he shifted in response.

"Is everything okay?" he questioned.

Nancy took a deep breath and tried to relax her body.

"Everything is great," she said with less conviction than she felt.

It occurred to her that while the Benjamin brothers were identical twins, there *was* one thing that could tell them apart—a two-inch birthmark that Barron didn't possess, but that

Theodore, apparently, did. Typically hidden by their respective mops of messy curls, it took getting them both into bed to tell which one was which.

Her heartbeat began to quicken and she tried to formulate a plan. It was imperative that Teddy, the man she suspected was *actually* half-naked with her in bed, not catch on that she knew. It was anyone's guess what he would do to her now that he knew she had proof of his crimes. After all, she alone had the evidence to take him down and a man with nothing to lose was a danger to her health.

How had Teddy gotten into Barron's condo? She thought back to Barron's front door. He had a digital key on his phone and, she realized, so did his brother.

But where *was* Barron? she frantically thought.

Probably out on the party circuit as was his MO. She could only hope that he would cut his activities short tonight and head home early.

Teddy seemed to sense that something was bothering her despite her saying everything was great.

Nancy used the pause in their activities to tell him she had forgotten to grab a condom out of her purse.

"I'll be right back," she slid out from under him and stepped towards the bedroom door.

"Larissa," Teddy said authoritatively.

She paused and slowly turned around. How did he know her fake name?

"Yes?" she asked innocently, hoping that he was going to toss her her earrings and tell her to put them in her purse.

Instead, Teddy got up from the bed and walked towards her. She tensed up as he strode past her to the bedroom door, which he promptly locked.

Fuck.

Nancy tried to think fast and dashed for the adjoining ensuite, but Teddy was in hot pursuit. Before she had the chance to close the ensuite door, he was on her, and seconds later, had her pinned to the ground.

Nancy struggled against him as she tried to wiggle out of his grip—no small feat given the size of his hands. She grabbed at his shoulders and pushed, but he lifted up his torso and took the opportunity to grab one of her wrists and then the other, before grabbing hold of them together with one hand.

The next thing she knew, Teddy slammed her head into the marble floor and everything went black.

*

Nancy felt the pounding of her head before her eyes flickered open. It wasn't the pain of a hangover, she thought as she struggled to recall what she had been doing before finding herself with an aching head—it was an injury. She opened her eyes and looked around Barron's bedroom.

It was empty and she was sitting on his bed, against the headboard with her back propped up by pillows. Between the pain in her head and her confusion about how she had wound up there, it took a minute for Nancy to realize that her hands were tied behind her back. She gave a slight tug and realized that they were tied up by ribbons of leather.

The butt-plug flogger.

*Jesus.*

Apparently, it had more than two uses, she thought sardonically. Her fingers felt around the leather strips before finding the ones that were tied together and then it all came flashing back.

Teddy, not Barron, and the struggle that they had had on the ensuite floor. She remembered Teddy slamming her head into the marble and surmised that he must have dragged her to Barron's bed before tying her up.

Her fingers explored the knot further. *Professional*, she thought to herself, feeling mildly impressed. If the aggressive foreplay hadn't clued her in, she was now certain that Teddy was also into hardcore domination. But, unlike Nancy's clients, Teddy, like his brother, preferred to be the one doling it out.

She couldn't tell what kind of knot he had tied, but if Teddy was into BDSM, Nancy knew one thing—all of the knots came with an easy escape. Safety first—that was one of the rules of the game.

Not that she fooled herself into thinking that Teddy was playing at anything. He had been stealing millions of dollars from investors, was planning to flee the country, and Nancy was the only one who could stop him.

That was enough to make any man murderous.

She wiggled her hands a bit to see how much the leather would give, but her hands were tightly secured. Her fingers searched frantically for any loose bits of leather that could be pulled to unravel the knot. She gently pulled on the various pieces until she felt one give.

Jackpot.

Nancy braced herself as she heard the bedroom door open and footsteps echo across the floor. Seconds later in walked Teddy, looking fresh as a daisy, confident, and secure.

"Ah, Larissa," he said with a cold smile. "You're finally awake."

She glared at him.

"How's your head?" he asked without a hint of sympathy. "You were out for two hours."

"I think I'm having problems with my vision," she said sounding groggy. "Instead of one of the sexy and successful Benjamin brothers, there seems to be a sleazy piece of shit standing in front of me."

She may have been at a disadvantage being tied up in bed, but she wasn't going to go down without getting a few shots in.

Teddy scowled for a moment and then his features took shifted into something lighter.

"I've been on to you for a while," he said, clearly pleased with his incapacitated and, literally captive, audience. "I saw you in the lobby of our office building one morning when I was talking to a friend," he continued. "I thought you were incredibly attractive."

Nancy thought back to the day that she had pretended to be on the phone while eavesdropping on Teddy and his friend.

Damnit. She should have gone full troll makeup that day.

"I saw you again standing on the sidewalk outside of my house," Teddy went on, clearly amused by her displeasure.

"How could you have seen me? You weren't home that day," she said, scowling.

"I wasn't home that day, you're correct. But my Ring camera caught you on video. I really need to recalibrate that thing's range. Anyway," he leaned against the wall, "I wouldn't have even checked the footage if my neighbour, Clarence, hadn't told me that he had seen some woman loitering outside my house for an unusually long period of time. I checked the recording and what did I see?" He paused and Nancy shot him a glare. "The same woman who had loitered in the lobby of our office."

Nancy screwed up her face. Unfortunately, it seemed that Teddy was one of those rare sorts who was very aware of his surroundings.

"When Barron told me that he'd met a dark-haired woman named Larissa, I didn't know for sure, but I had a sneaking suspicion it was you." Teddy's eyes bored into her.

"Your brother is much better than you in bed," she said cooly. "At least when it comes to foreplay. Is that what this is about?" She kept needling him. "Barron is better than you at everything—more personable, more appealing. He attracts women like a 75 percent-off sale at Saks. You just cant stand it, can you?"

Teddy scowled. "My brother is a lazy fuck."

A humorless laugh escaped Nancy's lips. "So that's it? You're in debt to the Mob and want to stick it to your brother." She shook her head in disgust. "You're pathetic."

"Shut the fuck up!" Teddy's anger spiked. He stormed over, grabbed Nancy by the shoulders and slapped her across the face.

That was her moment. Nancy yanked the loose piece of leather she had been working free, and the knots in the flogger fell away. Using her now-free hands, she grabbed the flogger's tassels and swung the butt-plug end at Teddy's face. The stubby metal piece struck him on the cheek and Teddy, caught off guard by Nancy's attack, stumbled off the bed, hands held to the side of his face.

*Make that* four *uses for the butt-plug flogger*, she thought, bracing for Teddy's retaliation. If she got out of this predicament, she was going to send the manufacturer a thank-you email. She couldn't speak to its effectiveness when it came to sex, but as a weapon, the sex toy did its job and then some.

"You bitch!" Theodore's growled, lunging towards her.

Last time, in the ensuite, he had taken her by surprise, but this time, Nancy was ready. Teddy might have the advantage of strength and speed, but Nancy was purely fueled by outrage.

Sure, she had wanted to get both of the brothers into bed. But she didn't like being tricked. And she especially didn't like it when a man had the upper hand. Teddy had also given her one hell of a headache, and that *really* pissed her off.

*Three strikes and you're out*, she thought, maneuvering away from the sadistic but oh-so-sexy Teddy—snatching up a hefty bedside lamp as she did so.

*

Minutes later, police and hotel security came screaming through Barron's bedroom door with little old Mrs. Jones hot on their heels.

Nancy was relieved that they were there, but they had arrived a little too late. She had already taken care of Teddy and had the bruises to show for it.

She hadn't known how Barron was going to take the news that his brother was a criminal, and just in case he took it badly and turned on her, she had texted strict instructions to Mrs. Jones to call the police if she didn't check in with her by 11 p.m.

"Hands up!" one of the officers yelled, pointing his gun at Nancy and her captive. Teddy Benjamin was definitely looking the worse for wear.

Nancy raised her hands and answered their questions calmly before one of the police officers, a hulking man with a bald head and a mustache, grabbed her arms and put her in handcuffs.

"You take those handcuffs off of her!" Mrs. Jones hobbled over and ordered in her most drill-sergeant-like voice.

Officer Mustache, taken aback by Mrs. Jones's commanding tone, which belied her little-old-lady appearance, did just as she asked.

Fortunately, the police also put cuffs on Teddy, whom Nancy had tied up with the flogger using non-professional knots. He tried to plead ignorance and assault at the hands of Nancy, but it didn't take long for the cops to unravel the truth.

Paramedics were brought in to tend to both of them, but Teddy's medical attention was completed while he was handcuffed to the stretcher. Nancy had hit him over the head with Barron's bedside lamp and hoped she had given him a nasty concussion. If nothing else, they would have matching headaches.

While the paramedics shone a flashlight into her eyes and checked her pulse, Nancy explained the details to the officers as clearly and quickly as she could.

The officers had then escorted her and Mrs. Jones to the police station so Nancy could give them a sworn statement. She was assured that her name and contact information would be kept anonymous and for that she was grateful. It wouldn't do to have her name plastered all over the media when the shit-storm—she knew it was coming given the amount of money, the connections to the Mob, and the devastatingly attractive defendant—broke loose.

When the police had walked her out of Barron's building, she spotted one reporter who had clearly been listening to the police scanner, and she hid her face from the reporter's camera.

"I've always wanted to go for a ride in the back of a police car!" Mrs. Jones sounded delighted as the officer opened up the back passenger door. Nancy heard him chuckle at the old lady's excitement.

"Well, I'm happy I could help," Nancy said wryly as she slid into the back seat. "Despite my bruises and the headache, I'd much rather you go for a ride this way than committing a crime."

"Oh, I'm so sorry, dearie." Mrs. Jones looked at Nancy with concern. "I didn't mean to be insensitive."

She patted Mrs. Jones's wrinkled hand reassuringly.

"It's okay, Mrs. Jones. All in a day's work," she smiled. "And trust me—I've had much worse."

At the police station, while Nancy sat in one of the small conference rooms and spoke to the police, Mrs. Jones worked her charms on the officers at the front desk. Somehow, she managed to convince them to let her sit inside one of the cells and had then pulled out her phone and asked one of the officers to take her picture. Charmed by the feisty little old lady, one of the officers obliged and Nancy nearly doubled over laughing when she emerged from the conference room and got a glimpse of Mrs. Jones's jail-cell photo.

"I tried to get them to take my mugshot, but they wouldn't do it." She sounded wistful.

Nancy had thanked the officers and then ordered her and Mrs. Jones an Uber home. On the drive back to their building, Mrs. Jones had insisted that Nancy come back to her place for a meal. Like the police, Nancy was unable to resist her neighbour's charm, so she obliged and Mrs. Jones fixed them up a 2 a.m. meal of hearty soup and sandwiches.

"I was so concerned when I didn't hear from you," her neighbour confessed. "I called the police but they said it would take several hours for them to get there because there were other calls that took priority. So, I told them that there was a murder," she said proudly.

Nancy was shocked, but also grateful.

It almost was a murder. If it hadn't been for the flogger, Nancy had no doubts that her body would have been thrown down Barron's garbage chute or laid out in the bathtub in a pool of her own blood.

"I insisted on coming with them," Mrs. Jones said. "But they wouldn't pick me up, so I called a taxi and waited in the lobby of the Ritz until they arrived."

Nancy almost spit out her soup.

The little old lady had insisted on being the first inside Barron's condo, but the police had held her back.

"You're the best, Mrs. Jones." Nancy flashed a grateful smile at her neighbour.

When the soup and sandwiches were reduced to crumbs, Nancy headed back to her place. After the activities of that evening and Mrs. Jones's hearty meal, she needed a solid eight hours of sleep. Nine or ten wouldn't even come amiss. It was nearly 3 a.m. and she turned her alarm clock and ringer off before she went to bed and didn't wake up until 3 p.m.

*

Groggy but feeling refreshed, Nancy lay in the soft confines of her bed and reflected on the previous evening. Then she reached for the nightstand beside her and picked up her phone.

Her screen was a flurry of news and social media notifications. It seemed that, overnight, or in the wee hours of the morning, the case against Teddy had officially broken. Not all of the details had come out, but because he was such a high-profile individual, there was a lot of buzz, speculation, and conjecture. Angus had texted her early that morning after reading the news, eager to hear about her part in the case.

*What happened!!!????!!!* His text message to her had contained nearly twenty exclamation marks and question marks and was followed one hour later with strict instructions to call him as soon as she had a chance.

She fired off a quick reply telling him that she had just woken up and that she would give him a call later that evening. Well, later that afternoon. That evening she planned on having a quiet night in—mind-numbing television and salty snacks were on the agenda. With all of the excitement of the case and especially the excitement in the last twenty-four hours, both her brain and her body craved junk.

Before she got to any of that, she cancelled the dungeon session she had for 6 p.m. that evening with sincere apologies and a request asking her client to reschedule. Then, she got out of bed and dialed Ms. Elena Fineberg.

In addition to the text messages she had received from Angus, she had three missed calls from her client.

"Ms. Fineberg," Nancy said when Elena breathlessly answered the phone. She spent the next ten minutes explaining to the woman what had happened and apologizing for not informing her of it before she went to bed.

"I knew there was a good chance that the press would find out and run with it immediately, but I also thought I would leave you with more questions than answers if I had left you a voicemail, email, or text message. And, to be honest," she said practically, "I'm thinking a lot better after twelve hours of rest."

The older lady graciously assured Nancy that she understood and gasped when Nancy relayed the details the previous night. Leaving out the bits about the foreplay and the sex toy, of course. Elena was her client, yes, but that didn't mean that she needed to know *all* of the dirty details of her work.

"The police will be in touch with you," Nancy continued. "And I think there is a good chance that they will be able to recover most of your foundation's money."

"I don't know what to say," Elena's voice was trembled with emotion. "I can't thank you enough."

# CHAPTER 20

News about Theodore Benjamin's $120 million theft was all over the country. Radio stations, podcasts, television shows, newspapers, and magazines—they were all discussing the twin financier's downfall, and it was the talk of Bay Street. Nancy wasn't surprised—the case had all the makings of a Hollywood blockbuster. Attractive twins, millions of dollars, offshore accounts, and ties to the Mob. Scorsese couldn't have asked for a better story.

Nancy had managed to remain anonymous despite being the one to uncover the fraud. The only ones who knew about her involvement, aside from Mrs. Jones, Angus, and Elena Fineberg, were the cops. Which was exactly how she wanted to keep it. After giving them her statement, she had handed over all of her evidence and let them take it from there.

Contrary to the cliché about the slow speed of the wheels of justice, the cops had moved quickly and so had the Crown Attorneys. She had cut off communication with their offices and got her updates through gossip, social media, and the news.

Clover Capital had ceased operations immediately. Nancy felt bad for the staffers who had been laid off, but word was that Barron had provided each of them with six-months of compensation. Not all of the money from Clover Capital's investors had been tracked down and Nancy knew that the force's forensic accountants would have their hands full for a very long time to come.

Brian, Clover Capital's thieving analyst, had been charged with wire fraud and had taken a plea deal in exchange for testifying against Teddy. It was the best the twenty-three-year-old could have hoped for. Not that it would do much for his career prospects. After facilitating the theft of millions of dollars of investors' money, he would be lucky if someone trusted him enough to run the checkout till at a grocery store. For his part in the scheme, Brian claimed he had done it to pay off his student loans. He also pleaded ignorance with regards to knowing all of the dirty details about what Teddy Benjamin had been doing.

Nancy kind of believed him. She didn't think that Teddy was stupid enough to tell Brian his plan. But she knew that Brian was well aware that what he was helping Teddy with was not above board.

Barron had initially come under scrutiny by both the cops and the media, but he had eventually been cleared of any wrongdoing. Reportedly, he was taking his brother's betrayal worse than those who had had their money stolen. Understandable, of course, when your own blood, your brother, your twin, had double-crossed you and planned on leaving you high and dry.

Financially, he would be fine—he was wealthy before the inception of his and Teddy's investment firm and he would be wealthy after its demise. One thing he would be unlikely to do, however, was work in the financial industry ever again. Teddy may have been the one who committed the crime, but the stain of it had rubbed off on Barron.

There would always be those who believed that Barron was wise to his brother's ruse, and even being cleared by the courts wouldn't convince them otherwise. Which wasn't entirely surprising. It was a little difficult even for Nancy to wrap her head around the double-crossing crime.

Interestingly, Barron had put the brakes on his playboy behaviour as soon as the news about his brother broke. She wasn't sure if his brother's actions had caused him to reevaluate his life or if he knew that it would tarnish his reputation on the social circuit. Goodness knows that when you are up, everyone wants to know you, be you, date you, and be around you. And when you are down? Friends are scarce.

He had called Larissa, of course. Not that Nancy had answered the phone. From the voicemail he left, it sounded like he had spoken with his brother after he the arrest. It was interesting that the one call Teddy had made from the police station was to Barron—the brother he had so badly betrayed.

She wouldn't see Barron again. As much as she wanted to. Their time together, as fun as it was, was mostly an illusion. Nancy wasn't Larissa—she had merely been playing a role. And Barron was attracted to that character, not to Nancy.

It was a shame, really. She imagined Barron probably thought she was just like everyone else who abandoned him after his fall from grace. And while it stung a little to think he might group her in with those people, she came to terms with it by reasoning that it was just one of the downsides of her job.

Still—she had seen the tender, caring side of Barron and a small part of her hoped their paths might cross again one day. But not as Larissa. If she ever met him again, she wanted it to be as herself.

Not all of the money from Clover Capital's investors had been tracked down—it was something that the investigators would be working on for months.

Teddy, Nancy read, was facing fifty-two charges, which ranged from wire fraud, money laundering, to racketeering and more. He had hired one of the country's top criminal defense attorneys—thankfully, not her client Vince—and, unsurprisingly, had pleaded 'not guilty'. Photos of him leaving the courthouse had made the front pages of both local and national newspapers. Teddy, a veritable god in person, still managed to look like a model in the grainy, gray-toned shots. It was unsurprising, perhaps, that he had amassed himself a sizeable fan club amongst some single women. 'Teddies', as they called themselves, popped up all over social media to defend the fraudster. They were, she supposed, taken in by his devastating good looks. Combined with his power and sizeable offshore account, it was a heady enticement for some who felt they could be the one to change him.

The judge presiding over Teddy's case, Judge Chantel McCracken—known in legal circles as 'The Cracken'—had set his bail at $5 million, which didn't quite break the record in terms of the highest bail ever set but came close.

Teddy, of course, had access to the funds in his Caymans account, which couldn't be touched by the Canadian cops, and he had posted bail almost immediately.

It was an unusual move on the part of the judge, requiring so much money to secure a release. But then again, Teddy's case was anything but typical. It was speculated that Judge McCracken had ordered it because Teddy had both the means and motive to flee the country.

As a condition of his release, Teddy was forbidden from contacting Brian, the analyst he had roped into his scheme. Which wasn't a condition that she could see him breaching. He had also been ordered to surrender his passport, wear an ankle monitor, and check in with his bail officer every day. He was also, for all intents and purposes, under house arrest—allowed out only between the hours of 9 a.m. until 8 p.m. Hardly strenuous, but likely the harshest conditions the judge was legally allowed to impose.

It eventually came out that Aaron Wallace, the mystery Cayman Islands investor, was a fake identity that Teddy had created. As far as Clover Capital was concerned 'Aaron Wallace' was a high-net-worth investor that Teddy had brought into the firm. Spreadsheets showed "Aaron Wallace" had given Clover Capital $1.3 million, but in reality, Teddy, hadn't given the firm so much as a dime.

The account that Teddy had opened in the Cayman Islands turned out to be exactly what Nancy had suspected—an offshore avenue to keep the money siphoned off from investors that couldn't be touched by Canadian cops.

The two numbered companies were kept to hold the stolen funds without tying them to Teddy. One of the companies with a $60 million balance had had every last dollar diverted to Teddy's Caymans bank account. The other company's $60 million account had been diverted to the Mob. Clearly not content with receiving the money Teddy owed them plus interest, the Italians had persuaded him, under the threat of violence she was sure, to cut them in on the deal.

Illegal activities and shaky morals aside, the Mafia were never a group you wanted to owe. Once they had something on you, you were at their mercy.

Nancy suspected Teddy's plan had always been to siphon the money and leave his brother holding the bag, but his plan had been hampered a bit by owing money to the Italians. She didn't know how much money he had originally intended to take for himself or when he was planning on pulling the proverbial trigger—disappearing from his life in Toronto and reappearing in the Caribbean as Aaron Wallace. It was one of the blandest names Nancy could think of, which seemed fitting for uptight Teddy. Although she knew if someone was trying to fly under the radar and start a new life, reinventing yourself as Montgomery Tuckwell wouldn't exactly help you to blend in.

*

She opened a new tab on Chrome and searched for 'X'. Nowhere did information travel faster than on the rebranded Twitter site, and today didn't prove any different.

News about one half of the Benjamin brothers was spreading like wildfire. Somehow, Teddy had skipped the country; he was a trending topic worldwide. She almost couldn't believe it. Not only was it a blow to the justice system, it was a personal blow to Nancy. Her sleuthing had solved the case for Ms. Fineberg and had ensured that he be placed under arrest, but with him gone, the investors would still be out their money and all of Nancy's work would be for nought.

Posts with Teddy Benjamin's name were everywhere on the social media site. On the 'Top' posts tab, she saw several news articles and clicked on the one from the *National Post.*

*Teddy Benjamin, Financier Charged with $120 Million Financial Crimes, Flees Country,* the headline read. The article itself was short on details but was being updated in real time. From the little information that was there, Nancy pieced together what had likely happened.

Somehow, and this was one part of the story that eluded Nancy, Teddy had managed to remove his ankle monitor and had thrown the authorities off by attaching it to the collar of his dog. With the help of someone or several someones, he had obtained a fake passport and chartered a private jet out of the country. How he had escaped from his home was another mystery, but it didn't take a genius-level I.Q. to deduce how easily he could have done it.

Teddy was under house arrest between the hours of 8 p.m. and 9 a.m. and had a police cruiser stationed outside his house to monitor him for any activities that might break the conditions of his bail. Where there *wasn't* a police monitor, however, was anywhere near his backyard. Which meant that after he had attached the ankle monitor to his dog, he could have cut the backyard lights, and slipped into a waiting car.

Embarrassingly, it had turned out that Teddy had been gone for more than twenty-four hours before the police even noticed that he was missing. To maintain the conditions of his bail, he had been required to check in with his bail officer every day, but Teddy had managed to get around that by leaving his personal cell phone at home and setting a timed text to send to his officer that morning claiming he was ill.

It was a good cover for the ankle monitor to not be moving for much of the day, and for spending all day inside of his home. His lab, after all, spent most of his time sleeping and lacked the thumbs needed to open the door on his own. Because of this,

Teddy's absence was only discovered the next morning when he failed to check in with his bail officer. Another officer who was stationed outside his house had knocked on the door and tried calling him several times before he had gotten the okay to break in. The police feared that the accused criminal might be in some kind of medical distress.

Instead, the officer had been greeted inside by a happy black lab who had an ankle monitor dangling from his collar. An immediate call went out after that and Teddy's photo was plastered on the local and national news, urging anyone who saw the financier to immediately call 911. It was orchestrated to perfection and was, perhaps, a more stunning caper than his financial con.

The company that chartered the private plane for Teddy had pleaded ignorance and Nancy believed them. They merely took the money. It wasn't their job to verify who was on board and whether or not their identification was real. That was the job of whichever country the plane was landing in. Which turned out to be, in Teddy's case, in South America. A literal jungle one could get lost in, where bribes to officials made vanishing easy. It was the perfect place for a criminal to evade capture.

Nancy picked up the phone and dialed Elena Fineberg's number.

"Nancy," Ms. Fineberg's voice came through her mobile.

"How are you doing, Elena?" Nancy asked, her voice full of concern. "I'm sure you've seen the news?"

The older woman let out a sigh: "I have. It's a shame, but Teddy will get his comeuppance eventually. Sometimes it just takes a little longer."

Nancy had no reply, but she hoped Elena was right.

"Have the police told you whether they will be able to recover any of your foundation's money?" she asked gently.

"They're working on it," Elena said regretfully. "It looks like some of the money didn't reach Teddy's Caymans account," she trailed off. "I don't pretend to understand the intricacies of it, but they told me there is a high likelihood that we will get some of it back. Which is better than nothing," she said optimistically.

*Which is also more than some of the investors will get back*, Nancy reflected on the $60 million Teddy had in his offshore account.

"Very true," Nancy said instead.

"I'm so glad that I came to you when I did," Elena gushed again. When Nancy had broken the case, the older lady had showered her with thanks. "Always trust your gut," Ms. Fineberg continued.

They exchanged pleasantries before Nancy hung up the phone. A few days later, a couriered cheque for $37,585.19 arrived at her office.

Not bad for one month's worth of work.

# CHAPTER 21

*Larissa . . . just let me know you're ok.*

Nancy glanced at the text message. Her heart—and stomach—dropped.

It was from Barron.

She couldn't reply. His brother may have committed the crime, but Nancy had been the architect of their firm's downfall. He didn't know that and it was too complicated for her to explain.

As much as she liked Barron—his company, their conversation, the sex, she wasn't ready to dive back into dating. Not to mention, her and Barron's entire relationship had started off with a lie. She had thought about reaching out, reconciling, and starting over, but the more she thought it over, the more it seemed ill-advised. Barron had had enough turmoil in his life the past few weeks. She didn't think it would help him to know that she had been lying and investigating him the entire time.

Besides, she wasn't over Jamie and she wasn't going to gamble what was left of her heart by taking a chance on a seemingly reformed playboy.

She left the text on 'read', and closed the app.

*

"A toast!" Mrs. Jones raised her champagne glass as they soaked up the sun on her patio.

"To you." Nancy tapped her flute against her neighbour's. "I couldn't have done it without you, Mrs. Jones."

The old lady waved it off with a modest shrug.

"To us," she countered and clinked her glass back.

They took a sip of the champagne, which was sparkling in the sunlight. Fine bubbles burst in Nancy's mouth as the citrusy brut touched her taste buds. She had brought over the celebratory bottle to share with her neighbour, along with a gift to thank the old lady for saving Nancy's life.

At first glance, the two of them were an odd pairing. Nancy with her straight black hair, serious expression, and closet full of disguises; Mrs. Jones with her curled white hair, glimmer in her eyes, and lace and floral outfits.

But they worked together well and Nancy wouldn't have it any other way.

The screen on Nancy's phone suddenly lit up and she glanced down at the table. It was an email from someone—an anonymous Gmail account—and it had been sent to her P.I. email address. There was no subject line, which was a bit strange, but from the small snippet of the email that she could see, she could tell the sender was serious.

She stared at it for a second until Mrs. Jones interjected.

"Is everything okay?" she asked.

Nancy glanced up at her neighbour.

"I'm not sure," she said honestly. "But it looks like I've got another case."

If you enjoyed this book, please leave a review on your chosen platform! Reviews are helpful to other readers and allow authors to continue sharing their stories. If you would like to know when I release more books, please sign up for my newsletter at janelaboucane.com/newsletter.

# ACKNOWLEDGMENTS

First and foremost, my mom, dad, sister, and brother-in-law who spent one boozy Christmas night brainstorming storylines for Nancy Screw. I appreciate you always entertaining my over-the-top asks. I owe Trevor an additional 'thank you' for coming up with the twin premise and title for this one. Brooke for being a great editor and Bailey for her fantastic illustrations. Additional thanks to the myriad of friends and family who are always encouraging me.

**Keep reading for a look at**
***50 Worst Dates***

# I SEE DEAD PEOPLE

I met Jimmy at a restaurant when a friend and I were out for dinner one evening. He was a tech worker in his mid-fifties and had pretty blue eyes and an easy smile. He and his friend, Rick, were sitting at the bar, telling entertaining stories to those seated beside them. Rick's stories were hysterical. He embarked upon a fifteen-minute-long monologue about how he had been fired from different jobs while going into detail about each termination, which was always owing to something sexual.

"I worked in the meat department at Publix and then I got fired." He paused while everyone eagerly waited for the punchline. "I got fired for beating my meat!"

The stories continued with jobs that included being a bait master, an arborist, and a mechanic. By mid-to-late evening, helped along by the liquor, his stories had everyone in stitches. At some point, we all decided that we should go for drinks one night. Numbers were exchanged and we promised each other that we would make plans one night soon.

Fast forward three weeks and Jimmy texted me to go

for drinks that same day at a hotel pub near my place. I was not aware that this was a date and only realized that Jimmy considered it to be one when I showed up and he said that he would schedule something ahead of time for our next date instead of asking me at the last minute.

I was not interested in Jimmy as anything more than a friend but I also didn't want to be rude so I said nothing. After a couple of cocktails and general "getting to know you" conversation, we decided to go for dinner. We went to an upscale steakhouse and sat at the bar, which is when things took a turn for the weird. Jimmy was a nice enough man, to be sure, and the conversation was easy, but after he opened up, I felt like I needed a young priest and an old priest . . . and a therapist.

Jimmy turned to me after we clinked our glasses together and took a drink.

"I can see dead people," he said seriously.

I stared at him and waited for the punchline.

It didn't come.

Dead relatives were all around him, Jimmy claimed. He also had premonitions.

"Oh?" I took a sip of my drink and said nothing else.

Jimmy went on.

"Yes," he continued. "I saw my mom being murdered in my dream and when I woke up, my dead relatives were all around me telling me that my mom was in danger."

I kept my face neutral at this point but I was wondering if Jimmy was maybe off of his meds.

"Then I found out that my mother was murdered," he said matter-of-factly. "In real life."

It turns out that Jimmy might actually have some sort of psychic powers. It's a terribly tragic story—Jimmy's mom was murdered by a troubled teenager that she had taken into her home. In trying to be a good person and provide the teen with a stable home, love, and care, she had become his murder victim. It is beyond horrific.

We sat in silence for a few minutes after this. I didn't quite know what to say. Jimmy had told me something that I would not expect someone to reveal on a fourth date let alone on a first. And besides, this wasn't even a date.

The bartender topped up our drinks and our conversation carried on.

"Have you ever been married?" Jimmy asked me, to which I shook my head "no." "I have one ex-wife," he said before launching into what went wrong with his marriage. Which was, chiefly, that his ex-wife had cheated on him. With three different men. All of whom were named Brian.

I fought the urge to chime in that maybe things could have lasted had he only opted for a name change. Instead, I crinkled my eyes and tried to arrange my face into some semblance of sympathy.

"Last year I found out that I have prostate cancer," Jimmy went on, adding that he had been on chemo and it was currently in remission.

I tried to offer up some condolences on everything shitty that had happened in his life, but Jimmy brushed it off and continued.

"I found out two years ago that I have a 20-year-old daughter," he said, revealing that he was now trying to get to know her. "She had had a baby four months ago and now I'm a first-time grandfather."

I sat there mostly in silence and let Jimmy talk. And talk. And talk. The poor man had had a rough few years and it seemed like he needed someone to talk to. I only began to get uncomfortable when Jimmy grabbed my hand. I typically eschew affection until I have really gotten to know someone and we have established that there is something between us. Hand-holding on first dates when I wasn't even aware that I had agreed to go on a first date to begin with was a no-go. Although I did kind of get it—Jimmy had shared a lot about himself with me and it had forged some kind of connection between us. I think it's known as "trauma bonding." Regardless, I am not into holding hands with strangers, so I tried to keep my hand on the bar at all times.

"Why aren't you married?" Jimmy asked—the question that every single woman in her thirties just loves to hear. I could be his next wife, he speculated, seemingly out of nowhere. I wasn't sure if this was information that his dead relatives were giving him, if Jimmy had had a fever dream the night before, or if the mere act of using me like a therapist had forged some kind of matrimonial bond in his mind, but I disagreed. I would have to come and see him at his ranch, he said. After all, we were going to be spending a lot of time together now.

I went home afterwards and told my family about my date. I felt really awful because he had shared so many personal things with me, but I just wasn't into him and I didn't know how to let him down gently.

"Surely you can just turn him down," said my brother-in-law practically. "Let's be real—it sounds like it wouldn't be the worst thing that's happened to him."

Touché.

## ABOUT THE AUTHOR

Jane is an Indigenous writer who lives in Toronto, Canada. She writes rom-coms, chick-lit, and satire, and often draws from experiences in her own life. In addition to writing, Jane is a wine and fashion enthusiast. She enjoys volunteering and supports several animal rescues. She is also the author of *50 Worst Dates*, which gained national television, radio, and newspaper coverage.

www.ingramcontent.com/pod-product-compliance
Lightning Source LLC
Jackson TN
JSHW031854060725
87234JS00007B/22